Giovanni Calvarese or Gio as he is known by his family and friends is a native of Philadelphia, PA. He enjoys writing stories and poems that would make a difference in people's lives. He received his BA in Literature from Saint Joseph's University. He recently received his EdD from Drexel University. In his spare time, he enjoys hiking, running and keeping healthy. He is passionate about making a difference in the world.

This book is dedicated to Jonny, Gabriella and their families and friends for making my visits to Venezuela possible and enriching. Through my fruitful experience with them, I have come to create this fictional novel of their country, Venezuela. May the people of Venezuela and of the world forever be inspired to follow and live fully their dreams without penalty of imprisonment, hindrance of their God-given liberties or of fear of who they are or become.

Giovanni Calvarese

FORGOTTEN AMERICA

THE UNTOLD ADVENTURES OF VENEZUELA

Matt,

May You Find inspiration to always Follow Your dreams and heart. Thank You For all that You do.

Giovanni Calvarese

AUSTIN MACAULEY PUBLISHERS™

LONDON * CAMBRIDGE * NEW YORK * SHARJAH

A CIP catalogue record for this title is available from the British Library.

ISBN 9781528905169 (Paperback)
ISBN 9781528914574 (Hardback)
ISBN 9781528957915 (ePub e-book)

www.austinmacauley.com

First Published (2021)
Austin Macauley Publishers Ltd
25 Canada Square
Canary Wharf
London
E14 5LQ

I would like to acknowledge my family and friends for their support in my writing of this novel. Without their support, this novel could not have been written. I would also like to acknowledge all of my professors and colleagues at Saint Joseph's University and Drexel University for their continued support in my personal and professional success.

Chapter 1
Inception

Forever haunted by a boom that sounded red smoke in Caracas. You still smell the stale burning sulphur lingering ubiquitously in the dusk-lit sky. That's the smell of our bolivares, our blood, our future and our wealth ruined and destroyed. Nobody forgets this. How can they? This day was like all days to come – the day of the end of the butterflies. This day is known as the insurrection of the 4-F Program – the reign of the Chavistas – the beginning of an end – the Red Scare.

Much of Lake Maracaibo, like all of our bodies of water, were once ocean blue, but now are oil black. The very abundant sustenance, water, a necessity, has become with many of our other staples, scarce commodities. Water became undrinkable. Our plains, *Los Llanos*, became infertile – much of our land uninhabitable. The 4-F Program deprives its people of life, opposite of what it claimed to do – create wealth, opportunity and equality.

When was this insurrection? I – we asked ourselves (those of us who still remember and those of us still alive), why does it matter now? It happened – that's *all* that matters. It happened and this cannot be changed. No matter how much we want to turn back the clocks, go back in time, we can't. We cannot go back in time. The clocks don't turn back. Time only goes forward. There is nothing more we can do. What is left for any one of us to do? Once you know, however, you'll understand all of it and will understand how the Chavistas would have deceived *you*!

In our current reality, we have become complacent, that this virus is life. Life or surviving the next day is not certain, but what is certain is death. Surely, if you have not died from the virus then the fear of the virus would consume you – living out your days as a zombie. Either way – living or dying – we have become complacent to this. Hell, we know not of any reality or of a world other than the one we encounter every day. So then the question remains, shall you want to know how *it* happened and when *it* did? Before we begin – there's no sure way of knowing that you may or may not contract *it*. Because today, *it* still lurks in the deepest shadows of our country, our life, our spirit and our government. Sometimes *it* resembles our families, our friends, or what we want most – happiness, surely *it* is not what *it* is.

Nonetheless, *it* all began on February 4, 1992. Red smoke loomed in the air before it became a permanent stain. A stain nobody forgets – a stain forever embedded in the environment – staining the very country we forgot. *It* consumes what is and will be alive. The *Uva de Playas* were once plentiful, but now they have become frail and brittle on the blackened ground where they tirelessly rest on. The *Uva de Playas* helplessly fight to live as they gasp the tainted air and drink the oil-ridden water. These were the first, but not the last, to fall victim of what the V's call, the Red Scare.

Those of us who haven't intentionally forgotten, utter, *we live in a majestic country that has been abandoned.* What was an idea became a virus; a plague rampant indiscriminately among our borders, but it wasn't just restricted to them. A virus, inhospitable to life, that's what everyone remembers it as – the Red Scare. This poison slowly burned our veins then eventually morphed to a parasite hibernating in our brains. It restrains any opposition to the Program. We become programmed to nourish it much like computer programs.

Why wouldn't anyone want to remember how a virus attacked and eroded every aspect of life? Feelings, thoughts, memories were once enjoyed, but now are the things most afraid of. Since the Red Scare, your life cannot be called your own. You live the life of the virus. No one is immune from its restraining clasp. Though almost twenty years since the inception of the virus, it grows stronger and stronger in and among us, especially on every Liberation Day, (or Harvest as the Firsts remember it), so forgetting becomes an impossible wish we long for.

People began to believe in the Program and the honest lies it offers, so then it became truth – a way of life – a way of survival from *them*. Our country wasn't supposed to be abounded from the Red Scare. It wasn't supposed to be toxic. It was supposed to give everyone a better life. It was supposed to make our lives less challenging to live. They were lies, but it became much more than lies. It became a way of life for some, but for many, a fight to survive.

Chapter 2

In Retrospect

Hola mundo. Mi nombre es Carlos Christian Santos. Por favor, llámame CCS.
It's Spanish, which means – Hello world! My name is Carlos Christian Santos.
Please call me, CCS.

We are going on a journey. A journey you will get to know as my home.
What if I tell you a story about this journey? How it is my home. This is a story
and only a *story*. It could be fictitious or authentic. That's for you to decide,
world. A story created through my journey. It illustrates the life of Venezuela
and as Venezuelan, for me yes, for all, certainly.

Well, you see, my home is a distant and blurred image of what it used to be.
My home is DEAD! Figuratively speaking, of course. My home isn't really dead.
It might as well be, given the corruption, political disqualifications and wars that
have saturated her spirit and blackened the weary hearts of her inhabitants.

There was nothing left after. Just nothingness. If nothingness is darkness,
that's what you or anyone would see today. My home is stained with red smoke.
It looms ghostly in the air, occupying the very sustenance we need to survive.
The water is thick and black as if someone wanted our water to be tar-viscid and
soppy. The ground is also painted with red smoky ashes that dwell over what
used to be *Uva de Playas* and nature. This is part of what you or anyone would
see now if you visit my homeland. My homeland is part of my journey; the rest
of it, are my travels. You may ask, are my travels a search for answers about
myself and about my home? Quite possibly, there may be answers – somewhere
beneath my memories, beneath the entire distorted and disordered rubble, there
may be answers. Answers I sought out, not by choice, but by circumstance.
Answers, I never found. I strive to this weary present of ours, fathomed how
possible could the life I live be reality or be a reality any different than yours – a
reality you live every day? Through much pondering, answers *I wanted* – I'm

unsure if I have found them, I'm not sure if I would ever find them or if I have, I am unsure what they are or afraid of what they could be. Another plague incurable or a future we all wanted, yet so unattainable and unreachable to live.

More on this later – we have much to discover!

If I tell the story right, much of our time together will be spent in the third person. The third person means my consciousness. My consciousness seems to jump from one topic to another. My mind gets the better of me. Why you may ask? It's quite odd coming from me, a member in the Opposition, the V's and a former member of the Bolivarian National Guard or *Guardias* as they're named, as Captain Santos. *Infiltrated, that's a word that sticks with you. The Red Scare infiltrated my life and the lives of others.* In the Opposition, we use initials. I am CCS (Carlos Christian Santos) of the V's. Call me CCS for short.

Here we go. *Thoughts* – too many thoughts. *Memories* – too many memories. It's a whirlwind of utter chaos – like shoeboxes over packed with pictures – *disorganised and cluttered.* Remembering it's something that I can't escape. *It won't allow you to.* It's happening again. I'm going off topic. I will try my best not to get lost and confuse all of you, but it's not guaranteed. When I get lost in my thoughts, I get *lost.* I become catatonic. My body remains motionless and speechless while my mind enters another realm, a realm I have no direction over. My mind moves, but my body is stationary as I enter a trance state somewhere in the past. When I'm there, all I know is that I want to leave but I can't. When I'm there, I'm well beneath my thoughts, struggling to piece together that one broken puzzle but unknowingly all the pieces are never there. I am trapped until the trance ends – enslaved in a shattered time – a time that has no place or purpose. What's on the other side is unbearable. So unbearable, even the Boogieman would be afraid; so afraid to even confront its own shadow.

Now, as I think about it, it is paralysis. It's a temporary inability to move or speak. My mind is fully aware of what's unfolding, not just in my memories but also to the outside world. I'm, however, unresponsive to any stimuli. My body and speech remain motionless. I want to move, but I cannot. I lose full functioning of my limbs. Though, I am not asleep. I can quite assure you I'm awake. It's as if I'm between consciousness and sleep.

You're wondering right about now, am I crazy? Well, that's for you to decide, world. Crazy, that's a word overused in my government. A government operated by lunatics.

Back to why my conscience gets the better of me and why I jump from many topics. I have two severe mental deficits: inattention and loss. So, then what about my deficits? It's odd for me to lose track of my thoughts because military officers, such as myself, aren't supposed to be that way. They are supposed to be altogether and have a good head on their shoulders, right? Let me explain what these disabilities are. This way, you'll have a better understanding to judge whether I'm crazy and to judge me holistically.

Where should I begin? One at a time, okay. I will explain them to you, world.

So, the first mental deficit is as if my mind travels zillion miles per second and the brakes are worn out, so stopping is nearly impossible. Just imagine making left turns in traffic blindfolded. I don't know if I'll make the turn or if I do, I don't know what street I'll be thinking of or turning into the next one. But because my mind is also a broken GPS, I won't remember whether I previous made left turns in traffic, blindfolded. So, you see, I have little control over my thoughts. They come and go like people travelling to places. You don't know where they are going, or why there are so many. You just know they are travelling somewhere; that's all you know!

I get distracted easily. This is why I have to focus on one task or one thought at a time. It's strenuous. Ask children to sit still and ask them not to move an inch or even speak for five minutes. It cannot be done, right? I mean, look at my country's education system. We ask children to sit and listen – to listen to the propaganda of the Program so that they too are programmed to follow blindly and not to think or be aware. But, anyway, that's how my mind operates, of uncontrollable, spontaneous thoughts and behaviour.

You may want to ask me at this point, why am I in the military? This is for you to decide, world. I will tell you how I was *pushed into* the military and the rest of my story truthfully but with a sigh. You must make your own conclusions. You formulate your own opinions. I can't do this for you. I can't make you think one way. Though, you will learn how my government may be successful at making people think as drones; as a catalyst injected with a virus that makes them think and feel one way – the way of the Chavistas – the way of the Red Scare as the V's call it. *Conformity dressed in disguise. We didn't know it at the time we were taken away. It was nonetheless conformity disguised as what we all wanted, freedom and security. Once we were adopted, we could clearly feel conformity, but we didn't know what it was. We were blind to our training and because of our training. It consumed our freewill and we had no idea what was happening to us. We were a herded, unnoticed, to our communities, to our country and to our world until we mindlessly followed orders. To our communities, to our country and to our world, they didn't know us by our names. What names did we have other than the collective one – the Guardias. That's what everyone knew us by – the Guardias.*

The other mental deficit is loss or despair. A person gets this by being exposed to severe repeated traumatic events over time. Afterwards, the symptoms can appear in any moment such as in the shower, eating dinner, having sex, arguing with people, sitting in a park, or sleeping with your pet and partner, which are onset by specific stressors. Later on in our journey, I will gradually reveal these stressors and how these stressors have a great impact on me. However, these are subtle, as I will not explicitly say this is a stressor.

I know what you're probably thinking; this guy has few marbles in his head. Screws are loose. Not all the tools are in the attic. If they are, they are nowhere to be found. You might as well call me schizophrenic. By the way, the inhabitants of my home, Venezuela, are all like this. Not knowing what's real or imaginary. This schizophrenia is a fragmented nightmare that continuously plays around and around, for me and for them. Ingesting a piece of you each time the nightmares happen – a part that cannot be returned. It's forever in a void – trapped! Escaping? That's what we all want to do. It's impossible to escape the hellish reality of these nightmares. There's no escaping. These nightmares I have are certain dreams that once were a reality that I experienced. Unfathomably, these nightmares were experienced by many other Venezuelans and non-Venezuelans who were there at the time.

What is most frightening, these nightmares still appear presently. I quite assure you they are real, not imaginary. We don't know when these nightmares appear. We are uncertain whether they will come back or not. We do know that they are not nightmares that you dream and when you awake, they are gone and then shortly forgotten. These nightmares are not easily forgotten. We just hope when we sleep through the violence, that the next day if we awake, is not worse than the previous day.

I often have hallucinations of my home too – back during the conflicts, when I was an undergraduate student at Simon Bolivar University. You will discover the nightmares, at least for me, started much earlier. My home isn't much different today than it was during these conflicts, when the nightmares began for many Venezuelans. Some argue that these are wars that still happen, but subtly, between the government and the Common People. It's a game really. Soon enough, you'll see how. It's a game where *they* always win. A game where the Common People always lose. The odds are always against the Common People but are always in favour of the government.

If I'm going to say this story correctly then this should be the part where I tell you, world, who I am. Don't worry. I won't give any specific details that would comprise your imagination – just enough for the world – you – to create a picture of me.

As you know, I am a military officer – Captain Santos for the *Guardais* and CCS for the V's. After the failed 2001 and 2006 coup of putting an end to the Chavistas, I shortly left Caracas to study in the States. In the States, I studied politics and education where I met my only American friend, or bro, as I call him, Ezekiel. While I was studying in the States, once a year I travelled to my home to be *there*. Why did I do this, you may ask because I had an indescribable compulsion to go back – to witness the magnitude of the red smoke and how much it has invaded my people's lives. Let's say, every time I went back to my country, it wasn't a warm welcoming. It was very much a cold one. I then came back to Venezuela after 6 years to covertly work with the Opposition Force in a non-military capacity. It is from there that our present journey begins.

To truly know and experience not just how my country became a fragmented bombshell but also how my people live decrepit lives, you have to have gone there. It's a majestic place, where they survive not live. It's a fragmented bombshell because of what happened to every child and what continues to happen to every child – myself included.

It's like there's something inside of me that calls me back to where it happened. Though I strive to search for an answer to this, but there isn't one yet. I suppose everyone who successfully left, has this similar feeling – a compulsion that eats at the depths of their minds. It is perhaps a compulsion to return, to understand or to make a change for the better.

Soy un Venezolano tipico. What does this mean? I'm a *mestizo* or to more accurately say, I am a *rambo*, which means mixed skin colour. I am a typical Venezuelan, a mix. Many Venezuelans, if not all, are mixed. Many are from different origins of races. Mama's parents are immigrants. Grandma was from Spain and Grandpa was from Italy. She is a beauty, Mama. She has a round face with high cheekbones. Every time she smiles, the people around her light up. Every time she walks, her silky light black hair sails in the wind effortless

15

passing her porcelain face. Papa's parents are also immigrants. Grandma was from Africa and Grandpa was from Italy. Papa, on the other hand, is muscular and had a face you know you wouldn't want to take advantage of. If you do…let me say, you'd be a changed person – physically and emotionally. I look like both my parents. My closest friend tells me, I look more like Papa when I'm angry and more like Mama when I smile. I have moderately copper-toned skin just as both of my parents do. I am around one hundred and seventy-seven centimetres tall, weighing around eight-four kilograms. That's me. I hope I didn't reveal too much.

I should mention my family. In this journey, you won't discover much about them. That's a different story to tell, for a very different time. They too can write their own story – a story much like mine that could be fictitious or authentic. A story depicting what happened to them and what became of them after everything that happened on the day of my disappearance.

I come from an average Venezuelan family unit. I'm about thirty-five now. But my brothers and sisters vary in age. I have two brothers and two sisters. Each brother and each sister either has a different Mama or Papa. My oldest brother, Jorge, now lives in New York. He left shortly after the economy started to plummet in 2007. My oldest sister, Arianna was born in Nebraska, so I have not seen much of her and little to say only because of what happened to me when I was just in my second year of high school.

A day I thought wouldn't ever happen to anyone again, let alone to me!

So that leaves my youngest brother and sister, Luis and Lucia.

They both still live in Venezuela, one in Maracay and the other in Margarita, I think. Like every other Venezuelan, they do not live every day; they fight to survive every day. Both have better careers, but all better careers pay an equivalent of five hundred US dollars a month. Now that's 350.000 bolivares. I think that is what they do and where they live given the intelligence I have puzzled together over the years. As I have said, what happened to me caused a gap in my not knowing much of my family.

Which means for non-mathematicians, one US dollar is about 7.00 bolivares. However, this *black market* exchange rate changes – for the worst and only for the worst! I wouldn't be surprised to see if it costs 6.000 bolivares for one US dollar. As the dollar strengthens or other foreign currency strengthens, our bolivares decrease in value. This is one of many factors of course. This is due to years of our sinking economy, but worse now as *Maburro* is president. So, as you can gather, our exchange rate for one US dollar is astronomical and will continue to be. How then can any of us survive? I assure you, you wouldn't be able to either.

Every time I mention or hear his name, Maburro – I want the donkey or jackass gone. Dead, you mean? I can't really say that and I can't really say, I mean that either. I only can say, *I want him gone – at least not in the position of our president! Go to Colombia, you jackass.* His policies and political ideologies are drunken. We have a phrase in Venezuela when a person drinks too much and acts foolish – *Vuelto Verga,* which means *drunken ass. That guy makes anyone jump out of their skin!*

Keep in mind, the structure of the story while you read. Its structure has two parts – the past and the present and with two people – myself CCS and my American friend, Ezekiel Ian Masefield. In the past chapters, you will read about my country and myself. In the present chapters, you will read about my friend, Ezekiel and myself.

REMEMBER – REMEMBER – REMEMBER – PAST AND PRESENT – PRESENT AND PAST! THIS IS YOUR ONLY GUIDE THROUGH MY THOUGHTS AND MY EXPERIENCES!

You may also ask why I have structured the story and our journey in this way. Remember, this is because of my disabilities. I have little control over my thoughts. I also don't know at times, what's imaginary or reality – and I may be unreliable – or then again, *am* I? Do I function because of some form of medication or I don't function at all. World, this is for you to decide.

You should always question when you read the present chapters. Are we, Ezekiel and myself, different people or are we the same person? Is Ezekiel another part of my consciousness, or is he really my *only* American friend that I have studied with for six years in the States?

Honestly, I don't know what's imaginary or reality sometimes. Why? I have hallucinations of the past and I believe these hallucinations are as real as the present. I am, however, functional enough to truthfully lead you and travel with you on my and also your journey. I can say with confidence, whether I'm hallucinating or somewhere in the present or the past, the experiences and events that I describe have happened. That's for certain.

Let's begin our journey and our travels through time. If you get lost, remember every chapter from here is structured PRESENT – PAST – PRESENT – PAST and so forth. If somehow through our journey you get lost then I am lost. Then it is on you as much as it is on me to stifle through the collective disorganisation and piece together some coherent meaning.

Chapter 3
Departure

Ezekiel becomes consumed in his thoughts about travelling to Venezuela for the very first time, but it is his fifth time to South America. He's not new to South America by any means, but new to a tragic and *red* culture that has been despondently crushing Venezuela.

Ezekiel glances over to his friend CCS to ensure himself that this is happening – that this is reality and not a dream or something like it. He anxiously pats CCS on the back, as bros do as a form of a friendly gesture. He does this to be sure he actually *feels* his friend and the moment where his hand touches his friend's back, it further reassures this is reality, for him and for CCS. Momentarily, Ezekiel nervously glances at his turned over black wristwatch reading 4:25 am. It is intentionally turned over so as to signify his poor relationship with time.

Carlos Christian Santos eagerly waits to board the 8422 local Airport Line. The trains wrestle with the brownish and reddish rusted tracks as they fight for their release. They screech in pain as they worriedly find enough momentum to stop. They roar and zoom in excitement as they push off. These constant sounds resemble the amount of apprehension, confusion and chaos in CCS' head. These are also the constant sounds echoing in the empty night – in the deserted train station, both of trains and of people.

Though the crescent moonlit sky glittering isn't prepared for a storm, it is calm after a thunder and lightning storm. The calm you know when the vehement storm has completely ended. The clouds stretch thin over this sky reaching for the crescent moon. The weather tranquillises anyone in its path. The wind briskly breezes restlessly too calmly and coolly as it positions itself everywhere. They are unaware of how gentle the breeze is as it touches their faces. While their faces feel the soothing touch of the night breeze, they somehow know it would be a long time until they feel this again. This cool pleasant breeze may be the thing most tangible to them, but it won't be long that this cool, pleasant breeze may be well forgotten. Surely, part of the world has forgotten.

Carlos thinks to himself, it's quite a distinctly cool, calm night. Not too hot either. It's perfect. Not a cloud in sight. You could not see the stars, but blue, yellow and white ghostly lights looming blind them. But who wants to see the stars anyway. I mean, who would pay attention to them anymore? People used to pay attention, but that's before…

Remember when we were children (looking over at Ezekiel thinking to himself), I don't mean you and I. I mean in general as children (CCS thought to correct himself). We would stargaze into the night and number the stars. Afterwards, we named them as they appeared to us. Our friends would point out anxiously, the North Star. The North Star is the guide HOME! Well, today in our heavily technological dependent and lit up world – we forget this. We forget the existence of the North Star. We focus on what's in front of us or what's in our hands. We don't look up! We fail to think ahead – to question. We are so busy with technology or better yet, we are so absent minded to…We become part of the masses and agree and think as one people. Not for ourselves or as an individual, but for a PROGRAM!

Stars are but bright shadows in the night sky – memorised at the empty world. In my country, the stars quietly overlook a world inundated with red smoke that slavishly seeps into her every last pore. She is consumed by the very fuel that feeds on her inhabitants' life – their soul, their individuality, their conscious and their thoughts. As the red smoke savagely ravages on her inhabitants repeatedly, it becomes more enraged and hungrier each time. Her inhabitants' spirit becomes hopeless and lethargic, and their heart blackened with hatred and loneliness. The stars in the States don't memorise at a world inundated with red smoke that slavishly seeps into her very last pore. These stars memorise at a world inundated with opportunity, and her inhabitants are free to capture whatever opportunity they want. They capture any dream dreamt of; any creative idea they desire to create or any possibility to be whoever they want. This is freedom my country once had but has been defeated by a red and dark monster. A red and dark monster that even Annemarie Johansen would be afraid to confront, let alone accept as a real monster, not as something imaginary in fairy tales. Though, Annemarie Johansen persevered in a hopeless, dark time – when Hitler murdered Jews and others in concentration camps in World War II. It was through community, faith and hope that Annemarie Johansen survived to tell her story. I suppose it will be faith too that will give people the courage to tell their story.

The stars are bight shadows in the empty night sky and much – much more too! Stars in the States are a hope for a brighter path to travel on. It is so in my country; stars are *hope*. The only difference is here, we see them; in my country, all you see in the sky is nothingness – just darkness – a darkness of red smoke. Hope is hiding or *dead* behind this treacherous red smoke. This red smoke is now a permanent stain much like blood on white shirts that cannot be washed away. It doesn't even fade. No matter how much you wash and scrub these shirts – the *blood* doesn't wash away! It serves as a reminder of the event that created the bloodstained shirts. Forever tattooed in time and in our memories. It becomes the thing we are most scared of…if it were our blood – our precious *blood,* what would have had happened to us, *death* or something worse? Just as Lady Macbeth attempts to repeatedly wash the blood from her hands and the spots from her clothes, so too do Venezuelans' blood not wash out from their hand, their clothes and their families' minds.

This is what Carlos and Ezekiel's eyes see as they look up in the sky towards the heavens and beyond numbering the stars. Ezekiel views a world filled with potential and opportunity for all people. Carlos sees a world filled with potential and opportunity but masked by red smoke that has caused enteral pouring blood and enteral plaguing torment.

The sky is freedom. It's not bound or changed down by propaganda, lies, deception and emptiness. It is limitless – freedom waiting to be experienced.

Carlos briskly stands upright while the cool soothing winds gently touch his face. This is the first time he is aware of the wind.

"Ahh…I need to stand for a minute. I have been sitting on this rash, splintery bench for exactly 22 minutes and forty-one seconds," he announced to Ezekiel.

Ezekiel replies with a smile in return. His simile is a contradiction. It means to be pleasant, but awkwardly resembling his anxiety going to Venezuela.

"Are you nervous, Ezekiel?"

Ezekiel hesitatingly answers Carlos' question, calculating his next words precisely.

"I'm a little nervous. I don't know what to expect. I have been to South America four times before. But this time it's different. I haven't been to a country that has folded or as you put it, *turned red*. Both by blood and smoke."

Carlos Christian Santos cautiously sits down as if he was being careful not to aggravate the left side of his chest. On an occasion, he favours the left side of his chest indicating pain still lingering from his past. While he sits on the rash, splintery bench once again, he faces Ezekiel to let him know that he is ready to listen and that he can return eye contact. Ezekiel's deep hazel eyes, filled with much thought and anxiety, engage with CCS' determined and confident eyes clouded with years of sadness, as the two friends shortly begin conversing.

"Yes. It's quite normal to feel anxious. Venezuela is a beautiful country, little Venice as tourists call it. You'll see. Then, on the other hand, I don't know how much you'd get to *see*. Remember, you wanted to go to have this experience," stated Carlos.

"I know. I want to go. I need to understand. After all, Venezuela is our sister country in the Americas of whom calls for help in distress."

"You have any doubts?" responded Carlos.

"No. Will we be safe? I mean when we get there, should I expect the worst?"

"Expect the good and the bad. You've been to other South American countries before. It's similar in culture. We are friendly and happy people. Maybe a little too lazy. However, it's different I'm not just talking about the culture. I'm also referring to our system of government. It was not always like this. We used to be like the United States. But what the people remember for 25 years is our current government, the insurrection of the 4-F Program, the birth of the Chavistas."

"I'm well informed about the tainted and tragic system that is called a government there. My mind is clear and waiting to be filled with possible adventures. I'm here to be objective. At times, I guess, it will be fair to say I can expect and other times, I won't be able to expect. Is this fair to say?" anxiously remarked Ezekiel.

"Keep an opened mind. But also be aware of your surroundings."

"Like in any culture or foreign place you visit, you should always be aware. It doesn't matter where you are or the time of day. You should always know who's who and what's what," stated Ezekiel.

"Yes, but here, in Venezuela, you have to be extremely aware of your surroundings. Like all Venezuelans, they don't take one step before thinking twice…they are sure that's the step to take. Any misconstrued words or miscalculated choices will lead to a bullet in your head or if not a bullet, the thought that you wish you were dead," responded Carlos.

"You mean, be especially cautious of the Collectives," whispered Ezekiel.

"Why are you whispering?"

"I thought, we shouldn't mention *them*!"

"That's true, but only when you're in Venezuela or on the border of Colombia," remarked Carlos.

"I understand, bro."

"Remember though, the Collectives are only one part of *them*. Keep your eyes open, ears at the ready, head clear and quick to react smartly if needed," responded Carlos.

"Get ready!"

"Don't worry. I will."

"I mean to say, are you ready to board the train; it's already here."

"It's four-thirty. The train is early. It's not usually early," replied Ezekiel.

"We don't want to miss our flight, do we? So it's a good thing that it is early. You know how airports are. Security checks are exhausting. You need a pot of coffee just to get through them. How about the flights? There are always problems. Remember while I was in Venezuela working with the V's, you were travelling to Chile."

"Yeah, yeah, I remember," stated Ezekiel.

"And you haven't quite told me what have caused the frequent visits after you have left in 2008?"

Carlos hastily re-accounts when Ezekiel missed his plane to Chile to avoid his question.

"Your plane was delayed two hours because of fuelling issues and because somebody wanted to smoke in the plane's laboratory."

While Carlos hastily follows up on Ezekiel's travels to Chile, he looks down at his hands quickly, (just enough to avoid Ezekiel's attention of his actions) to a locket that seems to have a picture of a woman.

"Yeah, fuck that shit. That was irritating," exclaimed Ezekiel.

"Because of the stupid asshole, I missed my connecting flight. So, I spent the night in a dinge, prostitute and roach-ridden looking hotel in Miami. The only one apparently available, claimed the airline company. Which of course was untrue. The airline just didn't want to spend the money. CHEAP BASTERS! Then I missed a day and a half in Chile."

"Yeah and…" nodded Carlos.

"No, now I'm pissed off. Now, you had to bring that shit up. Because Chile meant everything to me because of my partner. He was visiting his family. I was supposed to surprise him. But all that shit just fell through because of the stupid plane and the stupid asshole."

A long pause followed. Carlos knew not to interrupt. *Americans*, he thought, *they are always emotionally attached to the past. They should live life more in the present. See, this is why Americans are always unhappy because they dwell on the past and that they always work. They seem not to have time to relax or have time for their loved ones.*

"But all was good in the end," calmly stated Ezekiel.

Both Carlos and Ezekiel thought, perhaps it might be a great idea to actually miss their flight. What they don't know is, they'll be entering the mouth of hell where its furious reddish fire has engulfed much of CCS' homeland; where Ezekiel will forever be lost in time when he enters the *capitol*. Ezekiel will lose himself there. If he makes it through alive, he will be a changed person. Not for the better, only for the worst. Carlos, on the other hand, was already forced to sell his soul to his maker's counterpart – *Diablo*. So he has nothing to lose, only his life. But what's his life worth without his soul, anyway?

Carlos and Ezekiel's feet feel the rough and prickly ground as it trembles with fear of the passing train. Their feet taste the pungent and spoiled taste of the ground that has been victimised by both people and trains. Not realising any of this or the musty stench of rotting lives soaking in the air, clouds of ambiguity, insecurity, rage and pandemonium begin to deluge unwelcomingly in the night sky. After *it* happens, the enraged sky looks down to the empty ground to only see footsteps left behind.

"Goodbye 30th Street Station. Goodbye Philadelphia. Goodbye, the United States. Goodbye to all," stated Ezekiel as he and Carlos boarded the train.

One of the middle-aged, scruff ticket inspectors stated jokingly, "Alright ladies! You can finish your dull conversations on the sleepy train as one of my colleagues or I come to collect your ticket. All aboard to the airport!"

The black and red colour steel-plated monster stretches its claw legged feet on the aged rusted tracks, as it growls to a halt at the next platform. It overlooks you with intimidation as its evil, sinister laugh darkens with anger while it nears you. Do you continue to stand with pride and your head held high towards the stars and heavens or do you falter into a cradle, falling beneath its endless shadow, while it surpasses every fragment of your body and soul, as many Venezuelans fall *victim* to?

It's a ferocious beast too, that snatches anyone who approaches its wide, pitiless, enormous mouth. It'll devour you whole once you've entered inside without second questioning, whether you're tasteful or tasteless. Its only obligation – to shred into nothingness, molecule and atom, any person it comes into contact. To devour as many people at every platform its bottomless stomach holds. When inside, it seems to be gentle and soothing, as if it were a mother tending to her hurt or sick children. But once inside, there's no escaping until your final destination. It's fine. You begin to rationalise that it is not all that bad to show confidence to the other passengers. Though, who knows if you'll ever reach your destination? Sometimes or almost always, the monster stalls and rests its black and red ageless and boundless body longer and longer at each platform to ensure its passengers or *victims* panic, until they are absent of confidence.

Sitting in its jagged toothed seats, you don't feel it ripping and tearing your emotions to shreds. You think you're comfortable sitting there while your thoughts wander through your listening of music, reading a book or engaging in a scintillating conversation with a person you've met for the very first time. You falsely know, you'll reach your final destination, which you call sanctuary.

It rashly and harshly shuts its enormous mouth sounding, *BOOM! BOOM! THUMP! THUMP!* The monster hails in excitement as it zooms from the platform and into the distance, fading into the background of time. Their departure represents the lives they must leave behind, because who knows when they will see those lives again.

Chapter 4

Harvest

BANG! *BANG*! Shots fired. The door to my home shortly crumbles to the ground.

"GET ON THE GROUND – DO IT NOW!"

Giant and ceaseless *Guardia* voices shout and bark at Mama, Grandma, my brother and my sister as I am ordered to fall on my knees and interlace my fingers behind my head.

These voices are faded echoes for my family, but for me, these are silent sirens tattooed in my head – a constant reminder of what happened *that* day. What happened *that* day – it doesn't let you forget. I am constrained by its memory; troubled that it may happen once more.

They have stripped me, kidnapped me and brutally snatched me from my *familia*. I am a rabid animal longing to be put down after a violent string of attacks, feeding off of bystanders in public parks, or a ruthless murderer who just had escaped maximum-security prison to go on another rampage because some voice inside his head told him so. To *these* voices, that's all that I am – a rabid animal and a ruthless murderer.

I am none of these things!

This was the last I saw of my family and my last day as a child. This is what I remember of my childhood, as the training and being a soldier forges a new me – a new Carlos Christian Santos.

It was like any ordinary morning in the Santos house – *desayuno* or breakfast as North Americans call it. Being a Santos means you can't be lazy and miss out on any opportunity to eat. *Desayuno* is especially a sacred time you don't want to be late for. When Grandma and Mama shout, *Desayuno esta listo*, you better have been prepared to run to the breakfast table before any other Santos. If just one Santos gets there first, forget it! The *arepas* are already gone!

Grandma and Mama always make the best *arepas asadas*. Grandma, before she married Grandpa, had spent much of her time in Maracaibo. She and Grandpa immigrated there. The *arepas* in Maracaibo are known as *frito y dulce*, which means fried and sweet. On the other hand, the *arepas* Mama makes are traditional Caracas ones, which are cooked on a griddle until golden brown. Mama and Papa spent much of their time here, in Caracas where I'm from. Mama moved from Maracaibo to Caracas to find work. *Esperanza en la ciudad grande*, as Mama always says, which means hope in the big city.

DELICIOUS GOODNESS! That's how I describe Grandma and Mama's *arepas*. When you put the flaky, firm cornbread inside your mouth, it explodes with robust flavours. Its smooth and full-bodied texture blissfully satisfies your mouth instantly. After one scrumptious bite, your mouth painfully craves more. The sight of them alone, makes your mouth salivate and taste buds sing like *Las Turpiales*. You can't help yourself to have just one. How could you?

And Grandma makes the best ones too. I'm not just saying this. And I don't just say this to win her good side because if I do, she would always give me 20 extra bolivares each week – to buy something nice for the ladies. She would always whisper that in my ear, *compra algo hermoso para las niñas*. But truthfully, she makes the best ones. From what I remember – what Grandpa always used to tell me before I go to bed is that Grandma always played in the casino and she would give whatever winnings she had to the people who lose. Well, there was this one guy who Grandma always gave money to and whom Grandma later caught on to, would intentionally lose. Grandma would always deny it, but the guy thought she is *bonita*. Because of her generosity, he one day taught her how to make *special* fried sweet *arepas* that only a few Venezuelan elders knew. Grandma would never reveal this to any family member, not even to Mama. She would always say the secret is in one *special* ingredient. Trust me; these are the best-kept secrets. Nobody minds what the *special* ingredient is; the only concern is that it's delicious.

Mama's *arepas* are the best too. They are always crispy. Each time you take one bite, they melt in your mouth into soft, chewy pieces that make your stomach experience ecstasy. This high is but a millisecond. You know after one, you can't help but have another and experience the same ecstasy. Only this time you will think it is more sensational and intense.

Both Grandma and Mama's *arepas* are orgasmic. It's bliss in your mouth. Any *arepas*, *con queso* (with cheese), *con arroz* (with rice), *con carne res* (with beef) or *con pollo* (with chicken) and many more, is bliss waiting to be bitten into. Your stomach always experiences ecstasy from its orgasmic flavours every time your teeth sinks into just a piece of *arepa*.

Traditionally, in the Santos house and in much of Venezuela, during *desayuno*, we eat *arepas* with butter in the left hand and in the right hand; we have our fork filled with food. The food at this time usually varies. In our home, we have eggs, rice, black beans, chicken, beef and vegetables. Afterwards, we eat pineapple, cantaloupe and watermelon to digest the breakfast we just have eaten. The fruit pleasantly cools your stomach after the blissful experience. Fruit is always eaten last. It cleans your palate, that way in a few short hours it's time to eat again.

The smell of freshly brewed coffee always wakes up any Santos. You know if the pot of coffee is brewing, *desayuno* is near. Bold, zesty, rich aromas invite your taste buds to ache in pleasure. These aromas permeate throughout the house like guests at parties mingle with each other. It rhythmically hovers gently through each room to wake each Santos from their deep slumber. Its tender, motherly touch caringly glides through each Santos' soft skin as it slowly and rhythmically hovers back to the kitchen where Grandma and Mama's presence is alive. Each morning, the pleasant aroma differ from the person making it. Each brewed coffee has its personal flavour.

Every morning, music plays in the background. This morning, Romeo Santos' music is playing. It must have been Mama's turn to choose the music. I thought to myself, as the lyrics become familiar memories – love, conflict, and family. She, since I can remember, chooses the same song – her favourite one – *Yo Tambien*. It pleasantly reminds her of how she met Papa; how he swept her off her feet with one Venezuelan hot dog and a night at one of our national baseball games.

Papa seduced Mama with *Bachata*. That's how he got her to have a Venezuelan hot dog with him. *Bachata* has many variations today, such as *Bachata* Salsa, *Bachata* Urban, but then it was a traditional eight beat dance with two measures. Every morning they dance together before Papa goes to work. I hear the beat travelling down the hallway (1, 2, 3, tap, 5, 6, 7, tap). *Bachata* became a traditional dance at nightclubs in Venezuela. Every time I go to one, I see a different variation, a variation I can't help but learn and master myself.

Music in our house uplifts the soul and soothes the wounds of yesterday. It frees the mind from all obstacles and troubles that may lead it astray. Music is our quiet place – a place nobody enters but ourselves. Today, somehow, was different. I am estranged from what is happening around me. I'm isolated in a world not of my own, a world I know nothing of, and a world I know not how I got there. *Something is wrong*, I thought to myself. I don't know what it is. All I know is that it is an annoying splinter that won't go away and each time I attempt to answer what is wrong, the splinter becomes more maddening to itch. My body is here, ready to run for *desayuno* but my mind is elsewhere – *detached*. You know something is bothering you, but you don't know what. You feel something *strange* is going to occur, but you let it go. Only thinking that it is the remnants of the ten *Solera Verdes* and the three vodka drinks you ingested the night before.

Is it a hangover? I thought to myself. I didn't drink much. I know what hangovers are. Trust me, I drink more then I should, but YOLO! So, I'll tell you this one story. It was last summer when I turned sixteen and when the government announced its new policies. I was over at my friend's house and it all started out with some *vino*.

Then Jonny said, "Let's do vodka shots," so I did. We must have had at least ten shots. Then I said to myself, *I need some Solera Verde to make me not drunk anymore*. Truthfully, after ten shots they started to taste like sour apples freshly baked in apple pies. So I had about five *Soleras* to wash the pungent stale taste from my mouth.

Then Rafael said, "Let's go to the nightclub."

From there, I don't remember. I remember from what Jonny and Rafael told me, once I got home, I was sleeping in Jonny's bathroom with my head by the toilet. Rafael told me, though I can't doubt his story because it sounds like me. After I had the Cacique with coke while dancing, in the herd of people, I started to pass out. Luckily, I was next to Jonny who caught me. Hangovers are punches to the head, POP – POP – POP, that continue to throb in tormented agony after an hour. No amount of medication could ease its throbbing.

It's a weird feeling and not the good kind of weird either. I feel as if I had this same exact experience, waking up where my body is here, but my mind isn't. It feels familiar, but I know today is a different day and I know that it would be impossible for me or for anyone else to have experienced the same exact day, twice. We, like North Americans, call it *Déjà vu.*

Something is going to happen today, but I don't know what. Every time I feel this way, I usually vomit the *Solera Verde* and vodka I had ingested the night before. I thought to myself while getting out of bed to get dressed, *Great! I'm going to puke at Desayuno. That's all that needs to happen. I'll be in bigger trouble. More trouble than listening to my older brother, Jorge who said I should take the car for a joy ride and I did. If this happens, forget it, I'll forever be a prisoner in my home. I will forever be a prisoner in my own life.*

It's zero six hundred. While looking out my window, *another perfect day in Venezuela*, I thought, in spite of the honking, beeping, zooming and rumbling outside. We *Caraqueños* like to try to start our weekdays early. The weekends, well, that's different. So, the endless traffic begins to disperse throughout the city.

The sun is out this morning, unlike most mornings. Grey blankets the sun, only to watch rain trampling on the people. *Los Caraqueños*, which means people of Caracas, carelessly go about their business as if nothing is happening any time it rains. The fact is *los Caraqueños* pay little attention to any change. The only thought they have every morning is finding work. Today wasn't like all other days in Caracas. The sun is behind thinly stretched clouds. No one can see much of it due to the monstrous giants that cover its view. All that anyone sees are the bright rays glittering off of the monstrous giants.

All the family is together this week. Jorge has spent the weekend with us and Arianna is travelling back to Nebraska today. This is the second time I have seen her. She visits occasionally. I have an hour to get ready before Grandma and Mama call *desayuno*. I want to be the first today as usual. Yesterday, I missed out on the *arepas* because my oldest brother and oldest sister did a prank on me. They decided to barricade my door, but once I got it open, a half-filled bucket of sour milk poured on my head. So I spent another thirty minutes washing up and changing. By the time I got there, there were only a few left. So, I decided I would give the last of them to Lucia and Luis. This time, I'm ready. My door's open. I will have my *arepas* today. Sweet, sweet *arepas*! Nothing will stop me. No pranks will get in my way. Not today.

I looked down the hall stealthily to see if Jorge, Arianna, Luis and Lucia are sleeping, as a soldier who is passing by enemy territory to get to his combat outpost would do. With much caution and discernment, I turn my head to see whether they are still in their rooms. They are. This is great. I can get ready in peace, without any disturbance.

The hardest part about waking up is deciding what to wear and making sure my hair is perfect for Fernanda, a girl I'm going to ask to go to the nightclub with me this weekend. I have to make a great impression today. So, what should I wear? That's the first obstacle I have to defeat. What I wear determines how my hair has to go. Messy, spiked, flat or somewhere in the middle or something new.

My room is a mess. Mama is going to have a fit, tell me to clean it then kill me and then bring me back to life so that she can give me a beating. She always says, *voy a golpear su culo*, which means, I'm going to beat your ass. Maybe that's why I have a difficult time staying focused because my room is cluttered – always! Or I just can't seem to find where all my shit should go. It's easier for me to have my clothes out than away. I know where to find them and I know which ones are the nice clothes. My not so nice clothes are hidden in my closet. You know the ones that you will wear to a nightclub or casino or to relax with friends. The ones, the nice ones, are always on my bed. These ones, I always want to wear, especially when I want to ask a girl to go to a nightclub or to get something to eat – like Fernanda.

Ah, Fernanda. She's my *esperanza* (hope), my *diosa* (goddess). She's like *Susy*, but unlike *Susy*, she wouldn't melt in your mouth, especially when you kiss her. Her jet-black hair would make me lose consciousness. She could, if she wanted, be a Venezuelan model.

I have to make a great impression. I try to every day. This day though, I have to sweep her off her feet. She has to say yes. Do I act this way towards every beautiful girl? Yes, but with Fernanda it's different. All guys say that it's different, but with her, it is. I mean it; it is different. Every time I converse with her, I feel connected. I feel like she and I met in another life or something like that. She gets me even my stupid jokes. And she stands up for me when my classmates call me Carlito. I tell them to stop, but they don't listen to me. When Fernanda is there, they listen to her. Fernanda is new to the school. She transferred from *El Colegio Christo Rey de los Estudios Academicos* to our school *El Colegio Cristiano de Academicos Medias* at the beginning of this year. I was the first person to say *hola* (Hi) to her because I helped her find where she could find her classes. At that moment, I didn't think anything of it, until recently. I now do – it must have been fate. Why you may ask? We have almost every class together, except for Math. That class is at a different period but with the same professor. So, you see, she isn't just another girl I like – SHE CAN'T BE! She and I connect. We get each other.

I should get back to deciding what to wear. How am I going to impress Fernanda today? You know, every day I wake up with that phrase in my head, *how am I going to impress Fernanda today?* But today is a special day. So I have to look more than my best, more than handsome. Well, I should decide on something to wear. If don't, I'm going to be lazy and miss *desayuno*. I don't want to miss out on the *arepas*.

Should I wear the light blue or dark blue Hollister jeans? *Dark blue,* I thought to myself. Now for the shirt. A black Hollister shirt or a white-and-blue H&M collar shirt or the red-striped long sleeve H & M shirt. Carlito thinks to himself, this is harder than cleaning his room and possibly harder than asking Fernanda out to the nightclub. Carlito continued relentlessly in his head what he wanted to wear.

For thirty-five minutes, Carlito tried on the outfits and looked at himself in his mirror each time to see which outfit would fit for today. After much careful thought about how he would present himself to Fernanda, he decided to go with a simple but confident outfit. He decided to wear the black Hollister shirt, the medium dark blue Gap jeans and white and blue Adidas shoes. Carlito thinks aloud, *I know I said I was going to wear the dark blue Hollister jeans, but the dark blue Gap ones look better on me as I continue to look in the mirror for this special day.*

My hair, he thought to himself, *is going to be a problem*. This is another obstacle, I'm going to have to fix. But I have an idea of how to fix it. I will use little gel first to see whether the hairstyle is appropriate for what I have on, then if so, I can begin styling. This is what I have to do every day because I can never decide on a hairstyle. My hair has to be just right all the time, especially this time! Sometimes both hairstyles go well with the outfit I have on. I compromise at that moment. I still think, after comparing the two, getting dressed and styling hair, getting dressed is more difficult. Carlito goes through this just about every time, but he tenaciously refuses to pay any mind to it.

Much of the time when Carlito wears a simple but confident outfit, he wears his hair up. After twenty minutes of meticulously placing each hair follicle in its correct position, as if one misplaced hair follicle would collapse the whole structure, he's ready to ask Fernanda to go to the nightclub. Carlito gives himself one more look in the mirror to view the entire ensemble, followed by a nod to reassure himself he's handsome.

He quietly leaps through the hallway, not to disturb his brothers and sisters. Cautiously, Carlito makes his way to breakfast before the *announcement sounds*.

He smiles brightly at Grandma. Mama attempts not to reveal his honest excitement and euphoria about Fernanda.

"Good morning, Grandma and Mama," whispers Carlito.

"Who's the handsome devil?" Grandma excitedly shouts.

Grandma reaches across to Carlito to give him a kiss. He childishly attempts to pull away from her kiss, but it was already too late. These memories, some disturbing and some memorable, make grandma who she is. The difference between her and younger Venezuelans is that she has experience in understanding her memories and how they make us who we are and how we changed. Grandma reflects on the time when Venezuela wasn't occupied or infected by the Red Scare. She accounts in the beginning that everyone believed in the Program, but now it changed – it changed into the Red Scare. This reflection is just brief.

"Okay. Grandma. I know I look nice. Love you too, Grandma."

"Who's the lucky girl this time? You have something special for her."

"No, there's no girl," Carlito states funnily as he tries not to laugh.

"I know that look on your face. You can't hide it. Your smile is too bright today. I smell the Aqua di Gio on you too."

"Yes, Grandma. There's a girl. I'm going to ask her if she wants to go to the nightclub with me," whispered Carlito. Carlito didn't tell her that the girl is Fernanda though. Everyone in the Santos house knows about Fernanda because Carlito rants about her but still has not yet told her how he feels about her.

Granma reaches in her pocket. Her hands rummage through her pockets as if her pockets were holding a lifetime of memories, careful to pull out the right one. She finds her money neatly tied together with a rubber band. She counts out two-fifty bolivares.

"I know it's a little much. But it seems you like this girl. Take her somewhere nice," Grandma stated. She quickly but gently touches Carlito's chin and kisses his forehead.

"Well, Grandma, thank you very much. You don't have to." He gives his Grandma a hug like it would be the last time he would get to hug her.

Carlito's mom interjects abruptly to scold him for taking money without earning it. This isn't uncommon in the Santos house. Grandma gives money to her grandchildren all the time. This wasn't the problem. Because Carlito hasn't cleaned his room and finished his school writing project, Mama becomes enraged.

"Mom!" exclaimed Carlito's mom.

"Carlos, have you cleaned your room before taking Grandma's money?"

"Sort of, Mama."

"Let me fill this in. You have tossed your dirty clothes in the laundry basket and shoved your clean clothes in whatever drawer they fit in to."

"Yes, but I neatly made my bed."

"Leave the boy be. He'll clean his room after school, right *papi*?" Grandma says.

"The first thing when I get into the door. I'm going to correctly clean my room."

"Alright, Carlos. You are always truthful. You can keep the money. But if you don't clean…"

"I will, Mama." He jumps from his seat to give his Mama a hug and kiss too.

The aged cherry wood table is bare until food keeps it company. Its tired legs manage to keep it standing after twenty-five years. Food begins to fill the table, much like furniture fills empty rooms. *Arepas* are always placed in the middle of the table as to attract everyone's attention and to symbolise its significance. Grandma and Mama always have an extra bowl tidily tuck away, away from the overwhelming crowd of hands that snatch them in two minutes. These are kept hidden until the first bowl empties. Three coffee mugs are always placed on the table inviting Jorge, Arianna and Carlito into the new day.

Carlito eagerly waits for Grandma and Mama's announcement to chime, not just breakfast but the beginning of a new day – a new day revealed through breakfast. Already his hands embrace the warm cup of *café negra*. It is acceptance and love in a cup. The friendly warmth of the cup brings his hands closer to it as it majestically soothes the muscles and bones of his restless and tense hands. The warmth is more vivid today than other days. This is the day he's going to ask Fernanda to go to the nightclub and a day he feels he has experienced before. While his hands begin to relax, his senses are invigorated by the bold zesty smell and taste. Each sip rejuvenates Carlos, so that he experiences this perfect day, a day familiar and mysterious to him.

Grandma and Mama shout *desayuno esta listo*.

Elephants stampede to the breakfast table. Their titan-like footsteps fiercely make the ground tremble, hurriedly sounding through each room of the house as they recklessly make their way to the breakfast table. Their voices begin to shout frantically, but cannot be understood as if these voices were part of many voices in an overcrowded room. You just hear the sound of chatter flowing abruptly. The sight of Jorge, Arianna, Luis and Lucia running is monstrous and chaotic. Race to the *arepas*. That's what Carlito calls it. Little did they pay attention to Carlito, who was at the table first, already accepting the new day. Little did Carlito know, a prank may await him. He thinks nothing of this.

"Good morning," everyone shouts with joy.

"Good morning, Carlito," Arianna shouts. While she passes by Carlito, she pets his head as if his hair is like a dog. Though, his hair is long enough that someone could mistake it for short fur belonging to a dog.

Carlito had no time to react when his oldest brother, Jorge, a few seconds later did the same thing. Luis and Lucia, opposite of each other, couldn't help but laugh. They knew that this was a prank. Arianna and Jorge's hands were wet with blue hair dye, conspicuously hidden from Carlito's sight.

"Quit it, *maricos* (gays). Why does everyone call me Carlito? I hate that," Carlito angrily shouts.

"You're hair looks worse than how you had it," Lucia laughs.

"Yeah, it looks like a wet dog," Luis shouts.

"Yeah, I think it may be turning blue too," Lucia giggles.

"You should check yourself in the mirror, bro," Luis quickly mentions.

"I see what this is. All of you are trying to make me leave the breakfast table so I wouldn't have any *arepas*. I'm not falling for it. I'll fix my hair later. If it's blue I'll kill all of you *micros,* especially if it doesn't wash out."

All shout out, "Carlito has wet blue dog hair. You look hideous."

"Stop calling me Carlito. So what if I don't weigh as much as you, Jorge or that I don't score as many points in football as all of you do. It doesn't make me small – oh, look fired eggs and peppers. These smell awfully great today. I'm sure they are even better once they are in my stomach."

Grandma precisely and sternly walks over to the table – her shadow overlooks everyone sitting. Suddenly, the room is silenced. All you could hear were distant and faded sounds playing from Romeo Santos. She knew, like Mama did, that Carlito's hair was hideous, but failed to mention it as to avoid a lasting confutation and feud. She, like Mama, wanted to laugh because the pranks remind her of her own distant but unforgotten long travelled childhood. She didn't laugh.

"You can joke around with Carlos. But don't make him go off topic. You know how easy he loses his train of thought. It's not healthy for him because you know what happened yesterday when you did that at dinner. His nose started to bleed, mostly from the medication."

"Yeah, but…" someone started. Their voice was interrupted by Grandma's soul gazing glare. This wasn't mentioned again.

"Carlos, don't forget to take your medicine. The doctor says you're doing much better on this strand than the one before," states Mama.

"I know, Mama. I'll take it right before I leave the breakfast table," Carlito hesitantly announces to avoid any comments that may follow from Jorge, Arianna, Luis or Lucia.

Their voices remained stationary due to Grandma's ghostly hold on their next words.

Jorge states with a mouth half full and coffee in one hand and a buttered *arepa* in the other, "little sis, *listo.* I'll give you a ride to the airport. After that, I have to go to the University because I have to go by the economics department to hand in my thesis on, *The dangers of a single hand in markets – why governments solely can't manage nor solve economic reconstruction and stability*, for review. I hope they approve it so I can get out of *here.*"

"Yeah. I'll be ready in just a minute, Jorge. Let me quickly finish my plate of food," Arianna stated.

"Always running around, seems like he's not Venezuelan at times," Arianna mutters under her breath.

"Jorge, don't forget to pick up chicken from the store if there's any. If not, I'll see if I can make some burgers from the little meat I have left. You can stay for dinner tonight if you like, Jorge," states Mama.

The room suddenly quiets down as Luis turns off the music and turns the news station on VTVX. The silence creates a deathly chill in the room that has everyone shivering for a few seconds. When the news is turned on, it's never worth listening to.

"Luis, please turn this off? You know how everyone feels about it," states Mama.

"I'm sorry, Mama, but my and Lucia's history teacher mentioned that the *government* is supposed to announce its new policies. It's in everyone's best interest to listen to it even if they don't listen to the president's speech tonight."

The news broadcasts the following announcement: *It has been several months since our humbly loved President Chava was sworn into office for his second term and the details concerning his country reform agenda were discussed. We like to pay tribute to his succession with a moment of silence before beginning his announcement this morning. This evening he will be announcing policies that will come into effect immediately – starting now. The policies that will be announced are on poverty, oil, education and defence. All Venezuelans are expected to follow. If any grievance to these policies should occur, they will be dealt with strictly and as a matter of terrorism.*

Has listening to the news made everyone in the house more or less prepared to what is about to happen next? Probably not. How can they? How can anyone be prepared?

"What could he possibly institute now?" Luis shouts.

"A further decrease in oil, more subsidies for the poor and more *Guardais* parading the streets," states Jorge, sarcastically.

"Sis, *listo.*"

"Let's go, Jorge. I don't want to be late."

"Late! When's your flight? Isn't it later in the day? And now you want to rush out?"

"Yeah. I know. You know airports! If you are not there two hours before your scheduled flight, they sell it. I just kind of just remembered that."

"Women, always thinking of things at the last minute," Jorge whispers under his breath.

"Feliz Dia."

"Be safe and have fun. Don't forget the…" Mom shouts, but couldn't speak the last few, but important, words regarding dinner tonight while the front door closes with rage.

Jorge and Arianna see the *Guardias* on the street as they make their way to the car. They, like many others, would supposedly never think of the unthinkable events that are soon to occur. The unthinkable would be a new written chapter in history – a history that would daunt Venezuelans for years to come.

Inconceivable history unfolds to a day that later everyone will know as *Liberacón Dia (*Liberation Day).

Buses, Humvees and SUVs that *they* drove in, blackened the sun and uprooted the ground. Nature once undisturbed, now disturbed. The earth soiled. The trees poisoned. The grass withered. Nature and its omnipresence were displaced from these uninvited guests. Their heavy boots occupied every corner of every street. Their red and blue bandanas marked their allegiance and cause to why they are here. It gives them purpose and empowers them to carry out their orders. Orders that they are hesitant to carry out, but unnervingly do. Their faces paint a different emotion, an emotion of sternness. Anyone could tell the *Guardias* reluctantly carried out their assignment of occupying the streets by their unhidden, yet subtle body language. For the *Guardias* were premature to follow the allegiance of Commandant Chava, but soon learned. These were the guardians that everyone knew. The National Army the government sent to safeguard the public. The first people who saw them swarm the streets whispered to their neighbours, *they are finally here. They are here. We are saved.* What a few people knew became many in the matter of a few minutes.

Jorge and Arianna didn't think about how they were the prosecutors and not the guardians that day. They just kept walking like everyone else – they keep walking.

It wasn't long after the announcement that this strange, eerie feeling Carlito had, became unimaginably real. Carlito didn't think much of this. While Jorge and Arianna just left, this gave Carlito the opportunity to take his medicine and fix his hair. He disliked disgustingly taking his ADD medication, as one symptom is nosebleeds. These are brief and minor ones. Though he hasn't taken it in two days, he may skip another day. What use would it be when he runs out of it? Refills are hard to find. He was unable to fix his hair due to the unforgettable thump and bang at the door. Suddenly, the sky stopped moving; even the butterflies stopped flying. The sun eclipsed. Everything in that moment stood still. Time forever frozen in its position.

The sky blackened and erupted with furry, as a storm was about to explode. All you could see though is RED before Carlito was driven off in the diabolic, bleak monster.

BANG! BANG! Shots fired. My door to my home shortly opens without an invitation. "GET ON THE GROUND – DO IT NOW!" Giant and ceaseless *Guardia* voices shout and bark at Mama, Grandma, my brother and my sister while their hideous, monstrous shadows unwelcomingly fill the room.

They shout in unison while looking over at Mama and Grandma, "It is best not to resist. We are here for only one purpose. However, incompliance results in being shot or injured harshly. Don't think we won't kill you. We are given orders to do so, if necessary. It is best then to give in and not fight it."

It wasn't long until guns quickly were pointed at them to show their testimony to keep their word. They too were nervous and doubting if what they have done is moral. They didn't think much of it, while the thought of thinking it was brushed off as if it never happened. They were trained well to do one thing – successfully complete each assignment.

I nervously turned around from the hallway to see what was happening. I thought to myself, sure the government desperately needs their taxes this month. It wasn't like this at all. A sharp, unforgettable pain travelled through my heart. I was frozen. My legs stuck under concrete. I had no use of my limbs...I saw *them*! Blood ooze from my nose. Slowly dripping on my white-and-blue Adidas shoes. My shoes and my home stained with my blood as I watched a nightmare unfold in front of me.

"WHERE'S THE BOY? THIS BOY!" Fiercely showing my family a crumbled photo of my national ID without regard to my life. Without a heartbeat passing, their unnerving, intimidating presence located me with their dark deep eyes as if I were a rabid animal or a ruthless murderer. Without any time to react to flee or fight back in some way, the cold-forged metal touches the back of my neck as I am ordered to fall on my knees and interlace my fingers behind my head.

Merciless, callous beasts (that's what they are) pillage my home, abducting me from life. These men are without humanity. There's nothing I could do. I'm helpless. I'm held prisoner within my country and by a government who is supposed to safeguard my life, let alone any life. I am abducted by the Chavistas, who sanctioned my own abduction by the very laws they have solely amended. At this moment, I knew what it was like to be nailed to a cross – hand and feet bound and mouth sewn closed by barbwire. I am sentenced to crucifixion without a trial, much like Christ. This time it is different. God couldn't save me. The devil itself accompanied me to my cross. The DEVIL was there! NOT GOD! I wonder has God forsaken me? Abandoned me from family? This is how the gun and handcuffs feel as they press against my warm, naked skin. These are nothing less than shackles. These shackles are placed on me carelessly, as I am now a prisoner of the government, waiting to be executed.

Where's my trial? My constitutional and unalienable rights, I thought to demand. This would be no use though. *They* were the lawmakers, the judges, the prosecutors and jurors. I am a victim, not a citizen of my country, Venezuela. *They* are the warrant that prosecutes life and sentences it to solitude.

I am 'an unwanted child', as *they* claimed while they fixed a black cloth over my head and then exiled me from family and life. My nose continues to bleed through the black, dark cloth; you hear their drops staining the floor. I forcefully leave behind a life I am unwelcomed to return.

Chapter 5
Forward Thinking

On the 8422 local Airport line, CCS' empty and sad eyes stare perplexedly into space. His mind is somewhere in the past. Recalling a vivid childhood memory. The past feels more real than the present. Surreal, he thought, as he begins to sit and unknowingly listen to the loud closing sound of the doors – BANG – BANG – THUMP –THUMP. He's unresponsive to Ezekiel's words until he snaps his fingers in front of him. Ezekiel's fingers seem to act as a device waking Carlos from hypnosis. Carlos' eyes begin to fill with light once again as they make their way back to the present.

"Hey my brother, CCS! Hey, are you okay?" Ezekiel says calmly as he snaps his fingers in front of him to wake him up.

This is not the first time Carlos has fallen into a trance where his mind takes him somewhere back to his past. Ezekiel is familiar with Carlos entering this catatonic state. He, however, never knows how to approach Carlos' state of being. The wrong move and BOOM, Carlos could snap and then not know why he snapped. When Ezekiel attempts to exit Carlos from this catatonic state, Carlos is a bomb waiting to explode. Any mishap or wrong manoeuvre, VOOMP – KABOOM, Carlos becomes an enemy. With caution, diligence and patience, Ezekiel diffuses the bomb. Sometimes Ezekiel fears to approach Carlos, so he allows him to go through the past and come back to the present on his own as he did this time. Ezekiel can only imagine what it's like to be somewhere where you either have no other choice but to be there or you're dragged somewhere and don't know why you're there, but only for an unfamiliar purpose. Ezekiel just imagines the monstrosity of being dragged forcefully back somewhere into the past and not know of its purpose. In that, he too becomes perplexed and maybe just as perplexed as Carlos.

"Yeah, my brother, I'm fine. I just escaped reality. I took an unscheduled vacation, that's all, my friend."

"I'm good. All is well," Carlos indicates with hesitation and bewilderment.

"Alright then. I was worried about you man. I did not know what was going on. I thought you were in some type of pain, trouble or whatever, because of your episode. It was almost like you were all doped out on drugs or something, but I know differently, of course," Ezekiel mentions sarcastically.

Carlos' words and thoughts are lost. He begins to slur some of them. He's confused about where he is. This is the time where Carlos feels he's in between the past and the present. Reality for him is much like scattered pieces of a thousand-piece puzzle. This moment of his slurring of words is much like when he has too many shots of *Santa Teresa Rum*.

"Nah, Nah. You're right Ezekiel. I was in one of my trances. And yes, it was emotionally and physically draining. But unlike other times, this one was rapid but very vivid. Vivid as usual."

"Luckily man hardly anyone is here, well except for two families in the back and two elderly people, because man, a stranger such as myself would think you have taken a narcotic or something like it with how you were acting. Something like a person turning into a creature of the undead or some crazy shit like that," Ezekiel mentions with humour.

Carlos attempts to smile in return, but his smile is one of pain.

"Remember to concentrate on where you are. Feel what's around you."

"Yeah, yeah. I know how to do that shit. But can you please hand me that water bottle?" Carlos mentions with hesitation and impediment to Ezekiel while he points to his backpack.

"Sure! Here you go. You wanted to tell me something before we got on the train. The train rudely interrupted our conversation. I mean we never got to finish. When you're ready, of course."

Babble and crackle of voices lurk in the midst of Carlos and Ezekiel's silence and arguably their confusion. The half-fringe empty train car of pedestrians overhears the two charmingly mature ladies' sharp faint conversation on social welfare in Philadelphia. Their conversation reveals that they have professions in social work or politics. Their views are vastly the same and different. Their conversation never answers each other's questions; rather their conversation dismantles each of their views on the issue. Ezekiel becomes intrigued by their conversation, so his attention is on the conversation and not on Carlos. Carlos, though he would never admit it, his attention is on the two women's conversation as well.

"I'm not insinuating that social welfare policy in Philadelphia is hindering people's ability to take stewardship of their actions. I'm pontificating that it's a flawed system."

"So, you are refuting that politics should entrust social workers to run social policy locally, such as public assistant, food stamps and alternative funding and the dreaded, ignored issue of public education? You are defending that social workers have more influence on the politics of policy?"

"To have a lasting difference in society and a difference that is going to matter for future generations then, yes, they have to be."

"Well, you also mention there's too much red tape around politics for social workers and their social policy ideologies to have an impact."

"Yes. I recall my choice of words. Frankly, politics should take a few steps to the side-lines when it comes to enriching all people across all communities. Sure politicians can design programs with the aid of social workers or other relevant experts, but they should not implement them or manage them."

"I hate to be the elephant in the room, but it won't happen. Politicians see all these issues you are pontificating as a political matter that needs to be restructured either by more money or little money. It's really a sad attempt to a means to an end. But I didn't say that and it would be hypocritical of me to say if I did."

"Politicians are not going to solve the discrepancies of social welfare policy in Philadelphia if they do not heed the expertise of those who research and practice it. As America competes with much of the world, America will crumble on the ground where it stands if it doesn't put expertise first without making hasty decisions based on acquiring influence or fattening their pockets. Moreover, I have mentioned that the social service system in Philadelphia is flawed because of two significant aspects that aren't taken into consideration: the wealth and being of families and secondary public education."

"This is a story for another day, my stop Eastwick is approaching. See you around City Hall! Yeah, the business of social welfare policy in Philadelphia is political – I should know."

The train screeches in discomfort not wanting to stop. A jerk follows as it suddenly does at Eastwick. While Carlos becomes more coherent, he looks over at the trees in the distant background. He is reminded of the *Uva de Playas* back home, but for him, as for all Venezuelans, home is a forgotten burial. The *Uva de Playas* today are not much to look at, just hollow beings. They restlessly sit on the blackened, tainted ground.

The *Uva de Playas* branch out to feel alive. They extend their arms to smell and breathe the gentle wind blowing copiously. Their arms connect together so that they have strength as one. They stand tall, so their necks reach the warmth of the sun. Sometimes the sun is too harsh. Their wavy and curly hair protects them, much like hats protect people's head in the high blistering-beating tropical sun. Their bottomless feet sink in the ground unbrokenly to hold the roots of the earth. The roots cling to the earth much like temperamental children clinging to mothers, not letting nor wanting to let go. They eat harmful toxins from the environment as it converts them into energy from the earth then expelling clean air for everyone to taste for their lungs.

The *Uva de Playas* were once like this – abundant and fertile. Now, they have become something else, something resembling a skeleton of their selves. Carlos' eyes reflect this as he pays attention to a lady exiting the train. Ezekiel's eyes reflect the opposite. He views abundant trees that gracefully give everyone breathable air. People either knowingly or unknowingly recognise how precious and fragile they are, so they take advantage of life. Without trees, the earth would be uninhabitable. Without regard to the environment, trees are murdered, as Carlos witnessed in his country.

"*Gracias para la agua.*" (Thanks for the water). Carlos states as he begins to regain focus of where he is and what he was doing prior to his episode.

"You're completely fine now? You are not going to suddenly go into a trance any time soon, are you? You are not going to turn into Mr Hyde to come to think of it. Are you?" Ezekiel cautiously states as he manages to carefully choose his words.

"I'm fine. As you know, I get like this often. As always, I hope I have not scared you? And I don't resemble Dr Jekyll or Mr Hyde."

"No, you haven't. I don't know what to expect from you when this happens. And you haven't had a trance for a while, so I do not know what to think. It is sort of becoming scary."

"Due to, in part, my coming back to Caracas after eight years. I have them subtly though, more when I dream actually."

Carlos quickly changes the subject to avoid discussing his nightmares, which he never discusses not even with Ezekiel. He wants to avoid a long drawn out conversation about what the nightmares feel like and how this happens, but not what they are about.

"But I now remember what I wanted to finish talking about before we boarded the train."

"Yeah, and what was that?"

"Once we land in Caracas, for the first stop of our trip, you have to know we will be in the mouth of the beast. Things are not what they seem there. You are going to see, for the most part, how it is like any other city in the States. IT IS NOT, THOUGH! You have to understand, you'll be in the world of the *Capitol*. There's everything, nothing and anything in between. Of course, the safest place for us is in the airport because we are entering through the international section. Once we exit or go to the other part of the airport…it's different – a different world not of its own origin, you will see."

"I thought you have said that the airport is outside the Capitol. Venezuelans say that the airport is in the capitol because it is easy for travellers or tourists to remember."

Before Carlos answers, Ezekiel abruptly clarifies his previous statement.

Ezekiel states with clarity and surprise, "but it's really not in the capitol."

"IT DOESN'T MATTER WHAT TRAVELLERS OR TOURISTS SAY. The *Capitol* is always near. Once you enter it, it will embrace you. It won't let you go. You have to be careful every time, everywhere. The *Capitol* is always there, waiting, lurking, stalking for any moment to capture you – to swallow you whole."

"Carlos, okay! I got your point!"

"Acting like a bitch. He's a paranoid child asking his guardians to check under his bed and in his closet to reassure himself there are no monsters," Ezekiel says under is breathe while avoiding Carlos' eyes.

"I just hope you don't make a mistake. I hope nothing happens. Remember, once we land, follow my lead. Whatever I say to do or to say, no matter how stupid it may seem, just make sure you follow."

"I will my bro. Don't worry."

"It's always important that you don't get lost. Well, this shouldn't happen anyway because you will be with me at all times. But if we get split up, stand where you are, I'll come and get you," Carlos states with assertion and command.

"Why would I get lost? And I wouldn't disobey you anyway. You're saying this as if we are going into battle near enemy lines. If you say this is what has to be done, I trust that. I trust you. I always have, my friend. Hey, remember that one time I told you that I got lost just travelling on the New York subway lines because I had to visit the Venezuelan Consulate?"

"Yeah, I remember. Let's get back to what I was saying which was…"

Before Carlos could finish his sentence, Ezekiel rudely interrupts Carlos, not to get him mad but to finish his thought.

"So, your country or I should say your government," (STUPID MABURRO…VENEZUELA IS NOT A TRICK!) Ezekiel was about to digress, but quickly collected his thoughts and sorted through them as if they were going to be recycled.

"…Your country is the only South American country that requires a one-year Visa just to travel there for one day. I had to go to the Venezuelan General Consulate to apply for the Visa. I didn't drive because fuck the traffic in New York. Travelling to New York wasn't bad, but riding on their subway trains, now that was like finding out at the last minute I have to go into work on my day off. I was running around without any direction. In fact, running around like my head was cut off and I'm frantically and eagerly trying to put it back on. Later, I found out, though I didn't have to take any train, I could have just walked from the train station, which is near Times Square. I wasted two hours because somehow I ended in Queens," Ezekiel states with excitement, rage and relief.

"Yes, I remember you told me that but at the time you were angrier," Carlos states as he tries to recall what he wanted to inform Ezekiel regarding entering the *Capitol*.

"I'm sorry, Carlos. I didn't mean to…" Ezekiel states with an apology.

"It's fine. This is what I wanted to finish informing you about Caracas," Carlos states as if he was giving Ezekiel his next military assignment.

"Good. It's important you are aware that you'll be in the *Capitol*. Expect anything and expect the unexpected. Anything is possible in the *Capitol*. It's the most populated city in my country. With that being said, it is the most dangerous city in my country. Everywhere you go you will always see someone and that someone will attempt to stop to ask you – to demand – to insist on something. Just keep walking and don't look back. Whatever you do, don't look back. Don't engage with anyone unless I tell you it is safe. Don't ever deviate from my instructions. It's for your own good. The *Capitol* is alive. They are watching you. There's no place to hide, run or escape. They are always there. There they are, lurking in the depth of every shadow. There they come, beneath the darkness with their hideous and countless eyes. It's the most dangerous city in the world. Think about your worst nightmares. They all come true in Caracas," Carlos states as if he were about to recall a traumatic event in his past but he suddenly catches himself before he does.

"I'm completely aware. I understand fully the situation, the risk and circumstances."

"The one thing a Venezuelan will know after one glance at you is that you are a gringo. This is a good thing and a bad thing. Just remember in Caracas, I lead you and you just follow me."

"Okay, my brother. I'll keep my eyes open. My ears will be at the ready. I will think twice before I take one step. And of course, I will follow your lead."

"Good! Any questions at this point? Have your emotions changed? Are you nervous?"

"No. And I'm not nervous. Maybe when I get there. But in this moment, I'm so happy that I can't believe I'm going to Venezuela, the mountain country. It will be good times."

"In many respects, I hope you have good times but then again, I'm unsure how much you are going to see that you shouldn't see but inevitably you are going to see."

"In short, my friend, I am objective to what will, may and is going to happen, while I'm in not just the capitol but in any city or state of Venezuela," Ezekiel indicates with frustration to move the conversation forward.

"Simply put, yes," Carlos states for the last time to reassure himself that Ezekiel is aware and if possible, ready.

The matured face and unkempt conductor announces deadly, *Terminal A, get out now or if you dare to stay, you walk back to wherever you need to go. This train is not a chariot; so don't act as if it is one.*

Carlos and Ezekiel begin to stand as the red steel-plated doors inhospitably and coldly open wide as if they were being released from confinement. Immediately, the approaching dawn sky aggravates their eyes, like prisoners escaping solitude. They each carried a backpack and suitcase, which resembles the life they can bring with them and the life they have to leave behind – a life anonymous. Their backpacks are weights on their shoulders, sluggishly and steadily running them down. Carlos' backpack is packed with cluttered emotions and broken memories of his past and present, which he attempts to return, is heavier than Ezekiel's backpack. Ezekiel's backpack is cluttered and disorganised with anxiety and apprehension as if the choices he is about to make are undoable mistakes; mistakes that have deadly consequences. But it is too late to turn away from them now. Their backpacks embrace their shoulders as they step from the train and onto Terminal A, where what will be familiar and unfamiliar and what seems to be isn't.

"I thought I told you to leave your phone at home. It's no use once we get to Venezuela. Your phone will be pretty much dead once we get there," Carlos shouts in surprise.

"Ahh Ummm. About that."

"And who are you texting anyway?"

"About that…after this text I won't use my phone; it will be switched off and buried in my bag. It'll lie dormant throughout our travels. By the way, the person who I was texting is Santiago, my partner. I'm saying goodbye for the last time."

"I suppose."

While they exit the train into the Terminal, a new day dawns, a young dawn pale sky. Suddenly, tension tensely dims. Grey suspicion pervades perversely as furry begins to exploit the young dawn. Without haste, the sky once blue is now bleak and austere. Thunder stumbles and rolls across the sky. A roar escapes from it, announcing its arrival to the heavens. *It is here*, the thunder shouts in a tantrum. Ferociously, lightening viciously illuminates the heavens as it gives life to rain. Everyone remembers that distinct perfume smell. There's a moment in between the thunder and lightning, where the sky becomes a perfumery. Perfumes brew in the clouds but the perfumes become too heavy to hold. Water steadily begins to fall on the dry, undistributed soil.

A sudden slothful slender sociopathic storm intensely interrupts the young dawn sky.

"You smell that?" Carlos indicates cautiously to Ezekiel.

"Yes. That's the smell of petrichor or the earthy scent of water falling on dry soil."

"Let's quickly get inside before it starts to pour," Carlos anxiously mentions, as not wanting to get caught in the storm.

Sure enough, it begins to rain. You hear the raindrops hammering on the ground and sliding against the glass. All you can see is distorted and blurred images of the outside world –a world drench in water – a world submerged. The storm gains more speed as a sailor sailing the waves in the vast ocean. Ishmael is present with lunatic Captain Ahab, capturing or attempting to capture the legendary whale, Moby Dick. Wind howls and whistles upon the earth as predators do before haunting their prey. It forces the water to go nowhere and everywhere. The wind dissipates the fluid and swarming water onto the streets. The mix of wind-rain disseminates an eerie mist that penetrates the common people's line of sight. The storm is fog, blanketing the outside world, only to illustrate the mayhem it has begun to cause.

"You think our flight will get delayed?" Ezekiel asks with uneasiness while observing the unfortunate events happening outside the terminal door.

"There's always a possibility. You know better than I do; planes are often not delayed when there's rain and delayed when there isn't rain. We shall see soon," Carlos states with bewilderment.

The silent and empty Terminal A is but an interloper in disguise, masking its true identity as to why it is a stranger intruding on someone's premises. Somewhere in the shadowy-spooky vacant Terminal, a faint-keen projection of an astute voice impulsively mentions, *I doubt it. It's passing through rather unwisely as drifters do to remain unnoticed. It's peripatetic!*

Ezekiel and Carlos turn around to identify the mysterious comment but it was already too late. The voice has scowled away somewhere like a beggar thieving for food. Peculiar, they both start to speak as they approached the ticketing and checked bags counter.

"Good morning, and how do you do today?" A pleasant and innocent voice exclaimed.

Carlos thought to himself, it is way too early to be chipper like that. She must have had three coffees.

However, little do CCS and Ezekiel know, Liberty, the ticket agent was up all night trying to calm her seven-year-old autistic son from another draining, exhausting stint.

"So I see you two are travelling to the same place, Caracas."

"Yes, that's correct," Ezekiel states exhaustedly as if he had not had his coffee yet.

"So I see you are checking-in one bag. American Airlines offers one complimentary check-in bag per flight. Since you two have your own ticket, your checked bags fly free. I see you have a layover in Miami for 45 minutes before arriving in Caracas. Okay. Would any of you like to upgrade to first class for an extra 75 dollars?" the sales agent asks radiantly.

"No thank you," Carlos states.

"And you, sir? Sir, excuse me."

"Ah, yes. Sorry about that. I thought I saw someone I knew. Damn, they looked familiar. And no thank you," Ezekiel mentions perplexedly as if he was thinking about someone or something else that caught his attention for a brief moment. He thought she was a woman from his high school he had befriended.

"Okay, gentlemen, here are your tickets. The security checkpoints are up that flight of stairs, to your right. You are going to Gate F-4. Thank you for choosing American Airlines, your one-stop destination. Have a safe and pleasant flight. Enjoy."

F-4. They both look down uneasily at their tickets. To them, 4-F means something completely different. Though, they give little thought to it. Perhaps their conscious selves are giving them a subliminal message – that *it is closer than they think.*

The zenith point of the escalator overlooks Carlos and Ezekiel with intimidation as if it were mocking them to turn back while they still can – while they still can escape the grasp of the *Capitol*. From afar, it appears to be red. Painted red to read STOP – TURN BACK but it is all an illusion to the eye.

A voice of command, behind Carlos, exerts from behind him.

"Sir, stop. You need to come see me."

A robust TSA agent, Agent Langley, approaches Carlos. Agent Langley accepted a homeland security and immigration job to rekindle his relationship with his spouse and to spend more parenting time with his two estranged children who hardly know they have a dad. This is what Langley thinks about anytime he has to approach airport passengers. Nonetheless, he grabs his upper left arm where the tattoo is embedded. The tattoo that is as much on his skin as it is in his mind.

A disdainfully chilling touch, Carlos thought, as the agent's hand came into contact – a touch he far remembers too well.

Chapter 6
Discomfort

Every time I lie awake, it itches. The tattoo on my upper left arm always itches. It has been over a year since it was sewed into my skin like stitches fusing flaccid tissue back together because of deep, jagged abrasions.

The itch never wants to abdicate from our arms. It remains engrained in our minds. We relive why we are *Los Brazos Rojos* (The Red Arms) on the day. It's a day that haunts the gallows of our minds and the depths of our souls. The purpose of the tattoo is to remind us of the fear and that we were given a new life, a new identity and a new reality. It's the only reason why we are still alive and remain different among the Common People.

To show allegiance to the Chavistas, they branded us with their symbol. Permanent ink becomes one with our skin but also our blood. It slickly seeps its way in, inconspicuously attaching itself to our blood and our skin cells. We are tattooed with the Chavistas' signature and the day they were erected.

Every time we look over our left arms, it's there; every time we undress, it's there; every time we wash it, it's there. *It* won't allow us to forget. It persistently reminds us of how we became members of the allegiance, members of the Red Arms, willingly or unwillingly. For many of us, it was by force. We had no choice. How could we in a government that has total control? It's a permanent red stain bearing his name and bearing 4-F. We now are soldiers of the government, guarding President Chava and his right hand, Deputy President Frost! We are the *Guardias* or soon will be. Being sewed with the tattoo meant the coming end of our training and conditioning.

It hurt us until our pain numbed. Needles penetrated our skin one after the other. In a matter of seconds, our blood and the red and black ink fused a homogenous mixture. We had to watch. So we tediously witnessed how our skin was stitched back together with red and black ink. Afterwards, it itches, much like insect bites. They bandaged the freshly dyed ink so we wouldn't claw at it much, like deranged or feral animals. The first night or so, it oozes and seeps; a clear plasma is discharged from the wound. The bandage from underneath was drenched, drenched in a former life we witnessed dry up. After a while, it dried up like dehydrated raisins, much like our dreams that were once tangible. The first few days, our skin flaked and peeled to accommodate the new arrival. The itch remains a phantom after a day or so. The memory of itching remains with us like traumatic memories. Traumatic memories stick with you no matter how much you want to forget them. They linger in the very depths of our minds; to retell the stories of how we became different. This is what the itching feels like or felt like before the numbness sets in.

Some argue *it's just a tattoo*. We should get over it; forget it, like it never happened. If not having experienced the Program then they would never understand.

The virus was well implanted before the tattoo. The tattoo wasn't how we ingested the virus. The tattoo allows the virus to survive. It affects more and more people rapidly, every year because every Liberation Day more and more people, or victims as they become, are taken into the Program. Many of whom are unwilling participants that are persuaded. It's a better life than out *there*.

The tattoo grows with us as we age. All tattoos fade over time, as the colour of leaves do through the fall season in continental climates. Unlike all tattoos, this one, the colour doesn't fade. It becomes more distinct, much like our *Uva de Playas* as they mature. It further entrenches our skin and penetrates our blood every year. We forget a piece of who we used to be – a person with a childhood and a family. Eventually, a few years will pass and we won't know who we are. We won't remember being human. We won't know the very piece of ourselves that makes us different from all other living creatures. Soon we are going to be like *them*!

Our life is no longer ours to keep. The Red Arms and the New Bolivarian Republic are the keepers, so that our life safeguards the President and Deputy President and their philosophy of governing or their philosophy of reigning, as the Common People say.

We are now the proprietary of this syndicate, marked by their symbol. Forever, we are the property. Even in death, we still remain property to the syndicate and to the virus. The tattoo eats the flesh but eventually kidnaps the soul. This is why we eventually forget how to be human or that we are human.

It takes over our minds, much like an empty catalyst needing a host to survive. We become that empty host. We become no one; insignificantly erased from our lives and our families.

It's musty and dark. Four slabs of concrete encase me. Water desperately dirtily drips disgustingly from the decrepit depleting spout from across. This is what *they* call a room. I would tell you how long I have been in here but somehow, time has lost its way. It has no compass where I am. Defiance isn't funny around here. I know that now. This is how I arrived in this room, where all you see is absence. There's no sunlight where I am. After the first two days, I forgot what that is. What is sunlight? That question isn't a question anymore. That word, that substance doesn't exist any longer. Not to me at least. Have I lost my compass? Have I ever had a compass? Or is it just broken?

Every night the lonesome laagering light over my bed flickers on and off – off and on, as lightning bugs flicker their bulbs giving light to darkness. Unlike the lightning bugs, the room is always darker than it is lit. It passes back and forth, SWOOP – SWOOP – SWOOP, unendingly. It casts its shadow over my bed. Besides myself, on the nearby dilapidated and neglected wall, I read the same sign over and over again, while my frightened shadow struggles to synchronise with the flickering light. I read this sign every night before I go to sleep, to perhaps remind myself or try to make sense of why I am here, or to convince myself, I am here.

These signs are not just where I am. They are omnipresent – they are ubiquitous. You find them all around the compound – Nowhere Lost. You think you escape them in the shower, in the cafeteria, or in the stairwell but *they* always find you.

UNWANTED CHILDREN – that's what the dingy, warped sign reads. Below the sign, it further reads in unreadable print as medication labels list their side effects. Though this unreadable print is worse than any imaginable side effects:

A child must have met one of these conditions:

Exceptional in Academia
Balance Studies with Work
Outspoken towards the Syndicate
Parent Defaulted on Public Loans
Needs Better Life from Poverty
An Interest to the Government

Was this a symbol of some sorts that I adhered to every night transmitting a clandestine message? Just as the light flickers over my bed, transmitting the clandestine message of how insecure I am in this nowhere place. How I am among the unwanted children our parents never wanted.

Were we garbage disposed of then pick up from the streets by the government to be given a better life as soldiers? Did my parents really not want me? They didn't care whether I excelled in academics or blend into the crowd? How would *they* know that I voiced my opinions against their failed and senseless politics? So what? It's all true – *their* policies are futile. Did my family have a secret that we were poor and didn't pay the money back to the government? Why would I be an interest to the government? What do *they* want with me? I think these thoughts and so I am surrounded with frustration – as it's my *amigo* (friend) – my only lonesome friend. These were the questions I used to ask myself and on occasion that drift back into my mind, sporadically without any warning. From being encased in this room, this is all I know – a questionable life – a sad attempt to puzzle together why I have been neglected by my family, my parents, my country and my God.

Wasps swarmed in my stomach while I read these conditions over and over again. They sting with wrath as if I have disturbed and attempted to kill their queen. No matter how much I wanted to puke, I couldn't. The stings stung more drastically and more unforgivingly when I thought about every possibility of how any of these conditions apply to me. Zillion thoughts raced through my mind. I thought and thought in circles that it couldn't be – it couldn't be true. I didn't want to accept it. I refused to live my current reality. I reject it much like a transplanted heart. But it didn't go away. The stings became worse than a nuisance. Worse than your annoying little brother or sister nagging and poking you to play with them.

The wasps were a symptom of the virus my body isn't allowed to reject; a virus that has maliciously and meticulously encode every fibre and every cell of my body, so that my body becomes a servant to it. It consumed me like wasps hurdled around their cocoon to protect their home and their mom – not admitting any intruder inside.

Could it be that I'm an 'unwanted child' because of these conditions or was I conditioned to think this way? None of my asking these questions or any question matters, as in asking them I became numb like being frostbitten in the harsh, unkind winter night. There's no feeling in your hands or in any other part of your body afterwards. This is how we all feel, insensible to any pain or pleasure. It is not just because of this place but also, of what we are exposed to – the cruel, inhumane training and what we will have to do, unthinkable assignments. We are truly interlopers in our lives.

Perhaps this is nothing less than a vivid surreal animated dream, that in any moment I will wake up from. I just fell asleep at the breakfast table, which I hardly do. Well, okay, only when I have an unforgettable hangover because I had an unforgettable night because I have made unforgettable choices and now have to live with their unforgettable consequences.

It wasn't like this at all, not even close. It wasn't a bad dream. It wasn't a really bad prank. I wanted to cry, *Jorge I got the sick joke. It isn't funny anymore. You can let me out. I get it. I should have waited for you at the nightclub. Well, fine. I wanted to get back at you and Arianna for pranking me this week.* Or if it was a bad dream, I would have cried, *Jorge, don't lock me in there. I don't want to go in there. It will get me. Okay. I'll listen to you. I won't play around anymore. Please let me out. I plead with you – let me out, let me out, LET ME OUT!*

But somehow, it wouldn't work because it isn't a prank or it isn't a nightmare. Though, I wanted it to be that way. It'll all be over by now.

Sadly, I am incarcerated, a hostage in my own life, for what, for speaking my mind, for liking Fernanda, for knowing mathematics…FOR WHAT THEN?

It's true I tell you. It's true. And it wasn't fictitious. It was authentic, as real as I am talking to you (Carlos thinks aloud looking at himself in the slightly broken, lopsided, hanging mirror), as real as sitting on this bed and as real as kissing Mama and Grandma right before I sit down to eat SWEET, SWEET *AREPAS.*

None of this was fictional, surreal maybe, but it wasn't imaginary. You have to believe me, Carlos, you are trapped here. Your life is the New Bolivarian Republic. Accept the 4-F Program. There's no returning home. Home is not what you think it is anymore. It's time to become someone else – someone any person doesn't dare to become…EL *FALSO* (a DOUBLE FACE – PHONY).

This is home now. *They* are your family. *They* give you *la agua y las arepas.* *ACCEPT IT! IT IS the only option. Accept the invitation to be Santos. Accept it and it will be better. Accept your new life – a life you cannot escape and a life you cannot hide. The life is written for you. Accept it!*

Perhaps I have to *accept it* because everyone here echoes how socialism is the way, how socialism is the truth and how socialism is life.

I tell this to myself every night before I sleep. I repeat those words in my head as I see the reflection of my former self gently and uneasily fade into the mirror. I look into this mirror every day since my incarceration in the tombs. *I am Cadet Santos* as the mirror says back to me. I whisper faintly in my head – *Accept It,* while I sulk my way to sleep mutely!

I didn't know I had to grow up but I knew I could no longer be a child. How could I? I am a displaced child – displaced from home and family. For the first time in my life, I am abandoned. I'm alone in this darkness and desolation. All I could hear was absent silence. All I could see was absent sunlight. All I could taste was absent freedom. All I could feel was absent warmth. All I could smell was absent love. It was 'all austere'. I want to abscond from this life, a life not of mine, not of anybody but a life created in-between DEATH, in-between REALITY. A life, nonetheless, I have to claim. A life, nonetheless, I have to assume identity over. A life, nonetheless, I have to accept. A life, nonetheless, is mine.

I see from the shattered and fogged mirror, my life flooding away as tears began to flutter from my eyes, like withered snowflakes on the bare warm ground during innocent winter days. All I could see was impressed puddles of my life on the concrete floor – a life intangible now. This place is *nowhere.* That's what the wasp stings viciously whisper to me as I struggled to collect myself from where I am and where I need to be. While I sit on this makeshift bed, assembled by metal, plié wood and cotton, my hands fumble through my hair and all I think of is how my life is inclement in these dreary barracks they call Nowhere Lost. I am especially estranged in these tombs, desperately struggling to hold on to any rationality that could still be in my head.

Misery keeps me company here. It gloomily declares that it will only get worse. It indefinitely won't get any better. I have to lose a piece of myself to be another actor for the government but this time my acting has to be real. I have to be one more soldier to protect President Chava. But it is with cost, a cost that has no payment or forgiveness plan. It is a very bad loan that you don't want to sign your name to. I have to separate my humanity. I am no longer Carlos but branded as SANTOS. This is the only way I can get through it alive. I have to pretend very well to be *them*. I AM CADET SANTOS. My initiation is to become LT. SANTOS.

The sign, UNWANTED CHILDREN reminds me, all of us really, of why we were taken that day. The government justified appropriating children by designating it, *Liberacón Dia*. This was the day my brother and sister, Luis and Lucia, were going to talk about in their history class but the announcement came far too late for anyone to prepare. Like them, no one knew that it was going to happen. That *they* were going to, lawfully, as it is written, given the spirit of our liberator Simon Bolivar, the taken children will be given a better life, a life protected and nourished by the New Bolivarian Republic.

Was it a lie? None of our families would ever know. As soldiers or as cadets we have our orders and disobedience is never an option. Every Venezuelan knows this. The public, therefore, knows that soldiers are here to protect people. It is always within and by the orders to protect people. We are the *Guardias* as the public knows us by; because we safeguard the land from external or internal threats. This is what we are told. We are soldiers. That's what *they* say to justify our kidnapping to our family. They would never say kidnapping. For me to say kidnapping, will add three more weeks in this despicable, decrepit place. They would say we were chosen to live a better life, so others may live in a richer, safer and prosperous country.

Was I being protected that day? Was anyone else being protected that day? I knew at some point in time, like everyone, the answer but somehow it is a distant vision in the past, a past un-returnable and a past that never transpired. Is it a lie if we were told to believe something without question? Is it a lie to accept something without question? Is it a lie to do and say without question? Are they lies without warrant?

Carlos would know but Santos isn't supposed to think those thoughts. We are supposed to follow orders; that's all what we are told every day. The orders protect us and guide us to be better soldiers of Venezuela and to create better communities for every Venezuelan.

As cadets, there is no questioning. Questioning reveals weaknesses and limits our mind to accept the bigger concept. That we are being groomed as liberators of the New Bolivarian Republic preserving socialism, the only proclaimed path towards freedom and prosperity.

I sit and lay in this depleting room, on my final day, to reflect on the essence of the code of conduct, *patria, socialismo, o muerte Venezolano; venceremos vh ah!,* which means country, socialism or death Venezuelan. We shall overcome. I reminisce over *Liberacón Dia* as if I took my final breath before dying, luridly. It will always remain a day unforgettable for anyone who suffered its vehemence, a day we want to remove from happening, from our memories, yet, as all-grievous memories, they cannot be removed. These are always with you as the creases in your palms of your hands or scars on your body shrugging you to incessantly remember – it's rooted in us so that we understand and accept.

I have to accept my life because I'm branded with their symbol. The purpose of the tattoo is to remind us of this fear and that we were given a new life, a new identity and a new reality. It will always remind us that there is no point of return. We are the property. It's is our oath, our allegiance, our way of life to preserve socialism and protect President Chava. Though we hated to be reminded and we certainly hated protecting President Chava but we have to. It became the only thing we know how to do without question. Then we will forget hating to protect him and instantly wanting to die for him because of his wisdom, philosophy and programs that brought greatness to Venezuela and to every one of her citizens.

While my former self fades insignificantly in darkness, I remember distinctively the day I was taken, like movies with scattered-misplaced scenes. This day plays continuously without pause.

"Listo," (Ready) one soldier said as I was exiled from family and life. The restraints on my hands feel cold as the heat from my wrists escape my body. Their hands were tight, pressing against my arms like claws. All I remember hearing, through my family's pandemonium, were their ravenously ready footsteps heavily thrashing on the beaten ground. You could hear their cadence reverberating louder and louder as they march away from my home to the van. Their footsteps on the ground were like a recorded melody – trained and rehearsed over and over again not to skip a beat. The van purred as I got closer to its mouth. It sat idle until it was ready to leave. It wasn't until I was madly shoved into the van and the doors slam shut, BANG, that I could see again. My brother Jorge and my sister Arianna never would have thought it would be me in one of those vans, let alone any child. They probably thought, like any other Caraqueños, installation to update the government telecommunications network.

"Lo siento por esto." *(*I'm sorry for this) another soldier states as he unveiled me and unchanged me as a reformed prisoner.

"Mi hermano, porque?" (My brother, why) I calmly mention to establish a relationship with him and the three other soldiers in the back of the van.

"It's best to keep quiet for now. I have to handcuff you to this pole. This way you don't fall over. Trust me the other soldiers in the back won't hesitate to shoot you."

"Shoot me with what…for what?" Carlos strives to iterate without fear.

"Well, who knows what's loaded in those guns. We do have live ammunition though."

"So you are going to shoot me?"

"It's best to keep quiet. You don't want to find out."

"And if I don't keep quiet?"

"Then we have no other choice but to place tape over your mouth and put the black cloth over your face again. Or we may skip all of this and shoot you. We don't want to. We are not here to keep you prisoner." The soldier in the back states commandingly.

"So, I can't ask where we are going?"

"I'm sorry, you can't. All of your questions will be answered shortly."

"I'll just sit back and shut up then, just like a mad criminal going to prison or a madman being dragged to a crazy house."

They are impenetrable statues staring at you. The statues are abnormal; they appear not as other statues. They are dressed in green and brown fatigues with a red and blue bandana tied around their left upper arm. You won't see them move a centimetre or speak one syllable unless they have to. When they did speak, they were brief and to the point. Their speech was crisp and clear as if what they always say was carefully rehearsed. The soldiers were motionless. Their backs and arms were erect. Their hands seedily held their machine gun close to their chest, across their right shoulder, ready to fire. It is their new born child they hold. They carefully protect the new born child without letting anything happen to it.

Oddly, I was the sole prisoner in the van. I thought to myself anxiously, am I the only one? Were they after only me? Were there others? Are others going to the same place where I was going? Questions and many more, I wanted to ask so desperately but was reframed and suppressed from doing so. Wearily, I wanted to speak but if I do, what happens? They will place tape over my mouth or even worse, shoot me. It is not like I can see where I was going or know where I am. Taping my mouth doesn't matter. Nothing matters now, not even getting shot. What life do I have now, if you can call it that?

The van, I assume, is unmarked. It is a chameleon to the public. Its true purpose is to remain invisible to everyone. There were no windows to look out of, except for a small one in the back. It probably faces the driver but it's concealed, much like soldiers waiting to ambush their enemy. There's nothing to see of the outside world. The world is blind to me. I am non-existent. I only exist to the people standing in the van with me. My life has been erased…it's faded in time…faded where the indented marks on the page are unnoticeable. I sit on this metal bench, bolster by rusted screws that have been painted red. I sit and think of what my life has become – faded nonessential pencil marks. I am pencilled in on paper that soon will be erased. I am invisible. I am Todd Clifton, the invisible man unknown to society as a Negro.

Were we leaving Caracas? Were we being transported to a remote prison or somewhere like prison? Could I leave if I wanted to? Could others leave, if there are others wherever they are taking me? Is this place even in Venezuela? Are these real soldiers? Was it another rapid kidnapping? So many questions like this and more flooded and are held captive my mind. I have to calm down. I have to stay calm, so the medication can work.

Oh no! My medication! What am I going to do? How am I going to function? Thinking, an unconscious task becomes a conscious one and something excruciating to process. Will my brain be like scrambled eggs? Will I die from overthinking? Will I forever feel pain? I have to learn not to overact. Otherwise, these thoughts will be endless. You see, this is sort of a good thing because I didn't particularly enjoy ingesting the medication to begin with.

I have an idea, I thought. I'll look on the ground.

What shiny boots the soldiers are wearing. Their boots are like soft polished glass. The floor is marked though. They have neglected to clean it. It is scratched with black markings. It used to be white, I think, but now it is black. It has been torn and trampled on countlessly by feet and other objects that have passed through it. Objects and things like me have passed through it. How many children did they take? What are they doing to them? What are they going to do to me? Do I dare ask any or all of these questions knowing the consequences after I speak? Shall I disrupt the silence as they have disrupted my life – my sacred time – *desayuno.*

I have an idea.

"*Pardon, mi mano.*"

One soldier augustly announces, "Carlos Christian Santos what did we say about staying quiet."

They know my name. I don't know how. But they know my name. This is peculiar and all too real. It must be the *Guardias*. They must be real or very good actors. Or it is a ruse to think that this is not a rapid kidnapping, even though it is but they don't want me to think that it is not a rapid kidnapping.

"I'm sorry gentleman. I know you said I have to be quiet. But look, everyone my age goes to the club and drinks when they are not supposed to. Hey, *mano*! I tell you what, you let me go and I will wait eight more months until I'm seventeen. I won't go to any nightclubs or drink any liquor until July 28. What do you say?" (Even for me it's hard to believe. And it's a stretch to even not to have one drink but I had to try to convince them to let me go).

They started to laugh hysterically. Their laughs were like intoxicated hyenas after devouring their prey and then desiring more.

"Carlos, we don't care if you have been drinking or staying out late. We don't keep information on this. As we have said before, all your answers, despite how many times you want to ask, will be answered shortly."

Another soldier stated angrily, "I said to keep quiet! You were told not to speak! When we want you to, we will ask for you to speak. Otherwise, speak again and I will personally make sure you won't ever speak again. Do you comprehend?"

The enraged and demonic-looking soldier was about to come closer to me, ready to shoot me or hit me with the heel of his gun. I'm unsure which though. I can only think of the worst. Another soldier nodded sternly and clinches his shoulder with his rough, callous hands. This soldier stopped him immediately before he could harm me. By any means, it wasn't a friendly gesture but a warning of some sorts that he only knew not to proceed with his current choice of action. These soldiers know of one concept, collective thinking, following blinded orders and unjust commands.

I am frightened to even say yes. So I'll nod up and down. But I couldn't help it, I said yes anyway.

"Si, senor!" I exclaimed.

Two voices mutter in the background. They were far enough away from me, concealing something they don't want me to hear. This was their despicable intention. You know it's about you, but are unsure. It's like a feeling – a subtle but sour feeling that they are talking about you. Their conversation is faint; whispers drifting in the silent wind. I can hear but a few words. I attempt to stitch together a coherent conversation that I assume to be accurate.

"Why do the ones who always think they have something to say, always say something?"

"But this one is going to be difficult to conform."

"You think so? Given his background and his unlawful statements about the government?"

"Yes. And that he thinks and questions."

"We can't have that."

"You're right. We cannot have that. Not after how much time President C devoted."

The only word I could make from their faint, unsounding conversation, was conform. 'Conform!' What do they mean conform? What will become of me?

This just made it more difficult for me not to speak. What is going to happen? Will I become like those people on television who don't have a conscience and who don't feel any pain or pleasure? Will I become a shell of myself or a zombie of some sorts? I want to just…I don't know what'll do. I am chained to this metal poll. I have to leave; I have to escape. Conform. I fight so hard against it. What makes us unique is to have free thought? Take this away and you strip a person's humanity. Our government policies are intended to conform the community into thinking that President Chava's philosophy is the truth to solidarity and the path towards socialism. It's lies though. I fight so hard not to believe in them. I'm one of the lucky ones, but for how long? I don't know. I still have a voice. I still have a conscience. All this will be taken away to nowhere lost to a place that is dreaded by death itself.

"We are here," one soldier announces confidently.

"Prepare to administer the drug to the child," the soldier in the back states hurriedly.

"Can I just knock him out? It will be much faster than…That way we don't have to deal with all his weeping, all his claiming and all his annoying, dim-witted questions."

"No! Neither president Chava nor Deputy President Frost wants us to harm him or any other child. Not before…"

"Yes, sir. I'll administer the drug."

"Sargento Primero!"

"Yes, Sargento Mayor!"

"Hold the child down!"

Reacting was a mere thought beginning to process from my brain to my body before I fell unconscious. Unconscious is not sleeping. Sleeping is when you dream while unconscious, you are not dreaming. Nothing happens. It's just a confined basement of a house, dark and empty. It's a cold and unbearable place. Your mind is absent from stimuli, whether that be our projections from reality or figments of our imagination when we dream. Perhaps, it's the in-between or cross between life and death or death itself, as others have claimed. I misplaced time, time that I cannot treasure again. See, when dreaming you still have a sense of being. While unconscious, you don't have this luxury. You're absent from this luxury. All you experience is nothingness really. You're absent temporarily as you hope to be conscious again. Nothingness isn't darkness. At least, when you close your eyes ready to fall sleep that is what you'll see. Being unconscious is not like this at all. Unconsciousness is an impenetrable void.

Everything was hazy afterwards. Fog clouded my mind – it drifted in uneasily and relentlessly as wind entering from a cracked open window. Wind of disorientation and confusion cloaked my mind. It wandered in as an aloof guest intruding with its inane and rambunctious asides of candid gossip that people shy away from for as long as it's not about them. Undesired trepidation. That's what it felt like waking up from an unscheduled slumber.

We were all gathered on green, luscious pasture and what appeared to be a safe, open place enclosed by a rocky mountain and giant trees. All I remember seeing, blurrily, was *their* shadow. All I remember hearing was *their* static voice announcing our arrival and *their* agenda. It was alluring and the words captivated us. We felt welcomed and secured. On another surface, it felt cold, absent of warmth. Something wanted to tell me this place is not what it seems. They are not what they are. That's for certain.

Welcome. Welcome. Welcome, all to Nowhere Lost – your home. This is where all of you belong. Welcome home children. My sincere apologies for the restraints during your transport here, this was to protect you. While you are here, I promise – no – I assure you, there will be no such severe conditions opposed on you. Now, all of you are saved. In the words of Oscar Romero, we hear the cry of the poor and we know them by their names. This is why all of you are saved today – to be given a better life.

All of you are among the elite – the selected few who were chosen for great and humble duty. All of you will soon be a part of history. All of you will have a humble and great responsibility to serve and protect our Liberator, Simon Bolivar's vision, the New Bolivarian Republic. Each one of you have been chosen not in spite of your abilities, backgrounds or inaccuracies, but because of your abilities, backgrounds or inaccuracies. We will teach you how to hone, develop and supersede these. We know you are special. It's our obligation to instil this in all of you. It is our obligation to give you the confidence and knowledge to unlock the skills and abilities you already have inside.

Today your life begins anew. Today you are the recruits of this Red Arms syndicate – a syndicate that protects our homeland and our founded constitution from imperialistic factions such as the capitalistic monster, the United States. Tomorrow, your training begins. Culminating your training, all of you will become guardians of this beloved country, honouring our principal liberator, Simon Bolívar. It's in his name that all of you are the elite participants of this Liberacón Dia. All of you carry the torch that will brighten our country to greatness once again.

Let's begin to take to heart our code of conduct:

We are the liberators that give light.
We are the protectors that preserve socialism.
We are the guardians that defend our homeland.

We shall overcome imperialism.
We shall overcome deterrence.
We shall overcome iniquity.

We eradicate poverty.
We eradicate corruption.
We eradicate starvation.

Socialism is the truth.
Socialism is the way.
Socialism is life.

Our country, Socialism or Death
We shall overcome.
We are Venezuelan.
Vh Ah!

If nothing else, my fellow guardians of the Red Arms syndicate remember this from our code of conduct. These simply are rules to live by, Socialism is the truth, Socialism is the way and Socialism is life. Socialism is the only travelable path that leads to prosperity, security and freedom, where all other paths lead to imperialism. Imperialism is one of the devil's curses. Later, we shall turn to this. Much of your training will be physical but also academic.

We are all family and soon enough, you'll see how. Please experience our premises. Don't forget to eat – eat much. Food brings us all together. Our promise, you'll never go hungry here, just as every citizen in our beloved country. In his name, Bolivar, we are the Red Arms. Farewell recruits. May you ever be secure from imperialism!

While President Chava and Deputy President Frost were speaking those last words, they tapped their right hand twice cross their heart and raised their index finger pointing to the heavens before leaving the recruits. They point to the heavens, that God is with them eternally. He has not forsaken them nor would he ever forsake them. This movement always concludes any conversation, as it is a gesture of military command signifying their respect towards one another.

From afar, in the distance, none of us recognised it. It was concealed by nature. We were in a compound. Unending metal fences enclosed on us as we approached the outskirts of the grounds. Why is there a fence around us? Were we prisoners? Hostages? Animals? An experiment? What are we? What is this place? Is it in nowhere? One recruit, who has been here longer than any of us, gave us his response. We knew that he had been here longer than most because he wasn't wearing white and he didn't have a number on his forearm like all of us did. See the number on our forearms will eventually fade, but the number is always there only to be seen by ultra-violet light to indicate we belonged to the syndicate. Our number is our national identification number given to us at birth. Only the last three digits are readable. Mine is 154.

The older gentleman's response: "From what they told me, the fence is here to warn off any intruders or animals. So far, it's working. I have been here for a month. I asked though, could any of us or I could go out the fence – out of the compound? You know to go to a nightclub, pick up people or something. Well, they didn't like the question just because of the faces they had on – their condescending faces. At least they didn't ignore my question. They answered, eventually. They said we couldn't go out there right now because in the nearby town the police are looking for an escaped inmate from the prison that's five miles down the road. What am I going to do? Shrug it off, right? I have to believe them. They also said soon we could go out of the compound – we all can probably this week. They're supposed to talk about that today. I think right after dinner, I believe. I guess. One of the lessons they teach you around here is disobedience is disrespect and never an option. We have to keep this in our minds, especially once your training commences. Mine has already begun. We were allowed to see the new recruits. This is why you see me and everyone else today."

The closer we approached it we saw something – a sign. A yellow and orange sign on the fences read in bold black letters:

Prohibido el Passo (No Trespassing)
Electricidad (Electricity)

They all wondered where they were. It was a deep fascination they had dwelling in their minds. Everything was displaced to them – their minds – their thoughts – their bodies. Suddenly, it all happened. They were going about their ordinary lives moments ago, but yet, something unforeseeable, unprovoked happened. They were abducted. Today, they leave themselves behind. Today, they are given new identities. Today, they become child soldiers. All of this is unknown to the world but if the world opens its eyes and with careful observation, all of this can be seen.

Where have they taken them? *I too myself was more than just inquisitive. I was disarrayed.* Carlos silently thinks in his mind, while his eyes look around the barren pasture.

Chapter 7

New Arrival

The ground, in the distance behind them, trembled frenetically while Agent Langley struggles to catch up to them. It wasn't because he had an aloof figure. His figure is quite robust. His figure suggests he exercises by lifting weights and running untested miles. He does all of this to not feel some sort of insecurity about his self he ignores. He exercises unnecessarily to make up for lost time, not being with his children and his spouse. Though, the distance between them was an inaccessible obstacle to conquer that seemed to widen and widen with each footstep towards the gates. The distance behind them and the agent is faint and blurred as to turn back isn't ideal. His footsteps shout louder and louder as he nears Carlos and Ezekiel before they attempt to enter the security checkpoint. Carlos and Ezekiel remain deaf to the sound behind them.

"Excuse me, sir. You need to turn around and take a look at this." The TSA agent howled at Carlos as he begins walking through the path towards the security checkpoint.

Carlos and Ezekiel thought to themselves, *was he demanding us to stop. We would never stop. Our cause must continue.*

Carlos and Ezekiel stood still as travellers ignorantly pass them. They are frozen in time as if time wanted to stop them from something, from some situation. Their bodies were motionless while the travellers absently hit their right shoulders without any apology. Perhaps a few faint but unheard voices say *excuse me; sorry; watch out.* They are people coming and going in immeasurable increments, with unnamed purposes or purposes that is meaningful only to them. While they walk, they look down at their cell phones, look at their watches or talk to the person next to them. They do everything except look up and see what's in front of them. Absently, these people make their way to wherever they were rushing to next. Paying little attention to their surroundings.

Unaware of their surroundings, Carlos and Ezekiel was among these people, because they too weren't looking up or what is in front of them. Carlos and Ezekiel only give attention to an unfamiliar but captivating voice that was probably speaking to them, uttering, *you have to take a look at this.* They proceeded, regardless, to the escalators.

Cursorily, the TSA agent wasted no time. He grabs a hold of his left arm, like children running away from their parents because they decided to throw a fit over a toy they never received, or that their parents intentionally neglected to purchase.

A disdainfully chilling touch on his upper left arm, Carlos thought, as the agent's hand came into contact – a touch he remembers far too well. It unrelentingly brought him back to a past where he was abandoned as a child. A past unfathomable for any child to endure, and yet, reality to this day, that Carlos attempts not to accept. It's a touch compared with the experience of feeling a person's embalmed body waiting for burial. There's no life; it's cold and stiff – an integument of what they once were. Carlos was sent back into a bleak time in his past where much of his childhood is inundated with cold memories. It wasn't always like this but since then, his mind is consumed with many cold memories he strives to rewrite with the warm memories he still desperately holds on to – not letting go. He is as fearful to the person he tries not to become – Santos. He is as fearful as parents letting go of their child to accept responsibility of who they are. It's a battle he endures but never wins. These inhospitable, grotesque memories are the person he desperately struggles not to be. Compressed in the core of his consciousness, he was that person – Captain Santos.

Carlos hesitantly turns around to face what he sees as another *Guardia* of his past before realising he's in the present – there are no *Guardias* here. Carlos was about to take down Agent Langley but his mind came back to the present before his reflexes had done so.

"Sorry, sir. What's the problem?" Carlos mutters with slight clarity. His voice scrambles not to indicate any impediment. He fails to do so.

The TSA agent didn't recognise this at first so he continues with his statement.

"Sir, I believe this is yours. It's something you certainly don't want to leave behind," explained Agent Langley. His sternness and procession gives away his current or former military involvement. Perhaps he is or was a member of the Marines or a missionary.

Carlos thoughtlessly glances over at the TSA agent's left hand, and at the corner of his eye, he sees what appears to be a Venezuelan passport. Without wasting any time, he rummages through his pockets and pats his black leather jacket and his dark blue jeans as if he has misplaced an irreplaceable, invaluable object.

"Ah, yeah. I must have forgotten to pick this up at the counter when the ticketing agent handed me my plane tickets."

"You must be careful. This is your ticket to get back into your country. Without it, you won't be able to travel or return. This is your life in one document. No need for me to lecture. Of course, you know how invaluable your passport is, sir."

"I understand, Agent Langley," Carlos spoke commandingly as he reads his shiny nameplate, *Agent Langley, Chief Transport Security Officer*.

Carlos meticulously grabs his passport from Agent Langley's monstrous hands. He was careful not to drop it. A sense of relief flooded Carlos as if he had mistakenly received startling news that one of his loved ones was taken by the Red Scare and it was little too late to save any of them. As he took it from Langley's hands, it seemed heavier than before. Perhaps the ink from the stamps somehow seeped into the pages of his passport resembling the red, toxic soil of Venezuela. Yet, he was anxious but in the depth of his soul, he knew that if he accepts his passport, he would have to accept once again the invitation to become Captain Santos. Desperately, he strives not to become him but a part of him exists in the depths of his mind. With hesitation, confusion, anxiety, relief and assurance he secures his passport back into his hands and routinely puts it in his left inner jacket pocket. This time he won't forget it.

"Well, carry on. Have a safe flight."

"We will," states Carlos.

While the agent walks away, he instantly turns around as if he recalled an important but neglected memory. How he turned was precise indicating he too had military training.

Looking over at Ezekiel, Agent Langley utters with concern, "Your friend, Carlos, is it? Is he all right? Just because of how he was just speaking."

It took Ezekiel a slight second to realise Langley was speaking to him.

"Yes, sir. He will be fine. He just gets like this every time he travels. He's like a frightened child going to the dentist. The child knows he has to go but despises going. Carlos feels this way about flying, though he flies frequently. He still regresses back to a child going to the dentist. It's one of those fears that continue to haunt you; that you try to get over or forget but for some peculiar reason, you cannot. It stays with you like the very memories of your tragic childhood experience of going to the dentist. *It* simply won't allow you to forget."

"Well then, take care you two. Remember there's still time to turn back – don't go!"

"Excuse me! What was that?"

"My apologies, it must be the chatter over you. I said it might be slow, so go. The line is gowning in people."

"Okay. Thank you, I guess. Have a great day, Langley. And tell your spouse for me, have a great holiday."

"Will do, sir. You do the same. Safe travels. The United States will be here when you and Carlos return."

Before Ezekiel turns to Carlos once again, he gives a puzzling gaze in space. His eyes leaned to the left to make meaning from Agent's Langley words or the words he thought he heard.

"What was that all about?" Carlos asks Ezekiel.

"I don't know. Langley just wanted to know if you were okay. Then I thought he said don't go but it turns out, he said, we should go because it might be slow. Right now, I'm feeling peculiar, something puzzling my will much like Hamlet contemplating giving up on life."

"Well, I should be fine for now – at least for the moment anyway. You have to recite a literary reference when something estrange happens or when something is out of the ordinary you think has happened but simply it is your misunderstanding. Remember what I said about the *Capitol* and following my lead."

"Right now, you're sounding like a broken tune. Look, my bro, I realise how it might be dangerous entering the *Capitol*, but I assure you, I will do what you ask and I won't deviate from your instructions."

Little does Ezekiel know that he *might* face danger isn't by far the truth. Venezuela, or at least inside the capitol, the people's behaviours is comparable to escapees from an insane asylum.

"Good. It's just that no American wants to visit Venezuela, although they most definitely should. For an American to go to the Capitol, it is quite daring. It's just – I don't know… (with a heavy sigh as tears begin to fill his eyes) it used to not be this way. My country used to be majestic – filled with life, vibrant nature and passionate culture, but it's been ruined and saturated by red smoky ashes of the Program that promise something which never happened or ever will. The people though still believe and therefore have become lost by what will not happen. They don't know that, so they continue to believe. They still have hope – in the Program – in the Chavistas – in *it*. Perhaps they do because it's not worth having to believe in something that is impossible to occur under the Program. They continue to believe because the government has a game with them. A game where the odds are always against them, no matter how much they may fight back – we lose. So, we don't fight back – we accept the Program and have to believe in it because fighting never works or at least that's what many are conditioned to think, especially the Guardians."

"We have been over this before. I'm more than happy to write this article and gather evidence for my legal petition. Besides, I always wanted to come to Venezuela – to experience its nature – its culture – its language – its customs and its people." Ezekiel clarifies for Carlos, as to reassure him he's making the correct mistake to go into the utter chaos in the first place and to reassure himself, he will not turn away in this last moment.

"A part of me says, I shouldn't go back, but a large part of me says, I have to return. It's the right thing to do." Carlos mentions to Ezekiel as if he was going back and forth in his mind deciding whether returning to Venezuela would make it any different than what it has become now.

"Well, continue to debate on whether to stay in North America or go back home. This thinking will make you crazy – a lunatic. One thing is different this time."

"Yeah! What is that?" Carlos utters with uncertainty not of his words but of his question.

Ezekiel turns to Carlos and puts his hands on his head while Ezekiel's head is next to his as a sign of endearment to offer Carlos some form of closure.

"It's different now. You have me. I'm going this time. You already know why I have to go." Ezekiel utters with sincere confidence.

"I suppose you are correct on this one, bro."

"Don't mention it, my brother."

"Shall we go through security check? You know what to do." Carlos states to Ezekiel as if he wasn't paying mind to the fact that it is his turn to go through the security check.

Once they have gone through the checkpoint, they headed to F-4 Gate. Walking there seemed unnerving to both Carlos and Ezekiel. They both have their own apprehensive thoughts about a country that is unwelcoming – unwelcoming not from its people but from the Program. The Program is unwelcoming to any outsider. They are not apprehensive about going, though deep down in their consciousness, the part where their conscience speaks to them, to stop – look up – and stay in the States but rather, they are apprehensive to what they have to experience when there.

Every movement slowed; footsteps could be seen; people's words could be touched; heartbeats could be heard and breath could be felt. Time stood still in that moment as if God has stopped everything to make an unsubtle announcement meant for the world to witness. The world, ignorant towards the message because of little or lost faith, continues to go about their lives, whatever that might insignificantly include. For Carlos, God's message is not unfamiliar to him, for he lacks the faith to heed or even understand God's message. As for Carlos, he is concerned that God has forsaken him to become what he is now. For Ezekiel, unsure if God exists, acknowledges the message far too late without giving any thought that perhaps God has divinely intervened. Was this a sign, he would say after but gets lost in the same contemplation as the rest of the world – does God exist? For he and Carlos never could answer this question, as trying to ask that same question is frightening in its self.

"Alright, let's go to Gate F-4. We don't have much time. We have to make this plane to Miami so that we make the connecting flight to Caracas." Carlos states anxiously to Ezekiel.

"Wait bro. No rush to get there. We have about one hour until they begin calling passengers to board the plane." Ezekiel states to Carlos to assure him that there's no need to panic.

"I hate being in airports. I just want to get there and not wait. To not wait for any problems to surface." Carlos hysterically utters to Ezekiel.

Carlos, after being indecisive earlier, decides to disappear and get coffee.

"That's right. You hate being in airports, for I never understood why. Anyway, Gate F-4 isn't that far. Let's get there and maybe grab some coffee or whatever." Ezekiel mentions.

"I may have something on the plane or while we are in Miami. Right now, I just need to get there and have a seat."

"Then Carlos, that's what we will do."

While Ezekiel arrives at Gate F-4, he had about 45 minutes until the ticket agents make their announcements to board, so he sits and waits. Where they sit, their seats overlook the plans returning and leaving. Their plane, at Gate F-4, just arrived. Passengers of all sizes hastily exit the plane. The passengers' haste and red faces reveal signs that the aircraft is late. The aircraft crew shortly then begin preparing for its next adventure to Miami. From behind him, Ezekiel overhears a conversation that is very personal to him. He attempts with every last nerve in his body not to interject his thoughts into the conversation. His dissertation, *Education and Community: Bridging the Gaps between Politics and Social Policy in Understanding, Communicating and Educating Youths' Identity, Free Thought and Academics in a Changing Society* is indirectly being discussed behind him. Ezekiel, not too far in his thirties, decided after law school to earn a doctorate in educational leadership at Temple University, for he desires to change world education paradigms through law.

"The question, politicians such as myself, ask new lobbyists such as yourself, what children learn must be rigorous, relevant and held to the standards of tomorrow that will make them succeed as professionals. How do you plan on sustaining this?"

"It's not as much about what children learn then it is about how we teach children so that they have equal opportunities to attain whatever goals they yearn."

"So then, your premise is what teachers and the school must do in order to make this happen. Then I argue; the standards must be rigorous not watered down. Teachers and administrators have obligations to ensure the standards are met. I'm not advocating for content here, which is a thing in the past, but the skills each child need to have achieved upon their graduation. These skills, in essence, are the standards of tomorrow, I speak on."

"See, politicians, such as yourself, only see in one perspective, and that is the narrow one. Education is not just about the curriculum, which is both the what and the how of teaching and learning. Education is beyond classrooms that extend far between children's communities they live in and the cultures they experience."

"I will allow you to continue. So, please elaborate, lobbyist."

"If we are unmindful, or even to go as far as to neglect children's communities and cultures and then pontificate it, isn't a significant factor, then we will fail to educate them. Afterwards, we set them up for failure."

"I agree. Children need to spend time with their families. Their families have the utmost important obligation to ensure learning continues outside the classroom. Teachers and administrators can only do so much. All children's parents must instil in their children, responsibility. These children need to take responsibility for their actions, sooner rather than later. They are accountable for their learning. They unknowingly or knowingly make choices that both positively and negatively affect their education. They, either way, have to know the consequences of their choices – that there are lasting effects. We only can enforce these standards and ensure schools and school personnel are held accountable. That's what we do. The rest is up to the parents."

"You're not listening. I was discussing about building relationships with parents and their communities. Failure to understand their cultures, we improperly teach children and we certainly do not offer them an equal education. Look here (showing the politician an educational study). Parental resilience, social connections, knowledge of parenting and child development, concrete support in times of need and social and emotional competence of children are all factors that affect relationships with parents and their children's success in and beyond school. If we don't focus on studying and strengthening these factors then are we educating all children and are we educating them appropriately? However, community engagement is just one thread of education. Sir, you have to begin to see that the system is flawed and there's a disparity between educational law and social policy. For as long as there are gaps between educational law and social policy the system in which we teach our children under continues to widen the achievement gaps."

"Sir, this is a conversation that may continue that I don't have time for. However, we can discuss this a little further while I get some coffee in Starbucks over here."

"Alright, then. Don't forget the study I gave you."

The two didn't get far in discussing their ideas because little did they understand about each other's opinion.

Carlos sat down while the conversations ended. He didn't bother interjecting his voice to the last end of the conversation he briefly heard. He too was in his own clouded, jigsaw mind. At this moment, the only thing he is sure of is the coffee he is hugging in his hands.

Their conversation poked Ezekiel's nerve and evoked some of his deep emotions regarding community engagement, culture, curriculum, education and social policy and youth identity.

It was not long until they board the plane where their adventures, though, some new and some reoccurring await them. Anyone including Carlos and Ezekiel, couldn't anticipate what will happen following their touching Venezuela's naked, yet violated body.

Flight attendants call passengers by zones to board the plane. Anyone who either waits for their loved ones or friends to depart or to any outsider not travelling would think how these passengers line up, that they are herds of people attempting to snatch the little food left on the store shelves. What is oblivious to any flight attendant is that passengers have their lives in their luggage or whatever they could fit inside for their adventures. Duffle bags, suitcases, briefcases and book bags are over-packed than others. Some are practically empty. They decide which part they bring with them and which part they leave at home. Not every piece of their clothing, souvenirs or anything else can fit in their luggage. Some spend hours deciding; others spend a few seconds. You can see the difference between the meticulously packed ones and the unkempt packed ones easily. Memories, experiences and thoughts are held in these luggage pieces. Some positive and some negative memories, experiences and thoughts clutter their bags. New memories, experiences and thoughts, though, will be packed in these bags during their adventure.

For many, their adventures begin in Miami, but for others, their adventures begin elsewhere. Many travel for their annual vacation, express content or discomfort going. Children especially don't want to go, as going is a disruption to playing their electronic devices or computer games. Some return home after being separated by their loved ones. Some are anxious to return to a warm home waiting for them, but others are nervous to go home as they may not know what they find or if anyone is still there for them. Then there are others, where Miami is just another layover or a stop for them – another temporary shelter. Their adventures could begin at the next airport or even the one after that.

Carlos and Ezekiel's eyes fill with much bewilderment and begin to look ahead of the Venezuela they are about to experience. Would they witness protesters being shot? How about children begging for a few bolivares for their family? Shortage of cash in a city that only accepts cash as payment? Then there are the Collectives giving guns to children. How about the kidnappings or robberies while driving in Caracas traffic on Simon Bolivar Avenue? Would he see the Opposition developing change for both Them and They? Would we see President Maburro putting aside his antics to serve the people justly? Or would they see Deputy President Frost giving the order to the Sweeper Squadron to execute anyone on sight who speaks or acts against the Program? Would they see more child soldiers on the street? Would they see death pervading? Would they see happy Venezuelans making good from what little they have?

Mindlessly, paying attention to the flight attendant's announcement for zone two to board, the passengers routinely enter the aircraft, stow their belongings and take their seats just as the ones before them. Carlos and Ezekiel are among the passengers in zone two. Carlos has an aisle seat as he always does while Ezekiel has a window seat. Ezekiel's eyes glare at the plane as it prepares for take-off. Both Ezekiel and Carlos think silently, *might as well get comfortable,* as it may be one of the last times for them to feel comfortable. Their seats welcome them along with a short but necessary journey to Miami. With much worriedness blanketing their thoughts, they fasten their seatbelts. The seatbelts more than usual are heavy across their waist, where they feel tension and contentment from its hold.

The engines begin to roar in pleasure as they unhurriedly warm up. The body stretches its arms for one last exercise as it taxis around waiting for the signal to take-off. It struggles to pull away from the Earth's straightjacket, gravity. The tension pulls tighter and tighter on the ton metal object until it captures enough momentum to lift its giant metal body above ground. All rules of gravity have been broken at this point as it artfully ascends into the air.

Up here, everything is a distant and vague image. Freedom exists here. There are no restraints binding anyone's hands, mouths or feet. There's no anxiety of scouring for food or searching for cash. There's nothing to worry about because up here there are no boundaries. It's limitless. We soar higher and higher until we reach the Earth's stratosphere. Who knew that heaven would be so pillow-soft. Puffy cotton could be touched from here. It has a tickling touch and soothing voice – it hums soothingly.

While in Miami, Carlos came in contact with a Venezuelan. If you're Venezuelan, every Venezuelan knows that you are Venezuelan. It is not just how you look but also how you dress, act and speak. Though Carlos was unsure at first, so as any other Venezuelan went up to him and just started a conversation.

"Merico! Es tu Venezuelano?"
"Si. Y tu?"
"Si, merico."

"Can I ask you a few questions for a report I'm compiling? The report will be presented to the world to hear testimonies of Venezuela. The people's testimonies are the merit the world needs to listen to. Sadly, South America is the forgotten America. Venezuela is a country where its people are isolated and persecuted for their inherent freedom of life. With testimonies and other corroborating evidence, we hope to change this," said Carlos.

"Yes, I'm more than happy to answer questions and to get to know another Venezuelan."

"Let's sit over here. Our conversation shouldn't take too long. Like me, I'm sure you have a plane to catch."

"The matter of fact, I don't. I actually just got back from Caracas. I was tying up some loose ends. Here in Miami, will be my new home. It's unfortunate that I have to leave my country, but I won't forget where I'm from or who I am, Venezuelan. I had an opportunity to leave, so I did. I haven't had much choice in the matter as not all Venezuelans, who are leaving, have much of a choice. In fact, I'm here to apply for asylum. Some of my family actually is here, but for work, not to seek asylum as I am. Then there are other Venezuelans. Some of them will be coming to the States or going to Columbia or another developed country in the Americas, like Panama. If any Venezuelan has an opportunity to leave, they are not sitting on it; they are leaving. When they do, they are not likely to return as I am. The truth is, many Venezuelans cannot leave, either they do not have the financial means or they are afraid to lose their families. Sadly, Venezuela is lost. It has become a failed state. More so now, where there's a fog of uncertainty if people will survive another day or if finally, a civil war occurs between the Chavistas and the Common People. Nowadays, you are one of the lucky ones to get out of that uncertainty. Our money is not worth the paper it is printed on. It actually costs more to make the paper than the value of our 100 Bolivar. I'm sorry for ranting, but every time I look back at my country, I see a part of myself lost. This makes me sad – sad that I failed to help – sad that the people who can't help themselves have to stay – sad that the opposition became corrupt and allowed the current regime to continue – I'm sad, really, of all of it. So, you wanted to ask me questions for an interview."

Carlos' eyes douse with much perplexity. He almost went back to when he graduated from the military academy in Caracas. President Chava was there, illuminating the audience with his speech. The parrot he always had was sitting on his left shoulder to capture the audience. Chava congratulated the new cadets. They are now new lieutenants about to receive their assignment. Carlos didn't go back to this time because while speaking to him, he felt connected as if he was already there. He felt the same sadness as the Venezuelan sitting before him. Back then, when Carlos was Captain Santos he did not know what he was contributing to.

He didn't go back to this time because the medicine he has taken in Philadelphia prevented the relapse. Trying to go back in time on the medication is worse than getting shot in the abdomen. His mind pervades with trepidation and unresponsiveness. The medication floods his mind with sensations of cooling pleasure. With trepidation and pleasure fighting with each other, the two repelling forces become an exacerbating monster in Carlos' mind that he has no other choice but to allow avenge its fury. He's able to cope with this monster romancing restlessly in his mind because the medication has a sedative component in it to make him a little drowsy but aware of his surroundings.

"Yes. If you could answer a few questions that will be great." Carlos states with clarity.

"How should we start this?"

"I'm going to record you as I ask you each question. I'll tell you which question we are on. At any time you want us to stop recording, we will stop recording. At any time, if you don't want to answer any question, you don't have to. Just let me know my brother."

"Merico! Don't worry about it. If you say this is going to help our country then I'm going to answer any question you have for me."

"Yes. Sure. Before we get started, I have to tell you, I will keep your anonymity. Your name will either be excluded or be assigned a pseudo name. This is to protect your confidentiality and preserve your safety. Before we start I will record your name only for the purposes of the courts but your name will not be shared or revealed to anyone."

"Merico! Do not worry about it. Do what you have to do. So what's the first question?"

Carlos starts the recording. It is one of those high tech ones that omit any external sound or feedback. The recording device is small enough to fit in a pocket or another small space as to conceal its presence. Unknowingly, Carlos is putting himself in danger for recording. It doesn't matter if the person is Venezuelan or someone else; just because it is about the Program and *them*; he is putting himself in harm's way – the way of the devil. If a Venezuelan transit agent from a random bag check ever finds the recorder, just because he has it, can land him in prison. If any militarised agent finds this device, Carlos would have wished he had died from betraying his military and President Chava. Somehow, he forgot this in his frustration, bewilderment and apprehension of his country. He just wants to change Venezuela for the better or even possibly to better himself. In any event, the world will change just because of this one recording. Carlos doesn't know there will be many more recordings that share a similar, yet different dialogue of Venezuelans. It is a dialogue that speaks the same theme of loss, hatred, numbness, bewilderment, change, hope, solidarity and happiness.

"Please state your full name for the record, being mindful that your name is for the purposes of the courts and that your identity is kept confidential."

"Sure. My name is Romano Antonio Alvarado Raya. I am from Venezuela. I was born in the city of Valencia. I come from a family of one brother and one sister. When I was fifteen years old, my family moved to the city of Barcelona. Up until recently, I lived in the city of Caracas. I have been living there for 5 years. My youngest brother, Marcus Javier was shot dead by the military when I was 32 years old, which was about three years ago. He was shot dead because they had mistaken his identity with someone else's at a university protest. Will they ever admit this was a mistake, not likely. They never admitted to the crime itself. They always said *He wasn't shot by us but by one of the angry protesters, we were trying to disband.* Let's not talk about that. My sister, Arianna Nicole and her two children, Julian and Gabriella have moved to Miami, but with deadly, unfixed costs."

"How would you describe the Venezuelan government? Please provide some examples."

"The government is shit. My fault. I should try not to curse."

"Well, if you can leave the profanity out of your choice of words, the courts wouldn't get angry as much. However, they will also understand your frustration and intent to share your emotions. Again, I cannot elude you or directly inform you of what you should say. Just be honest."

"The government is corrupt. Sure, almost every Venezuelan who is not a Chavista says that. Well, okay some Chavistas sometimes say that too. I know this for a fact. We say we are socialism but we really are not. I don't know what we are. Maybe we are communist? Then again, the government doesn't act for the greater community either. All I know is President Maburro and Deputy Frost has total control. We are corrupt people. President Maburro's missions or programs have noble ideologies, but none of these missions or programs was ever developed. Then again, many of his programs were the same as other presidents before him. For example, housing for the poor. He started this wonderful program that provides housing for the poor where they pay little to no money in utilities or property taxes. In fact, they are given a monthly monetary incentive. His program is similar if not the same program as it was, under President Marcus Pérez Jiménez. To think of it, there's little difference except that Chava was subtler than Jiménez. They both persuaded the people of the housing programs. They will be well taken care of if they continue to vote and support them. Today, there are not enough of these houses. There are still 5 million people living in the slums of Caracas alone. Where are our brothers and sisters' houses going to be built? Where are they going to live? They are still living in slums. I was one of these poor people. This is why my family moved around a lot, and among other reasons. I said that we are corrupt people because we are. The housing appropriations don't go to building houses. These appropriations are funnelled through an intricate money-laundering network that benefits Chava's influence to keep him in power, now Maburro, and to benefit Russia and Cuba's immoral communistic programs, which continues, to an influence Venezuela and their people. This immorality is successful by the way. I have not begun to scratch the surface of corruption. The corrupt always stay in power either that be the Oppositions or the Chavistas. They stay in power, I suppose, Merico, because we Venezuelans are undereducated or uneducable, depending on who you ask."

"I hate to cut this short but you are describing another question. However, one of which we will return to."

"I'm sorry. Sure. Whatever you need for the interview. It is just that I start to see everything that has been happening and is happening in my country as haze. Everything is the same. You get a pit in your stomach when you witness this corruption happening or hearing it on the radio, but after a while, because it happens as routine as brushing your teeth before bedtime, the pit in your stomach becomes anaesthetised. You don't feel anything anymore. It doesn't affect you any longer. You accept this because this is the only certain thing left. We have accepted false hope. We no longer attempt to question anything."

"Can you describe the current situation your country is facing, its people and any surrounding countries it may affect?"

"You mean our economy?"

"You can mention the economy or any aspect of the country."

"Okay, so the economy of our country needs to bankrupt itself, so it can start from zero. From there we establish a credit system. It cannot get out of its debt. There's no way. We have the highest inflation rate in the world and with four different exchange rates. Today, for one United States dollar, it is eight hundred bolivares. Trust me, it will get worse. For three years, there has been a shortage of staples. Some staples include beer (because every Venezuelan loves their Soleras), cornflour, water, poultry, meat, vegetables, fruits, toiletries, baby formula or baby food and you can't forget about condoms. Much of our products are government regulated and imported from various countries. There's no telling which markets will have the same, any, or even different products. There's no telling which days the regulated products will be in the markets too. When the product is regulated (that's almost every time you go in the markets today), you just cannot buy those regulated products. Everyone is given a national identification number. It's six digits long. We have to wait for the day when the last digit of our national identification number is announced. The days are always the same. For example, on Mondays it's zero to one, on Tuesdays it's two to three, on Wednesdays it's four to five, on Thursdays it's six to seven, on Fridays it's eight to nine, on Saturdays it's back to zero to four and then on Sundays it's back to five to nine. You only can buy regulated products twice a week. That doesn't mean you can't go to the markets any day of the week, you can. It's just that you can't purchase any regulated product every day. In some places, the rural places, the National Guard writes your number on your forearm with a permanent marker. Don't expect it to fade until a few days later because once it fades it finds root in your skin. Even then, once it 'disappears,' you too would be scarred with the permanent ink. They may tell you to come back later. This way, they write on your forearm, not to remember your face, but to remember they had written your number on your arm. When you return, they look at your number and just give you the regulated products without fingerprinting you, or while you are standing in line, they will just give you the

81

regulated products without fingerprinting you. It's that chaotic, especially if we have not seen a regulated product for a while. When we do see a product that hasn't been in the markets for months, we transform back to primitive animals. I mustn't forget to tell you that when buying any regulated product we only get two of each. It doesn't matter if you have a family; not everyone only gets two of the same regulated products. Here's a short example, if you go to *Farmatoda* (a common pharmacy) and try to buy let's say toothpaste. Well, toothpaste is a regulated product. You happen to find one (but good luck finding toothpaste now) and try to buy it with unregulated products; the cashier is going to ask you to put it back. If you are not Venezuelan, you are likely to assume the markets would be flooded with people on Saturdays and Sundays, but this is not true. Every day the markets are flooded with people. It's a herd stampeding in chaos and confusion. Much of the time, the products you are looking for are not there. Also, expect to stand in the cashier line for two hours or even longer. However, if you are some sort of dignitary or military, you get to skip the line. That's right! You don't have to stand in any line. Not ever. Okay. What was I saying? Oh, yeah, about the long line. It's not just because of the herd of people stampeding but because of the products they buy. You want to buy as many products or a product that is heavily regulated the day your number comes up. You must hoard these. You'll never know when you can buy the products again. What's worse is being fingerprinted when buying these regulated products. They have to fingerprint you; otherwise, you do not get the product and likely go to prison. This is a different story to tell, about why you go to prison if you disobey getting fingerprinted that I'll be sure to reveal in our interview. I do want to say this though. I can persevere through being fingerprinted and looking over my shoulders in these markets to always see the heavily armed militarised police but what I cannot endure is witnessing the children. Children as young as eleven have to work in these stores. Okay, so you may ask what can they possibly do? Many of them bag our groceries, help clean up spills or help carry things to the shelves. The sad thing is the companies cannot pay them because it will be illegal for them to do so. The children then aren't technically official employees. Sure, they are paid something, but most of their money comes from the tips of the customers. You know the children that work there; they either live in the slums or on the streets somewhere with their families (if they have any). You know this because they are malnourished. Their ribs are easily seen under their chest. The bones of their spines stick out like a sore thumb from under their skin. You know this because of the soiled and damaged clothes they are wearing. You know this because of their rancid hygiene. You know this because there are tears dwelling in the back of their eyes. There are too many unfed, homeless children to count. There are likely to be more of them every time the inflation rate rises or any time the government decides to appropriate their families' land, their parents' business, or order their parents not to work at their current job. Why? It becomes that much more hard to pay for things because there is little money, or things cost too much, or their parents lose their jobs because their employers can't pay them any longer, or their parents have gone missing because they cannot take the pressure or situation any longer, or simply there are scarce resources their parents can't acquire. People do not know the poor are crying, let alone their names."

"Thank you. My next question is…"

"Wait. Sadly, more recently we have become more primitive than you think. People are at the point of being tired, so they do not wait in long lines anymore. They ransack (I think that's what Americans say) the stores without paying for anything or throwing two bolivares and hurry out of the stores. The armed militarised guards now have shot these people, which are almost many today. They either have died there or shortly thereafter because they were not given any medical attention. In response, Deputy President Frost ordered barricades of militarised guards to occupy the outside of all public markets. Also, in response, President Maburro ordered all stores to operate four hours a day and three days a week. So, this changes the system of buying food. Certainly, it is a lot more rampage and chaos."

"Okay, thank for these pertinent details, Romano. My next question is…"

Carlos yet again is interrupted. He will for the remaining questions of the interview just wait about a minute to ask another question.

"Wait, wait. I wasn't done saying… Alexis, Pedro, Rafael, Sofia, Gabriel, Adrianna, Adrian, Pablo, Johanny, Yolanda, Maria, Josephina, Jose, Nicole, Emanuel, Gonzalo, Jonny, Lucia, Luis, Alejandro, Carlos, Javier, Jorge, Sabrina, Mitchel, Micelle, Fernanda, Jessica, Freddy, Daniel, Francisco, Yadria, Karol, Marianne, Juliana, Mia and Debora. These are but a few names of the poor that cry for aid, help, support and change. There! Now, I'm done."

"Romano. Who are all these people you named? Why have you named them?"

"These are only a few children that work in the markets in Caracas to provide for themselves or for their families. I have met these children while I was living in Caracas. They are all probably dead now. If they have died, they are likely dead from starvation, suicide, or from a shooting. Like many Venezuelans, I hear the cry of the poor and know them by name but we are unable to give them a proper burial, let alone help them. If they are fortunate they are somewhere lying in an unmarked grave, but that's if they are lucky. Even the world governments cannot help them. People die in my country routinely. It's an expectation. People cried away their tears."

"I know, like any Venezuelan, this is a tragedy that our government continues to nourish and neglect to resolve."

"Yes, yes it is. Isn't? You would think more would be taken into the Program," with a heavy sigh, Romano says under his breath conceitedly.

"What was the last part you said? I didn't quite get that."

"Nothing! All I said was what's your next question?"

"Is it true heavily armed militarised police and National Guards occupy almost every street corner? Do these heavily armed militarised police and National Guards' presence on every street corner make Venezuela a safe or safer country?"

"You're joking, right, Merico? Come on brother! What kind of question is this?" Romano states with arrogance and frustration.

"As I have said my brother, these questions are for the world to see and for the courts to hear. I know the answer as well as you do, or as any Venezuelan, but you have to answer the question, so there will be evidence for the world to know Venezuela is another neglected, isolated and failed country where the Common People live in a prison of solitude. Your voice is among the many that the world will no longer ignore. Only if you feel comfortable though, you may answer the question. Do you feel comfortable to continue?"

Romano gets up out of frustration and starts to walk near the window before turning around to say: "You know what Carlito – no I'm not okay. Do you think I look okay? I don't think I want to finish this interview."

His frustration and anger has risen from the ashes of his past – a past much like CCS', but of regrettable choices that Romano remembers far too well, like a perfect-fitted puzzle. He recalls a time where he was fighting against Venezuela becoming a policed state, but he has failed. In his failure to save his humanity, he left and washed ashore to Miami. His eyes reflect the light off of the window, canting what were friendly protests, but became bloodshed conflicts between *They* and *Them*. Somehow, Carlos knew this, but he is too frail to intervene. This is the best solution – not intervening. On the other hand, Ezekiel encounters just another upset and defected person who has branded memories of a failed state. These memories haunt them from making a new life in North America. Romano sees through the blurred, unrecognisable window, a reflection of himself looking back. He looks through this window to remember something, something important.

"My brother. I'm sorry. I'll continue with the interview. It's just that that particular question revealed rejected memories that continue to force being trapped in my mind." Romano speaks calmly, as the static of the recording device unnoticeably keeps on playing. Carlos absently forgot to pause.

"It's quite alright. Take a deep breath and when you are ready just speak."

"Sure."

"Do you need me to repeat the question once more?"

"No! This is not necessary to do."

"Okay then. Romano whenever you are ready to proceed, talk. Just go ahead, whenever you are ready."

"What I was trying to say before I got angry was – no a policed state is not okay. It's never okay. Not with Venezuela or with any country. To say the police or military occupies every street is understating their presence. They are everywhere, even in your dreams. Well, I may have been too dramatic in saying that but they are everywhere. From the uneducated eyes, it may appear that the military or militarised police protects or safeguards them but things are not what they appear. Maybe for a short amount of time they have protected us. What they protect us from now, is from voicing our opinions. They stop free thought. Those of us, who know better, know that more police means more violence and more corruption. In the beginning, they stood on street corners, inside markets, outside of bus terminals, on state borders or outside of homes. They were meant to intimidate everyone. People were meant to develop a suppressed fear of them. Sure enough, they did. It also means more opportunities for corruption to happen. Sure enough, that happened too. The police are aggressive. Give them any opportunity – I don't know like stare at them, attempt to take more regulated products than you're supposed to, go near them, speak to them, start an argument with a stranger, talk about them, protest, accidentally knock into them, not answering their questions, not following their orders – any little thing is a reason for them to harm you or arrest you. People don't protest anymore in fear of being arrested or likely murdered in cold blood. Kluiver Roa, a fourteen-year-old schoolboy of San Cristobal was the first but not the last to be shot dead during an anti-government protest. I was there that day visiting my nephew, Luis Lopez. Not only was I part of the protests, but I was also there with them. Here's another time, when I was sixteen years old, military personnel flooded the streets of Maracaibo to appropriate my uncle Gonzalo's farm because it was rich in oil. Before the police arrived, people gathered out on the streets to protest because other people's land were being appropriated too. We became displaced and had nowhere to go. Signs read *stop the violence; you're killing them, stop acting as God. We deserve security, not policed. We can't feed the poor, but we can start a war, the government isn't broken, but it was created this way. Falsely educating children is falsely believing they are free. The government has failed us. Venezuelans are dying as you continue to get richer. We are not free but enslaved. We will not live a life unlived. What words do we have, when we are oppressed from using them, you're the monster who wants control.* Of course, I have translated what the signs have said in Spanish to English. A policed state creates fear – fear people live every day. We become so used to the military and police occupying outside our lives that we don't do anything anymore. I mean, what's the use anyway. No one hears our cries. Not even the Opposition, whose help that we hoped would be the change Venezuela needs to hear our falling tears and spilt blood from our veins. Let me ask you, do you know why a caged bird sings? Venezuela has become a cage and we, the Common People are the birds. We are trapped in this cage. See, caged birds sing for freedom and dreams longed for. Even though caged birds' wings are clipped and feet bound, their voice trills. Caged birds cannot fly now but they will. Once they fly, the bar of rage will wither away. So, then the caged bird flies away and its fearful trill will be heard. Venezuelans may be caged today but our voices will be heard."

"Have you been a victim of violence or have witnessed someone being a victim of violence? Please give a detailed account of when and where you were when said alleged violence happened."

"Alleged violence. Alleged attacks. Nothing in Venezuela is alleged. These crimes happen; I can assure you of that. Sometimes these crimes happen because of the Collectives, because of the police or military, or because of any person needing what you have or think you may have something they want, so they are willing to commit robberies to get it from you. However, to answer your question, I was a victim of a few robberies, like all Venezuelans. I will explain one to you. It happened when I was in secondary school at *Colegio Interncaional de Carabobo* in Valencia. I was walking home on the evening of March 21, 2007. Three people who I didn't recognise were walking behind me. I didn't think anything of it at the time because people walk behind people all the time. It's common all of the time in any city. However, I didn't know they were walking behind *me*. I also didn't know they were around my age, with guns. I did not know they were going to *rob me and with guns*. I didn't know it happened. It was normal for me to walk home from school but I left later than usual from a friend's house. Should I have thought the worst, or should I have been more aware of the time? I wasn't thinking this at all. I was thinking about going home to eat dinner with my family and my girlfriend. Which then I didn't know she would be there. I was leaving late because we (my classmates and I) were probably studying for a test or something like it. Of course, I forgot it was getting late. It was about 6:30 when I walked home. In Venezuela, there is an unwritten rule: get in before it gets dark or don't walk alone when it is dark. Well, I became the victim because I broke this rule. When I turned the corner, that's when *they* came up to me. One guy on the left of me ambushed me while the guy at the back of me pressed a gun to my back. The third guy came up in front of me and demanded that I give them my messenger bag, my wallet and my phone. I didn't want to. I had to though and when I argued with the guy in front of me this made things much worse. The guy in front of me pulled out a gun and the guy on the left of me pulled out a knife. I didn't get a good look of their faces because they were wearing clear plastic masks that distorted their appearances, you know. However, through the struggle, the guy on the left managed to cut my left forearm. Afterwards, they ran away. They were also afraid come to think of it. I knew they were around my age because of how they looked and how they talked. I was fifteen at the time. They were between fourteen to sixteen-years-old. Before the three of them left, the guy in the back of me cocked his gun. I thought I was going to get shot then but he took the heel of the gun and hit me in the back of the head while the guy on the left kicked me in my ribs and the guy in front of me punched me in my left eye before I fell on the ground. I didn't do anything because I was afraid and helpless. Every fibre of my body was shaking when I saw the weapons. So I became frozen at that moment, struggling to not shake and keep my feet on the ground. This wasn't the first time I was victimised but the first time I had been ambushed and robbed. You think the robberies were worse in 2007, you should see them now. It has become our life. You cannot walk alone even in the daytime. In some cities, such as Caracas, there's a certain time where you don't want to be outside at all, not in a taxi, not in a club, not on the bus or subway because it has become that horrifying. This time begins slightly before the sun sets for the day."

"This is some ordeal for you. I'm sorry, for you may have heard this many times before. You have mentioned corruption in some of your testimonies. Can you clarify this by providing any more information than what you already have given?"

"Sure. No problem, Merico. The government buys the people, especially the military. The military keeps the peace of the government not the people. In turn, the military and police buy the people. There's a perpetual cycle Venezuelans see, a network of corruption. Okay. I'm not saying all military is corrupt but more are corrupt than are not. For example, I have mentioned children can get guns from the police or from the military. This happens through a conversation of give and take. If children know someone in power, they can get weapons easily, or if the police ask the children to do something, they give them weapons afterwards. So, what does the police or the military ask from the children, which is what you are going to say next? I think you are going to ask me anyway, so I'll just explain before you do. The military or police may ask for information from the children that the police need, or they give them weapons so that the children and their families can protect themselves when the police or the military are not around, or sometimes the children or their parents buy the weapons from them. Then there are cases where groups of people, such as the Collectives, buy guns from the police or the military and give them to children or other young people. Other times, weapons that are discovered in crimes are really not destroyed. These are put in the hands of other gangs or children. Weapons are sold to anyone who wants them, no questions asked. The guns are from Venezuela, other South American countries, Russia, Cuba, countries of Europe, Africa and of course, the United States. Practically anyone in Venezuela can get guns or other weapons. You would argue *it is not like this in the United States*. In the States too, in cities, people can buy guns off the streets easily…well, from what I hear. Have I seen anyone buy guns? Sure I have. However, I don't have to talk about my friend Sebastian buying a gun from the border patrol officer, do I? Or when I can talk about the time where I bought a gun from my neighbourhood police station. After I was robbed on March 21, 2007, I decided to purchase a gun. I didn't know how to go about this but I assumed it would be easy. After all, it's Venezuela. For some reason or another, I went to the police.

I had a conversation with a police officer about how the robberies were worsening. Then I told her how I was a victim. Come to think of it, it was the conversation after a week I had been robbed. I decided to report it. Foolish of me, at the time, thought maybe they could help because there might be a pattern or something that the police could investigate. In the end, they didn't do anything. I was having this conversation with a police officer and she said meet me in the back parking lot in three hours. I did. I was then given a gun. It was a black 9mm handgun with a fifteen round clip. She gave it to me for nothing. She also gave me five 15-round ammunition clips to go with it. She didn't want any money. She said it was one of the guns going to be destroyed, so she said, I could have it. I took it and I believe I gave her about three hundred bolivares. You know, for the trouble of giving me the gun. I wasn't thinking at the time. All I was thinking was that I wanted to protect myself from *Them.*"

"Thank you for providing answers to these questions. I want to apologise for having you relive some of these memories, what I believe to be traumatic. However, this will support the cause and give us the evidence we need to continue to help the people of Venezuela."

"Well, I can't forget because it is with me, you see. The scar of me being robbed and having my national identification number branded on me forever allows me to remember how much I had to leave to save my humanity."

Romano takes off his jacket and shows Carlos his upper forearm where the scar lives and where his identification number was branded. It lies beneath the scar. The wounds when Romano was robbed and was tortured by the Red Arms Syndicate have healed but improperly. The time of this experience has passed but is still very much real for Romano. He can't stop these scarred and painful memories from hurting or continuing to remind him of the horrors he went through. These scarred and painful memories have stolen his love and hope for his country but not his humanity and his bond between his family. He still has a sense of individuality and purpose to make something out of his life and safeguard his family, here, in the United States.

While Carlos saw Romano's scar and his branded national identification number, it brought him back to the time where he was required to arrest any citizen on location who was not following the laws of the New Bolivarian Republic and he was also ordered to recruit potential cadets for the Red Arms Syndicate. These missions came to be known as Liberations, carried out by the Repossessions Squadron. These days were once written about in the Opposition newspaper, *El Nacional*, but were immediately silenced. In turn, the government newspaper had twisted and distorted these happenings to fit its image.

Chapter 8

Thoughts Unfamiliar

Soy el mismo. Soy el mismo. Soy el mismo. I am the same. I am the same. I am the same. Am I? Why not God? Why have you done this to me? How is anything the same anymore? How am I the same? How are any of us the same anymore? What is the meaning of life when we have a prescription to die? What is the meaning of life when we take it away from people who are undeserving of it? What is the meaning of life when *they* tell you not to feel pain or pleasure?

I don't know what I am anymore. I don't know who I am either. I am not what I am. I'm not this person they want me to be, but then again, I have become this person. At some point in my *previous life,* I desperately strived not to become this person but I am, and I continue to be this person. I had no other choice. The alternative would be wishing to die but not allowed to die. See the training or the Program didn't make me think this way (or for everyone else who went through it for the matter); rather it was what we had to do when we became soldiers. During our first missions, *they* warned us of these feelings of dying and doubting our behaviour being ethical, or the content of our missions being humane. It was what we were supposed to do – carry out our missions and behave without questioning. When we felt this way, we had to report it to our commanding officer and when we didn't, we were reprimanded, severely. Being reprimanded taught us how not to doubt. It taught us how to fulfil the duties of being a soldier – being the Red Arms.

In retrospect, am I responsible for my actions? Can I be held accountable for them? Would you still consider me to be innocent after what I have done? Who knew the people had so much blood. I used to say in the beginning, *the blood spots wouldn't come out of our hands or our uniforms.* I tried everything. Nothing worked. The red spots were still there. Stain remover did not work. Hell, bleach just made the blood soak more into our hands and into our uniforms.

Sangre por sangre. Blood for blood. This is the only way peace would be met. The Chavistas didn't want it to be this way. *Sangre por sangre.* Blood for blood. They were given no choice after the raid on the military bases.

Every right I have done is washed out by the wrong I have consistently committed. However, I don't believe my actions or choices are wrong not because I was trained this way but because I believe in the greater message, President Chava and Deputy President Frost pontificate – *socialism is the true path of freedom, prosperity and security where all other paths lead to imperialism, where imperialism is the rancid nation of corruption, devastation and poverty.* I believe that what I am doing to be correct and for the great glory of our country's vision. I believe in the greater good of all people, not just the greater good of myself. Then again, it is not wrong to believe in the common good but maybe I am hesitant of how we are achieving it. Just maybe – I am hesitant at the moment. Yet, doubt, hesitation and confusion drift back in my mind, like the cool Caracas December breeze. I ask again, to myself, am I the same person or am I not what I am? Have I transformed reluctantly to a different self that I accept to be who I am? Am I all of these things or none of these things?

Nobody forgets his or her first successful liberating mission. That's what we called them: liberating missions. It's something special about it. It transforms you like a caterpillar transforming into a butterfly. The caterpillar isn't the same creature any more. It's different. It changed. It became something new. It is something, perhaps extraordinary. A helpless creature that once crawled on sixteen legs long struggled to survive. It is now a powerful two-winged colourful creature that flies. The caterpillar, I suspect, is not aware of becoming something new and extraordinary but people do when they transform. I certainly do. Would you call my transformation extraordinary? Well, I do not know. I know the Program does. The Red Arms would say we are special. I would agree, now, with their assertion. We are the liberators that give light to our country and protect her from imperialism. We affect this change by establishing order in our country and eventually, abroad. This is why we punish anyone who creates disorder. We recruit those who have the potential to contribute to our order. Where there isn't order, there is chaos. Chaos simply cannot happen nor can it be rampant.

What I didn't know was what we had done and what we continue to do would have any effect and impact on our people. We didn't know they would retaliate negatively. I didn't know nor did I understand what effect the Program had on me and on the others who have been indoctrinated in our squadron,

Repossessions, or indoctrinated in other squadrons. I did not know it resurrected a long despised group, *Las Victorias* or the V's as they called themselves. They would once again attempt to topple the 4-F Program.

During the first *Liberations,* I told myself this very statement, *soy el mismo,* when we took hostage the Common People who disregard the laws of the New Bolivarian Republic that our President Chava established to better all citizens from domestic and international threats, so that Venezuela is secure and prosperous once again. It didn't matter whether they had a cause or merit to defy these laws. We didn't question anything. Certainly, we didn't question any actions against the Program. We just did, as routine as waking up from sleep. It's an unconscious task, merely thoughtless, that we just complete.

These thoughts, *soy el mismo,* still trouble me and weave in and out of my mind sporadically as inconsistent as the Caracas rain. I am standing alone on the overpass. My troublesome thoughts silently reveal themselves in Spanish and in broken English. The sleeping city of Caracas pouring with decayed rain, drenched with loneliness is unheard throughout every street corner, as we have raped the people of their inalienable right to peacefully assemble. I try to hear the rain cry. I don't hear it though, pounding profusely and freely on Caracas' bare, scarred body. I just hear my thoughts. I hear the pain. They are bounded with barbed wire, encased with dull, pointy blades. For some reason or another, I don't just think my thoughts but everyone else's who I have arrested, tortured and possibly killed. They don't leave my head. I live in the spirit of their agony. I feel I am being haunted and attacked by these spirit voices. That's what they are, spirit voices. They are much like the voice Hamlet encounters of his late father revealing to him, his murderer – which happens to be his stepfather and uncle, Claudius. Except here, there is no Claudius because I am the arrester, the torturer and the killer. I'm a Claudius. Their pain is immense, incomparable to the pain I inflicted on them. I physically feel the pounding rain, pounding hysterically, crying down over my head and painlessly dripping over my body. I feel it shrugging me to fall on my hands and knees as my own tears coldly and sorrowfully fall from my eyes as my thoughts jumble brokenly from what I have just done. Rain hammers hysterically and heavily as I hurtfully heave horridly. I heave and heave without solace, as the insufferable pain rots my moral judgment. It's almost as if it is ironic, the day I mean. *They* called for clear blue skies with a lot of sunshine and yet, it's greyer than my own bottled, taken thoughts.

I am too ruined with hatred and confusion to hear that the rain is God's message. The message that God is perhaps sending me that he apologises and it is time for me to come back to him, so he can show me the true way of life. My hatred and confusion prevent me from listening closely to God. However, I know now that it wasn't like this. God isn't speaking back to me. I know what I am doing has to be right because the Red Arms guide me on the right path to prosperity, security and freedom. In the beginning, these thoughts did continue to trouble me every time we'd take hostage, the Common People but eventually, I blocked them out and I am not able to hear them any longer. Thanks to the reactant injection I receive daily. I easily block them out. Momentarily, I don't hear any thoughts. As I suspect, God is absent from my life. Perhaps God doesn't exist, at least not in my life. *My allegiance is to the cause of the Red Arms. They, the Program, the Mission, President Chava and Deputy President Frost* is my God. At least *they* speak to you directly and with clarity instead of indefinable, mystic symbols. I have to say, *my allegiance is to the Red Arms* every time I doubt because doubting the Red Arms doubts the Program, which means we are failing our liberations. We cannot fail! After I say, *my allegiance is to the cause of the Red Arms*, those thoughts are numbed and I am unable to hear them any longer. I am ready to focus on the mission. I am ready to fulfil my creed as a soldier.

Lieutenant Carlos' thoughts cloud his mind as he continues to look over the bridge and into the vastness of the lit, polluted city and the barren, brown mountains. His thoughts become heavy and weary. He contemplates jumping to his death but doesn't quite make it. While he begins to weep in the rain, he falls on his keens with his handgun pounding back and forth on his forehead, stating *Soy el mismo. Y aunque la vida, tal vez hos haya llevado por distintos caminos, no somos súper humanos para controlar o cambiar el destino.* (And although perhaps life has led us along different paths, we are not super humans to check or change the destination). He states these familiar lyrics from Prince Royce's song *Soy el Mismo* to somehow console his self that it's just a dream. In any moment, he'll wake up in school with his friends and with Fernanda.

He just arrested Fernanda, a girl he knew in high school. While he weeps away a life already dislodged, he begins to regress back to a happier time – to his childhood before he was forcefully stolen from him. A life removed. The pain intensifies (perhaps from the recent injection) as he continues to think about her and so unknowingly, he begins to lean against the cold, damp concrete overpass wall marked with a shallow sketch of Chava ready to fall into the empty, pandemic Simon Bolivar Avenue. This is why his thoughts are jumbled and acting as if he was a new recruit who just has received the promotion to lieutenant. Fernanda meant everything to him but he had long forgotten about her, until this night. Encountering her caused Santos to blackout to a blurred wasteland of what remains of his kidnapped childhood.

"Carlito, can you come back for just a moment and finish your *arepas* before Jorge takes you to school. You can't be late again. Come back to us little Carlos. We are waiting for you – so you can finish your breakfast."

"I know mom. I won't. I'll finish my *arepas*. It will be a sin if I do not finish them. It's just that I have to fix my hair for one last time and change my shoes. I realised that I have red and black ones that match better with the outfit I have on."

"That boy you have raised thinks and thinks. He can't sit still can he? Sometimes I think he just has his head up his ass. He changes his clothes more than I forget my glasses, which usually are on top of my head. Remember that one time I thought I lost your dad's wedding band. I actually thought I baked it in the *hallacas*. After that dinner, I remembered that I forgot I left in in the bathroom by his picture."

"No Ma, he can't. But of all people, you should know why he's doing this."

"Yes, Adri. I know. Who was the girl he always talks about? Ah yes, Fernanda. When will that boy of yours ever ask her out? You know, when I was his age all the boys did not care. They just asked us women – all of us women out. But that was a lifetime ago. Nowadays, the guys and girls make it like a ritual. It's just a few drinks or a dance. Maybe you'll have sex but how else will you know if you like them and start a possible relationship if you just do not ask a girl to go out on dates. Well, how about this? The perfect way to meet girls is to ask them for a dance and then slip your number in their hands."

"Ma. All right! It's different. Okay. He and his brothers and sisters live in a different time than you and life that is getting much harder with the 4-F Program. Guys just do not ask women out from a hot dog and dance or after a drink or a dance."

"You know, Adri, I don't like politics in the kitchen."

"Ma, all I'm saying is that getting a girlfriend is different now from when you and I were his age."

"Mama. What did you say? I did not hear you," Carlos yells across the room.

"Mom, see Carlito is going to hear us."

"Will you stop worrying? He's not going to find out."

"Nothing Carlito. Just hurry up. Your *arepas* are getting cold, and it's almost time to go. Let's go, Carlos. And I do not want to hear you yelling across the hallway again."

"Yes, mom. I won't. I am coming now, mama."

Carlos hurriedly races back to the kitchen table before he gets reprimanded again. If he gets reprimanded again for disobeying his mom's wishes then he is likely to get smacked on the back of his head. The *arepas* are still flaky and tender, just the way he likes them. The table looks chaotic. Half empty plates of devoured food and half-filled glasses of water and juice loiter freely on the table. It has been left there waiting for the family to come back to eat but some will not return. In the Santos house, every morning is like this because the children are always lazy to get up on time, so they quickly eat. They always have something else on their minds other than finishing their breakfast. However, Carlito's seat welcomes him to finish eating, so the yawing Caracas day can embrace him.

"Carlos you know what you already had on was fine. I do not know why you continue to change your clothes every five minutes," Carlos' Grandma jokingly states.

"Ma, are we forgetting something?"

"Adri, what nonsense are you talking about now? Forgetting what, my glasses? They are on top of my hair, aren't they?"

"I do not mean your glasses. Though you should check the countertop because they are not on your hair. I mean are you forgetting something?" Carlos' mom suspiciously nods back at grandma as to give her a hint that it's Carlos' birthday.

"What, dear. What do you mean? Huh. Oh yeah. Carlos, do not become an old sack of bones and a forgetful mind, okay. *Feliz cuple, papi.* Happy Birthday, Carlos."

Grandma reaches over to give him a kiss and to secretly put a crumbled five hundred bolivares in his jacket pocket.

"Thank you, grandma. But back to why I had to change my clothes. Yeah, I know. But today is science class we get to work with our groups to experiment with creating both physical and chemical reactions. And guess whom the teacher assigned to be in my group, my bro Rafael and Fernanda. Today is going to be a great day. I have to be careful about what I wear," Carlito excitedly mentions.

Jorge had just walked into the conversation. Like everyone else, he knows that Carlito likes Fernanda but has yet to mention anything to her. She just thinks Carlos and her are very good friends. Jorge, the jokester as he is, cannot pass up a perfectly great opportunity to prank Carlito. Where would the fun be if he did not?

"Yeah, little Carlito, so about this girl you always mention. Is she your girlfriend or something? Oh, wait! You must be in love with her because you never shut up about her. Admit it! You like her. I'm sure I always hear you singing one of Prince Royce's songs, *yo solo quiero darte un beso…si el mundo fuera mio te lo daria* (I only want to give you a kiss…if the world was mine I'd give it to you)."

"Will you stop messing with me? Yes, I like her but only as friends. Okay. Jeez! We are only friends! She's a very good friend. She helps me out at school."

"Oh, she helps you out alright! I'm sure you two are just *friends*. Keep telling yourself that Carlito. All right, little brother. I will stop only because it's your birthday," Jorge mockingly states as he runs his hands through Carlito's hair.

"We'll celebrate after school since you irrefutably want to go today," Carlos' mom states lovingly and happily while trying to hold in a smirk.

It's a new day for Carlos at *El Colegio Cristiano de Academicos Medias* (The Christian School of Middle Academics). The school looks like a campus covered in green pasture and as tall bushy trees surround the stone paths that have been ill unkempt. Carlos enthusiastically enters the school grounds, knowing that he once again gets to study with Fernanda and Rafael. The school overlooks him as he unintentionally stares as its vast body in search of his friends. An echoic voice drifts in Carlos' ear, stating, *Oye, merico, mi hermano. Feliz cumple merico.* (Hey my gay brother. Happy birthday gay). It was Rafael.

"Hey, merico. How are you?" Carlos responds back.

"I'm well. Hey, man. Let me take you to Fernanda. She's already here. She wants to ask you a question about the science lab today since you know science and all." Rafael pleasantly answers while walking next to him.

Carlos doesn't know yet that Fernanda didn't want to ask him a question about the science lab, though she did have concerns about today's experiment, but to give him his birthday present.

Up ahead, Carlos sees Fernanda sitting on the concrete broken steps talking to her friends. She's probably reminiscing about which outfit to buy at the mall today after school or the surprise nightclub party for Carlos and his friends.

"Hey, Nina Bonita!" Carlos yells to get her attention.

"Oh yeah! Carlos! We are here!"

"Let's go, Rafael."

This fragile, incomplete memory is dissuaded by the negative reactant injection forcing Carlos' mind to come back to the present where he is unaware falling off of the overpass and into the frenzied traffic of Simon Bolivar Avenue.

At first, I didn't recognise her but it is Fernanda. Once I realised, I regressed back to an earlier stage of my life – to the time I learned to accept – the day I was abandoned from family and life. A time where God has forsaken me and this day forgets that I am still alive. I died that day. I am no longer the same person I was back then. Today, I am different – a different self in a very different time and life I forcefully live.

Fernanda, *la nina bonita*, and the beautiful girl I once knew and understood. I was going to ask her to go to the nightclub that day. However, that fucking didn't happen. It is a mature version of her now but she's just as beautiful as she was the first day I met her, if not more beautiful if that's even possible. It seems that time hasn't aged her. It's the opposite. She's more vibrant. I didn't get to ask her if she would dance with me – that did not fucking happen. I will never forget her jet-black hair – it's robust and full of potential. Potential I never had. Now, her potential withers away like dehydrated raisins as she is placed into custody. A part of me – the part that is buried in the cemetery still wants to ask her to go to the nightclub. This self is stuck in that day – a day waiting to be captured and happened. This is the pain I was doused and submerged with while arresting her and her family.

We arrested anyone who defies the New Bolivarian Republic laws. These laws prevented any Venezuelan and sometimes visitors or outsiders (as the Program claims they are – outsiders) from speaking against the government. This is necessary to protect all people from demonstrating any violence that otherwise would propose threats to the Program. We arrested Fernanda and her family because they were protesting without a permit. Her family was not protesting though. Many families do not protest because they keep their head held down and mouths closed. We detained them anyway, to get information out of them. We detained every involved family. We allow anyone to peacefully speak his or her mind about the government so that we can make it better. The Program does not infringe on people's liberty to speak as long as it is not violent. Speaking against the government or the Program is violent. However, she and her followers had spoken out against the Program and had done so by violating the laws. The laws are to protect every citizen. This is what we are taught. This is what I accept. This is what I follow as my orders. We arrested others that day that were also involved in the movement to speak freely, the Students Against Totalitarianism. This is what they call themselves, Student Against Totalitarianism or SAT. They didn't have a permit and were threatening our National Guards or the boots on the ground as we call them. We got the call and arrested them at the Central University of Venezuela.

The New Bolivarian Republic Laws:
There must be a permit to protest
All prices and costs are regulated
No employee of public or private businesses work more than four days
per week
No business shall operate more than 6 hours a day
Every citizen shall receive no cost medical and dental care
No citizen shall possess any weapon or firearms
Poverty and socioeconomic classes have been abolished
All public and private salaries are regulated
Women shall become sterile after birthing two children
All possessions must be given to the military upon request
All media and communications are regulated
There shall be public military exercises
Found guilty of treason is immediate release
For all capital cities, all citizens are in by 11:00 pm
There shall not be any form of violence imposed on our people
Any citizen who shall disobey these decrees shall be detained and questioned

The protest was in response to advocate for more funding for professors, more resources for students and better security within and around the Central University of Venezuela. These ungrateful people can't respect what they have and the dignity of all individuals. I thought these words and have said often to my squadron, the Repossessions when we get the call like this. Our founding president, Chava and his Deputy Frost has made laws that all professors receive the same amount of funding, every student gets the same amount of resources and everyone is protected. What more do these ungrateful, disgusting students want? They don't pay any money to public schools or colleges. They hardly pay anything for private schools or colleges. Fernanda, her followers and the involved were spewing grossly lies about the Program. These have no weight, value or merit. Because this was considered slander and the National Guard deemed their actions were disrupting the public, we came in to repossess them, re-establishing order. There's an unofficial word we the Red Arms call the protesters, infidels. It's unofficial because the Program has not yet classified them as infidels; they are still named protesters. They are infidels to us. We despise their disloyalty to the Program.

We had a drink or two to celebrate at our squadron or at the local bar, *El Ultimo Lugar* (The Last Place). At first, I drank to forget, as I suppose as any other lieutenant did. We drank to forget our morality and accepted that what we did was in fact moral. The alcohol is a powerful toxicant that lingers in our blood even after we have finished drinking. It made us forget. We forgot who we used to be, just adolescents taken away from family and life just four years ago. The drinks our comrades and I have indicated the type of liberating mission. We knew how everyone felt any time we walked in the bar or back at our squadron. When we drink Soleras, *verde, azul, or negra* green, (blue or black label beer), it means it is a successful celebration of our achieving the liberating mission. When we drink rum neat, rum over ice or rum and coke it means a failed celebration that either we have forcefully won with capturing many detainees or we have won it by encountering our past that we unfortunately dredged up. For me, at this moment, I wanted it to be one of the successful celebrations but that would not be possible. If it were an unwelcoming celebration, we had to report it to our commanding officer that our past is getting the best of us. Probably, after arresting Fernanda, her family and some other Students Against Totalitarianism (SAT), the Red Arms will have a few, maybe more drinks to celebrate a small but important victory.

In the chaos of the rain, a red and black Humvee roared over to him flashing its illuminating lights directly over the overpass where Carlos steadily is drifting over to the side of the shallow wall. Carlos thought to himself, it never rains in Caracas, not like this anyway. The rain is too heavy to stay on the streets. Due to Venezuela's poor irrigation system, the streets begin to flood with dark red mucky rain. The rain creates a slick, light blanket of water across every road. His tears immeasurably add to the vastness of the blanket of rain. Carlos unnoticeably begins to look up at the glaring light as he slowly hoisters his handgun. Tears continue to slowly and silently fall from his eyes. He could not make out who was approaching him because the light from the vehicle blinded him. From the close distance, another soldier steps from the Humvee and approaches Carlos firmly and confidently. *Someone* found him. God, he thought, but this mere thought was short-lived. He knew it wasn't God. It was someone else. Someone else found him on his knees, banging his handgun on his forehead in the red mucky rain. This aloof figure gigantically blocked the dim-lit street lamp instantaneously casting his inert shadow over Carlos. It was Lt. Rodriguez. He was not much taller than Lt. Santos. He walked over with a peculiar, unfitting presence to sternly and confidently find him having lost his way. *It* had found him to rein him back to finish this liberating mission. To remind him that the Red Arms and the Program are his family, that *they* would never leave his side as his family had done some number of years ago.

"Hey, my brother! You have to pull yourself together! You must get a hold of yourself! You're a soldier now?" Lt. Rodriguez shouted authoritatively.

"I can't! I can't continue like this anymore! Just leave me be, okay!" Lt. Santos states with sorrow.

"You know I can't do that, right? It's time to get on your feet! Did you take the negative reactant injection today as well as your stabiliser for your thoughts?"

"What does that have to do with how I am, right now?" Lt. Santos defiantly spoke.

"It has everything to do with it. You have come all this way – to what…lose your mind? This is not the Lt. Santos I know. Look here. We all have to at some point in our training or in our missions encounter the last personal connection we have but this will pass. I'm going to ask you again. Did you take the medicine today?" Lt. Rodriguez stated with frustration and annoyance.

"Affirmative, Lt. Rodriguez. I have taken my negative reactant and stabiliser today, sir!"

"Then stand up soldier! Are you shit or are you the Red Arms?"

"I am the Red Arms! I am a liberating soldier. My missions are to liberate Venezuela and to protect her from all forms of imperialism."

"That's right, soldier. Yes, you are. Your mission is to liberate and repossess those who need to fall back into order. Sometimes we have to do things that may seem unnecessary and seem unjustifiable. However, I assure you that what we do is necessary. The people need to be liberated. Our country's spirit craves for liberation. What we have to do is necessary. It's a necessary part of order. Our presence is necessary! Our military is necessary. We are a necessary part of order. WE create order. The *Program* creates order. We are the *Program*. We are necessary. We are order. You are necessary. We cannot have chaos. Those who commit to chaos need to be reformed. If they cannot be reformed, they are released. It becomes God's problem then. You know this. You have taken the creed as a lieutenant, do not forget this."

"You think I forget our creed. You think I forgot! I haven't forgotten. I remember. It is just that I need some time alone, okay. I just… I don't know. I need to…I need to think. I need to rest now. I need to be left alone. Leave me alone!" hastily shouted Lt. Santos with much fury.

"I cannot let you do that. You have to get off your feet. Fine then. Recite the creed. Go ahead, since you remember and claim you still worship it."

"I, Lieutenant, Santos, take this creed to reform poverty – to ratify our country for the better from the commands of our new founding President Chava and Deputy President Frost. I take this office to preserve socialism, to defend all people from imperialism and retaliate with necessary fortitude and strength. I solemnly swear to fulfil every liberating mission as the Red Arms Syndicate or die trying. Oorah!"

"Excellent soldier. This creed you have taken is the oath of your life now. We all are here to protect you. We all have been through what you are going through now, mind fucked. We all have doubted. This is why we have our commanding officers and take our daily reactant injections. It helps us. We become better every time. It's important that we talk about our confusion and unworthiness of being the Red Arms. In this moment, I need you to be the lieutenant that you are. You have to complete this mission. So, stop being mind-fucked and let's move!"

"Affirmative, Lt. Rodriguez. I am Lt. Santos, part of the Red Arms Syndicate in the Repossession Squadron. My primary duty is to carry out all my missions successfully or die trying."

Carlos limped back to the Humvee with Lt. Rodriguez in anguish and uncertainty. Abruptly, his mind snapped back to its current state, being a soldier. Something happened in his mind that caused him to leave the last bit of his humanity behind. He snapped back to his current reality where he will be driving Fernanda and her family to a remote location outside of Caracas to be interrogated. All detainees are interrogated for the purposes of obtaining information. After the interrogation, they are reformed. If reformation does not work then their intolerable actions are considered treason and then would be released by lethal injection. Many Opposition people, as they call themselves, despite which group they affiliate with, pretend to reform to stay alive. So, with this new understanding, we just release detainees within two hours of being tortured because after two hours they are not going to comply. After being captured, their only hope is to stay alive. Lt. Santos will be doing the interrogation, as it is customary for any arresting personnel.

Lt. Rodriguez reminds Lt. Santos of the procedures of his conduct in this mission. "When we return, we have to give our mission report. You also have to go immediately to Major Maburro for debriefing before you can start the interrogation process."

Lt. Santos gazes at the rear-view mirror checking if he needs to increase his speed. While gazing at the rear-view mirror, he can't help but think about what he left behind. Whatever is left of these memories of Fernanda are shattered, fragmented pieces of his past continuing to ride further behind him until eventually, these shattered, fragmented memories become distant, vague distortion of something far unreachable.

Carlos states wittingly, "wait you mean the guy who was a bus driver 12 years ago who decided to join the Guardias is now our commanding officer?"

"Yes, Santos, it's the guy. Yeah – funny thing right? Our devout President Chava promoted him to major two years ago."

"Well, it should be easy then. I mean, the debrief anyway."

"Carlos, I wanted to tell you that since your stellar performance and unwavering devotion to our cause, you are up from promotion to captain soon."

"Well, do not forget that I'm also the best interrogator and marksman the squadron has." Santos jokingly laughs.

"Now Santos, do not get ahead of yourself. You have only become the best marksman because Captain Rivera has shit for eyes."

"You may be right, Rodriguez! That is about Captain Rivera but I'm still the best marksman and interrogator. Three in the chest, that's what we are taught, but my last shot I always get the head."

"That's what I wanted to tell you."

"Tell me what, Rodriguez."

"You are probably going to be promoted after this interrogation. Thereafter, you will get to lead any squadron of your own choosing because Request for Reassignments happen then as well. Though, you need to keep it together. This interrogation will determine all of this, most likely. This means you cannot allow these superficial, doubtful emotions cloud your judgment and the way of the Red Arms' missions. However, the interrogation must be flawless. You know what you have to do after two hours if it comes to that. "

"I understand Rodriguez. This is why it is procedure first to go to debriefing. While at debriefing this time, Major Maburro will adjust my daily negative reactant injection and we will talk about what happened out there, in this mission."

"I need you to hear me."

"Yes! I hear you. Do not worry Rodriguez. I will not fail my mission. I realise this is an important one. The students we arrested, the SAT group and Fernanda may have valuable and pertinent intelligence on the group they are resurrecting, *Las Victorias.*"

"Excellent Santos. You do hear me. So then, do not fail us. Succeed! How does Captain Santos Sound?"

"I will succeed to preserve socialism and to protect Venezuela from imperialism or die."

Chapter 9

Disturbed Awakening

After a five and a half hour flight, Carlos Christian Santos and Ezekiel Ian Masefield arrive at the capital, Caracas. Their first stop from the airport is to check-in at the Venetur Alba, a government appropriated hotel. Before it was a hotel, it was a government security building in 1955, under the Marcus Perez Jimenez administration. In the early eighties, this hotel belonged to the Hilton Hotels, a private North American company. This changed, however, since the insurrection of the Program in 1992 – the birth of the red monster. The government in 2007, to retaliate against the imperialistic, Northern aggressor, the United States, bought the hotel itself. The Program bought out other Northern American companies during this time but many of these companies closed due to the Program's lack of interest or means of retaining the business. These buildings are empty carcasses wasting away from the elements of the Earth. The Venetur Alba is becoming like these decayed, rotting buildings. The decay, the rotting, the waste is a product of the Program's failure to upkeep these buildings and in some instances develop them. Their decay is nothing but notorious. Somehow, Venezuelans do not smell or see it.

Few tourists, merchants and politicians come anymore. Caracas has become a battleground of crime, darkness and uncertainty but it has the appearance of any developing city. It has the prospect of wealth, of life and of happiness. The Venetur Alba Caracas symbolises this prospect of wealth and happiness. It was one of the first established international hotels to benefit both Venezuela and other visiting cultures. The hotel captured the arts, the history and the culture of Venezuela, welcoming all who stayed for business or pleasure. Though its presence lives to portray a different story, a story where it outcries for help. It cries behind the walls, at night, in the silence of the falling water from the stale waterfall, *fix me, fix me, I do not want to decay because when I do decay I surely will die. Once I die the arts, the history and the culture dies with me too.* However, it has been far too long since the Program heard its cry of mercy. The Program did, however, once start *surgeries* to revive the Venetur Alba, but with almost all of its programs, the surgeries stalled and were left on life support.

"Ezekiel, I'll meet you on the other side. Do not worry. You will not have any issues going through immigration. Just show them your passport and visa. Remember what I told you."

"Tell me what Carlos?" he said as if somehow he intentionally forgot.

"Keep your mouth shut! I suspect it has gotten much worse since the last time I was here. It's an annoying feeling I have."

"Yeah, I keep my mouth shut alright," Patronisingly he states.

Ezekiel says under his breath, "Jezz, paranoid little."

Despite his recommendation, Ezekiel spoke to the immigration officer. He thought, while looking at the officer, *he looks friendly enough and about my age. So, why not? Here goes nothing.* Little did he know the immigration officer is a friend to North Americans but he would learn a valuable lesson in return.

Ezekiel casually and nonchalantly walks over to the nearest immigration officer's window, window 10, and states, "*Hola mi hermano. Hablo un poco de Española. Aqui esta mi passporte. Hablas ingles?*"

"One minute, sir," The immigration officer says kindly.

"Okay."

Through, Ezekiel's immigration process into Venezuela, he recounts his studies of how and why Venezuela is red, especially in the Capitol. President Chava, being poor himself, believed that privatisation develops hatred among people and that this hatred continues to widen poverty. As poverty widens, the few who have wealth continue to have more of it, which disconnects people from each other. Where there is disconnection, there is no unionisation of people. Why should some people have more than others? Why cannot all people have an equal amount of wealth, where a centralised entity such as the Program supports all people with any necessity? Chava also believed in the idea that people possess material objects for the necessity of desiring them, which causes people not to be free of their individual self. The absence of material possessions creates an opportunity for people to possess freedom. Simply, the fewer objects people own, the happier they will be. By possessing a simplified life, people are happier than possessing a complicated one. With this vision, Chava was able to move the people to form the New Bolivarian Republic of Venezuela. This *new Venezuela* would eliminate poverty, disease, hatred, murder, insecurities and famine. To do this, Chava believed in creating centralisation, where the Program would be the sole proprietor, so all private businesses over time were then bought out by the Program and controlled by the Program. After the centralisation of all businesses and programs, Chava created ministry positions to establish unified control. He did not appoint people who were necessarily qualified for the position but instead, he appointed his friends. Little did Chava refused to realise that within the Program, there is corruption among its ministers, its political offices and its employed associates. His successor, President Maburro continues to shape this deeply entrenched idea of centralisation. President Maburro too fails to realise the existence of corruption and failed political missions. Because he is easily persuaded, he turns a blind eye, unresponsively to the failing Program he has inherited. This refusal continues to perpetuate an inhospitable virus. Corruption is just one aftermath of the Program's inception but another is a policed state.

The silence becomes too disturbing. Both the immigration office and Ezekiel want to say something but do not know how. It was not because of a language barrier but because of the awkwardness of two similar, yet clashing cultures. The immigration officer hastily decided to pass the time and asks the following question,

"Ezekiel," The immigration officer says suddenly.

"Yeah," Ezekiel states as if the agony of silence is subsiding.

"Is your name from the bible or something?"

"As a matter of fact my name is from the Bible but I do not think my parents had religious reasons in giving me that name. They wanted to give their first son a name of strength and courage. In the Book of Ezekiel, Ezekiel means God give him strength. He also lived in a period of international upheaval; the development and collapsed of the Assyrian empire, the destruction of northern Israel and the resurgent of Babylon. Ezekiel was also one of many exiles who prophesised God's worldly sovereignty over all nations. As I said, my parents just wanted to name their first son something after strength and courage, not for any religious reason or something like that. I don't consider myself a religious person but to ask me if I believe in God is a different question. One that I don't have the patience to answer."

Both stand in the silence as the daunting question about belief in God pervades over them. Juan Pablo is sort of beside himself given Ezekiel's forwardness.

"Ah, okay then. Well, it is nice to meet you. My name is Juan Pablo."

"Nice to meet you. Hey, by any chance you know what's taking so long with my passport?"

"Just one minute and I will return. *Mi amiga. Donde esta el passporte* de, Ezekiel?"

"*Lo siento. Aqui esta*, Juan."

"You should be careful in Venezuela. If you are travelling with a Venezuelan, you should listen to him or her," Juan Pablo states as he stamps Ezekiel's passport.

"Yes, sir. I will be careful. I'm travelling with a Venezuelan."

"Good. Listen to him or her. And welcome to Venezuela."

"Thank you, sir."

"Ah, I see that you have made it through immigration. The easy step into the Capitol – the life of wealth," Carlos says somewhat loudly as Ezekiel approaches him from the seemingly empty distance.

"Yes, Carlos! I made it through fine."

"I hope you have followed my instructions, Ezekiel?"

"Well, I kind of did. Hey, it was not my fault! Juan Pablo wanted to speak to me."

"What do you mean you kind of did? And who's this Juan Pablo person? What are you talking about?" Carlos states astoundingly.

The vast majority of people coming and going around the streets of Caracas distracts both Carlos and Ezekiel. Familiar and unfamiliar faces walk by one another, going to places where their minds lead them. We pass by hundreds, even thousands of people every day, unaware of where they are going or what they are going to do next. We pay little to no attention to any detail about them or even to their own actions because we too are often part of the masses, going somewhere, blindly. Their faces may be imprinted in our minds, creating a moment to remember if the experience is novel but often their faces and the experiences aren't. The imprint of their faces instantly fades. They are mere random images that become hazy moments afterwards. Caracas makes New York City seem insignificant when comparing population.

"No, that's impossible. It cannot be true. It's her. It cannot be. There's no way," Carlos subtly mentions not realising he had just thought aloud to Ezekiel. Carlos suspiciously pulls out the same ring he had on him in Philadelphia. Carefully not to attract Ezekiel's attention he puts it away. He would recognise her jet-black hair because it was distinct from any other women who have jet-black hair. Hers was straight until almost at the end it waves sluggishly above her shoulders. Anyone who knows Fernanda would easily recognise *her* jet-black hair.

"Yo bro. Everything okay with you?"

"Yeah, yeah. Everything is fine," Carlos speciously states as he tries to hide his true emotions and thoughts.

"Sure, but who were you talking about a moment ago? Because a moment ago, you were just saying, it's impossible. It couldn't be her. So, who's the girl? Your mystery mistress or a long forgotten friend with some benefits attached?"

"How about this, let's not talk about that, okay? We have far more important things to discuss and discover than my flawed and unreliable thoughts. First, we have to visit Julio, at the hotel. Can you trust me, bro?"

"Yeah, I trust you." Ezekiel then silently speaks, in his head of course. *Carlos is being stranger and stranger.*

The hustle and bustle reverberates through every street corner as Carlos and Ezekiel ride on the red New Bolivarian Republic bus that was made in China. Voices pervade the streets. The constant flow of words spills and spews out of uncountable mouths. Venezuelans ask questions: *Cuantos tienes* (How much), *Que Passa* (What's up), *Donde es* (Where is), *Donde vas* (where are you going), *Te gusta* (you like), *Que hora es* (what time is it), *Que mas (*What more), or *listo* (ready). Sounds jump through these streets too. Beep. Beep. Zoom. Zoom. Roar. Screech. Honk. Honk. Ding. Boom. Chime. Eventually, all of these sounds and words merge together like Caracas traffic. It all becomes one.

Beyond the colossal noise, Venezuelans live in a prison of solitude. They don't live but fight to survive.

It's expected to not find any money in any ATM machine. *Excuse me my brother is there any money dispensing from this ATM machine? I'm sorry there's no money.* Imagine asking this twenty different times to twenty different people to find out the answer is always the same – *No, Lo siento. No mas mi pana.* (*No, I'm sorry. No more my friend*). Then after asking this twenty different times, you find an ATM. *Excuse me, my brother. Please tell me money is dispensing from this one? Yes. It is but you have to wait and stand at the end of the line, which is around the corner you came from. You mean, THIS CORNER. Yes. My brother. This corner. Thank you.* What do you do? You have to wait and stand at the end of the line. Now you have waited for about two hours. It's your turn at the machine to finally get your money. See, you just do not make one transaction. You have to make many to get many bolivares. You put your bankcard in the bottomless mouth of the monster to find out the machine is not dispensing. Not anymore! It just ran out of cash. Almost every *buhonero* or merchant-shops only accept cash as payment in Caracas. Credit is as rejected as freedom here.

The bus driver, unkempt and sloppy appearing like many Venezuelans, drives on the anarchic, mobbed Simon Bolivar Avenue. Up head, everyone on the bus or in their own vehicle sees mountains. The closer you get to them you notice that they are barren. These, at first, are despicable to see. You see that there are homes inside of the mountains. You assure yourself, from here it looks like any typical home, but further and further into the mountains, they are not. These are homes because people make them their homes. The inhabitants slavishly built these slums with abandoned materials to produce something resembling a home. Roofs forged together by rusted, shiny tin. Walls nailed together with splintered, robust wood. Floors paved together with mud and rocks called concrete. Not one, not two, but many of these constructions are built on top of each other in rows that go up and sideways. These constructions were built with sweat, blood and a false promise that one day these constructions would turn into opportunity. Some of these constructions were painted different colours to symbolise not the people's sadness but the happiness that they have a place they can call their own and away from the urbanised Caracas city – away from the Program – the Red Monster. No motor vehicle could ever make it up those frail hills to reach these constructions, so the people built rough-and-ready narrow paths. Be careful not to fall down or back into a bottomless blackened pit. However, the people know how to navigate their way around the paths and back to their homes. Laughter and joy fill these homes at night while the lighting sings brightly and where the music speaks gently. They are celebrating their sons and daughters getting jobs. They will be working tomorrow in a retail store, fast food restaurant or their own small corner stand in one of the *buhoneros*. They are happy that more money will stream into their homes, which means more *arepas* to fill the tables. They don't count 200 or 300 extra bolivares. They are just happy to have a little more money for a little bit more food. You see, not one or two people live in these constructions, but multiple generations. Extended families live together to support each other. These constructions are the slums to the public, but to the people who live in there, they are their homes. Where the sidewalk ends and when the street bends, you'll see where the slums begin. But here, the sun doesn't shine crimson bright. The moon bird doesn't rest from his tireless flight. There's no cool peppermint wind. It's just dim. To outsiders, this is so, but to them, the sun shines crimson bright and they smell and taste the cool peppermint wind. They may be poor but they live a rich life. Do we know them by name? Do we hear their cries of joy and wanting change too?

"Hey, Ezekiel, wake up?"

"Man, what are you talking about, I'm awake."

"Then get your head out of the gutter."

"What are you talking about? I was just looking over the mountains, at the slums."

"Yes, the slums. The people who live there are mostly happy. They are happy because they are thankful for what they have. As little as what they have, they are happy people. I can't believe I'm saying this, but if there's one thing good about the Program it would be that."

"It would be what Carlos?" Ezekiel inquisitively asked as to clear up his confusion of what *that* Carlos is talking about.

"I mean the people are not materialistic. They are happy in the worst possible situations. They do not need material possessions to make them happy. They are happy because they have each other and they have a great country – in terms of natural beauty, culture and people, and food when they can find any – not because of the situations happening nowadays."

Ezekiel condescendingly states to chastise the Program, "of course, they are not happy about the situations happening nowadays! Why or how could anyone ever be happy under *those* situations is beyond my own comprehension."

"Alright, bro! Enough with the sighs, comments and rude undertones."

"Cool man, cool. Hey, do you want to talk about what happened back there when you were saying it's not possible to see her."

"No, I rather not. Besides, stop joking around. We are almost there to see Julio."

"So then, Julio works at the hotel? What's so special about him?"

"All will be revealed, my friend! In time!" Carlos hastily says before standing up to jump from the bus.

"Okay," Ezekiel says calmingly as he is unaware that they are approaching the hotel.

Carlos taps Ezekiel on the chest with the back of his palm to indicate it's time to move.

"Let's go. We are here!"

While outside the hotel, Ezekiel notices more of the same national guards that were lurking, stalking and watching outside the airport.

There may be, in fact, more national guards in the city, actually, Ezekiel thinks to himself. He abruptly grabs a hold of Carlos's right shoulder, gently as not to make him react as if Ezekiel is some sort of enemy combatant, to ask him why there is a presence of so many military guards.

The sun blackened by a treacherous overcast. The sun dims out, consumed by the ghostly and grossly monstrous guardians. They march in unison, covered in camouflage fatigues. They are nothing but camouflage to the Common People. The sound of their boots and the click of their machine guns haunt the Common People well after they come and go on the streets. The fear lingers on the pandemic streets and in the deepest gallows of the Common People's minds. They only know of one thing, follow orders. Their thinking is not of their own, but the will of the Program. Their presence is tall and not as orderly as military personnel's are supposed to be. The National Guard and the National Police are one of the same – the product of the Program – the Red Scare.

"Hey, Carlos! Hey, my friend. Wait for a sec!" exhaustedly states Ezekiel, not because of the occupied book bag on his shoulders and the suitcase he wheels with his right hand, but because of going through a maze of people just to get off the bus.

"Yes, what is it?"

"What did I tell you about keeping a low profile until we get into the hotel and see Julio?"

"There's this one question that has been bothering me ever since we left the airport. I'm itching to ask it desperately. It is a splinter in my mind. It won't go away until I rip it out!"

Reluctantly, Carlos entertains Ezekiel once again by responding, "Alright. Fine! What's the question? What is bothering you! What is so important?"

"I can't help but notice the many military guards around. It's almost like they are everywhere preventing something from happening," Ezekiel curiously states.

"I understand the question. So okay…you are right about one thing. They are everywhere, but they are not preventing anything as if anything would occur. I mean, the people had it. Many of them gave up. They lost hope. So, they are complacent. But you are right. There are many of them. They are here more so now than at any time before to intimidate people. In fact, if you give them any reason they may just shoot you. Ah, wait. I know what you are going to say next. Relax. They are not going to come near you because they are more afraid of you and besides, you are not Venezuelan."

"But why are there as many of them now as before you mentioned."

"The Program believes that by mobilising more national guards on the grounds the people are more protected and the ones who want to start *trouble* by convincing the rest of the commoners to *rebel.* They simply won't do it."

While Ezekiel is baffled at this point, he automatically responds, "Oh, okay then." His response indicates his tired frustration of the lack of sense and awareness the commoners have.

Before entering the lobby, Carlos turns to Ezekiel and leans over to his left ear as if he is bending down to pick up something he dropped and whispers the following remarks: "They are always watching us. When you think you're safe, in your house, at work or with your friends, they always find ways to track you. You're never safe from the Red Scare. That's what started out as – a virus – an epidemic – a plague that was going to eradicate poverty and restore equality to all. This virus was disguised as the 4-F Program. These soldiers you see, and the many more you will see throughout any city in Venezuela, represents the omnipresence and grip of the virus. You are now in the mouth of the red monster. You are in the *Capitol*, so just pay attention to me." Sure enough, Carlos pretends to bend down to pick up some receipts that fell out of his pocket and to tie a loose shoelace.

Ezekiel suspects the usual from Carlos' message, paranoia but in his judgment, he will follow his lead, not because he said so but because he is in a different country and a country nonetheless that appears to be heavily occupied and armed.

Carlos and Ezekiel finally arrive in the lobby. The lobby is grand but obsolete. While the Program appropriated all of these private buildings, it failed to upkeep them, so they are dilapidating. The marble floors remain unpolished. The aged cherry wood counters remain un-waxed. Half of the ceiling lighting remains unchanged. For Carlos Christian Santos, anxiety and nausea drapes over his mind as to pull him back somewhere in the past while walking through the lobby. For Ezekiel Ian Masefield, excitement and weariness infiltrate throughout his mind while he walks through the lobby. Large oil paintings are noticeable that hang behind the reception desk. There are three paintings, one of President Chava, another of Simon Bolivar and the last, of President Maburro. Chava's picture is on the left, Simon's picture is in the middle and Maburro's picture is on the right. Their presence unerringly looks at you with trepidation, as if you are among the *Victorias* or if you are Chavista, their presence looks at you with comfort. Somehow, by looking into their eyes, you can feel the presence of their spirit. Though Chava and Maburro have the same spirit presence, of nationalism, valour and conceitedness, Simon does not. His spirit cries to the Venezuela he once knew, to what Venezuela is today. His spirit states, *the art of victory is learned in failures.* Yet, neither of these presidents have learned from their failures.

Typical Venezuelans. No one is behind the reception desk other than the paintings. Carlos Christian Santos rings the bell four times indicating a secret code or message. From the office appears a well-polished, professional hotel associate. It was nonetheless, Julio. Carlos immediately identifies Julio's well-kept demeanour and bight simile.

"Ah CCS. Is that you?" Julio takes a closer look. Looking at the faded scar on his left wrist.

"Old friend, JMS (Julio Marcus Santa), it has been a while. How are you?"

"CCS, it's you. It has been a while brother. But Chéreve!"

"Unfortunately, it has been, Julio. But Chéreve!"

"But hey, at least you are still one of the good guys."

"Well, thanks to Leo, I'm proud to say I am."

"So, how's the States? What have you been up to for these last four years?"

"Where are my manners, Julio? This is my Gringo friend, Ezekiel Ian Masefield. We studied together for four years, at the same University, Temple, but in different programs."

Julio shifts his eyes to Ezekiel and extends his hand for a firm handshake. "Well, it's nice to meet you, Ezekiel. May I call you E for short?" *Tu hablas Española?*

"No. *Un poco de Española.* Well, Julio…only if, I can call you J for short. Hey man! I'm just kidding. But yeah, if you want you can call me E for short."

"It's just that Ezekiel is my brother's name and I'll get confused. You know?"

"Yeah. Yeah. Perfectly fine man. No sweat. Alright."

"But Carlito…" Julio humorously mentions.

"Carlito, you know, I do not like that name. It just reminds me of how my brother and sister had always insisted on calling me that despite my urgency and desperate plea to not be called Carlito."

"I know. I'm just messing with you. Anyway, we have to catch up tonight. Same place as before?"

"Yes, outside by the pool area. That's where we will meet."

"How does 7:30 sound?"

"Our usual time, perfect. Hey, will Leo and the others be there tonight?"

"No, not tonight. But that's tonight. Let me check all of you in."

"Sure, old friend."

"Okay. I see that you have reserved suite 1015. Here are your cards. Ah Ezekiel, here's yours."

"Cool boss."

"Just in case you and Carlos may need a second one."

"Let me finish finalising the bill. So, you are staying for three nights. Carlos, can you sign the document?"

"Yes, for sure."

"Okay. Here's your copy. We are all set. See you both later tonight."

"Of course. And by the way, the States is well. The States, as always makes progress."

"Excuse me, Carlos. You have forgotten your newspaper. I believe it is yours – you want to take a look. Trust me, old friend. Anyway, it's about today's news."

"It's something I forget these days. As always, old friend, thank you."

While on the elevator, making their way to their room, Carlos begins to read the newspaper Julio just gave him. Ezekiel is mesmerised at Carlos for just what happened, he thought it uncharacteristic of him to act the way he did, puzzling. The elevator grinds in agony as its old bones – that are its chains, nuts and bolts have not been oiled for decades – helplessly stride to pull itself up and down each floor.

"This cannot be safe," Ezekiel exclaims as if he and Carlos were the only two on the elevator.

"Uh, well this clunker, timeworn machine here won't fail us. It never does," Carlos states quietly to Ezekiel, as to not disturb the other few guests riding in the elevator. Well, it would not matter because they mostly speak Spanish, so what they say, the people would not understand them.

Ezekiel waits for the three individuals with a red 4-F on their hat (different from the hat Ezekiel carries in his bag) to get off at the fourth floor to say the following cautiously, "What was that all about back there? As always my friend, I forget things now. Or how about the paper you picked up, oh you must have forgotten about that. Why is this puzzling? Why are you being peculiar all of a sudden?"

Carlos hardly hears him as he is too engulfed in the newspaper. Seconds later, Carlos states, "Julio, old friend, you never cease to amaze me (while reading the newspaper). Yes, Ezekiel. I'm happy you have waited for the Chavistas to get off of the elevator before you asked me about my discussion with Julio."

"Uh, wait a sec. They were Chavistas?" he states paradoxically. "Oh, that would explain why they have gotten off at 4F, because it is supposed to mean February 4 as well as the fourth floor. I got it now. But you have not answered me. What was all that back there with Julio, though?"

"Walk with me. We are approaching the tenth floor and I have to show you where our room is. Trust me! Anyone who is unfamiliar with this hotel can get lost without knowing they got lost. I have chosen this room because of the Victorias, the opposition. It has a symbolic meaning. This symbolic meaning is, on October fifteenth, Leo Emmanuel Lopez resurrected the group by marching through the culture and financial district of the capitol in retaliation of the massacre of protesters, shortage of water and food and no security around the college campuses at 10:15 in the morning. Also, it's symbolic for me. At 10:15 in the evening, Leo and Maria, the first leaders to revive the Victorias, brought me in while I was Captain Santos on the verge of being promoted to Major Santos. So, Julio is a member of the V's and he sends messages to me through newspapers or other written forms. I'm not the only person he sends messages to obviously. These messages are anagrams that explain what has been happening and any plans in the works. Don't forget the reason the *Guardias* recruited me was because of my math skills. Reading the anagrams follows the same logic. Very few of us can decipher the clandestine messages. I am concerned. Leo has been imprisoned for quite some time now. So, I'm sure it's one of the other Victorias."

The Venetur Alba's hallways are surely a maze – intricate to navigate through. There is no apparent pattern or at least one that is easily identified. It appears, however, the even numbers are located on the right and the odd numbers are located on the left. Numbers are missing on both sides of the hallway. Around every other corner, that part of the hallway is dark, absent of light. No light shines there. Then around other corners, there's light, but it's fading – it's almost out! But Carlos remembers the way to the room. He needs no light. Darkness is just fine for him to get there. After all, to him, walking through these dim-lit hallways is sense memory. The pattern he follows, of how to get to room 1015 is nothing but unfamiliar. The pattern pulsates angrily, much like the fading, silent dim dark absent illuminating light from the walls and ceiling. Up ahead, through the thickness of light's shadows, room 1015 flickers riotously.

"Okay. So Julio is like a spy or something from one of those United States spy movies?" Ezekiel perplexedly mentions.

"Hardly. No. It's not like that at all. Remember what I told you. The Program, here, controls the media and all of its forms, so communication is nearly impossible until Julio alters a few papers that he takes and gives to the opposition. Not all opposition members get the newspaper; so then, it is up to us to get in contact with the rest of them. But I'll tell you this…it is becoming more and more difficult to communicate with each other because the Program's grip or control is becoming tighter and tighter."

"So then, what is the message?"

"Well, you see there are opposition members all over Venezuela where some of them have government positions. Julio's friend works for the printing press. This is how Julio is able to get the anagrams to us. But of course, you mean the messages in the newspaper. It just says what we already know, but it also says who will be at tonight's meeting."

"So let me get this straight. What you already know is it's getting progressively worse and the country is on the brink of collapse. Its people will attempt to fight but not know how to fight or why they are fighting. They just will."

"Sort of, Ezekiel, sort of. Briefly, it states, *Leo Emmanuel Lopez is imprisoned; Maria Elizabeth Santana has been falsely detained, awaiting to be indicted; and the protests will happen at Central University, at the principal market and selected subway stops tomorrow.*"

"Okay. Yeah, so you already know this. Then the Program knows this, but they cannot stop them from happening tomorrow, right?"

"It will be chaotic. Just remember that."

"I will. But like you said, it may be far worse this time."

Once Carlos Christian Santos and Ezekiel Ian Masefield enter the room, they sparingly drop their bags to inspect the room. For Ezekiel, he is curious about the amenities and aesthetics of the room. For Carlos, on the other hand, he is in search of something; perhaps it is the handgun that the V's left for him (though the Victorias strive to practice non-violence) or perhaps he is determining whether his thoughts, experiences and emotions are even real. Has his mind gotten the best of him or the Red Scare's intoxicating grip? Both CCS and EIM, have moments of reflections.

There are eight million Venezuelans who live in the capitol, scraping to only have one solid hot meal a day, if that. Of those eight million, six million live in *los barrios* or slums, so for them, they plead with death not to take them – which they plead, death's rent will come the next day. They plead, plead to withstand just one more day for opportunity that isn't waiting by – opportunity to escape the barrios and live life, not survive or manage it. The slums are not just in the mountains; today it seems they are everywhere. People who live in apartments, houses – they too survive, not live.

That's the catch isn't. The Program promised better housing for all people, even those who live in the substandard conditions they call home. They spend generations in conditions like these to be given sporadic and inconsistent aid from the government. You, anyone, will be conditioned to believe and know this is life and that it gets better, eventually. Complacency collects in their minds. They become used to it, desensitised to any emotion to change the current government. It's a virus really hibernating in their minds deceiving them. I, as a tourist, should know after all. I feel the virus clawing at every cell and nerve of my body to compromise my immune system, that means that I too am becoming complacent and desensitised after only having been here for just a few short but long hours.

Venezuelans who live in Caracas, or eventually, move there are called Los Caraqueños. Venezuelans come to Caracas to make a living – for an opportunity at a better life. Caracas is the city of hope. Thousands of Venezuelans every week battle to come to work here. This is the city of hope for a reason. It's the *Capitol*. All who live here, well, government personnel anyway, feast on its luscious food, abundant resources and endless cash. Work and wealth live and thrive here. This is what Venezuelans and Los Caraqueños believe to be the capitol.

It's just a disguise – a mask that has many faces for the people. It's a face of comfort. It's a face of crime. It's a face of security. It's a face of chaos. Caracas is the illusion of work and wealth. Every sidewalk, every corner, every street there is poverty. Poverty has a smell and it smells of perished corpses, forgotten, dissuaded and removed. What lingers in the air is repulsion, the repulsion and stagnation of stale faeces, rancid decomposition and polluted perspiration. This is the smell of broken promises, of broken dreams. Failed and corrupt politics are to blame. Venezuelans are blind and deaf to the ubiquitous repugnant smell of Caracas but it is worse, where they live or where they came from. It's unbearable there. They come to Caracas because eventually, no one is able to smell the stench of poverty. They become numb to its smell.

Despite its smell, Venezuelans come to Caracas to make a monthly comparable wage of twenty-five US dollars. If they are among the small few, they make a comparable monthly wage of fifty US dollars. Unfortunately, these monthly wages are not enough and are often spent on obtaining two weeks' worth of food – well, that's what they hope for. If they are lucky, they ration their supply or sustain any of the little food they purchase.

Ezekiel reflects how Caracas is divided between the haves and have-nots.

Something smells rotten in the city of Caracas. It lingers in the air and never dissipates. I cannot get used to how walking over to one side of the street then to the other, the vast differences between the two. On one side, you see developed buildings, courteous and well-kempt people and well established and educated people then on the other side, you see depleted or underdeveloped buildings, people wearing rags as clothes, people living on the street, people begging for bolivares and non-established or undereducated people who fight to make a living. This contrast is easily seen. Walk to Este 1 or Barrio Enero 23, you'll clearly see.

Private businesses flourish on the right side of the streets and public programs deplete on the left side of the streets. As private businesses leave or are shut down by the red monster, they slowly become like the public programs, depleted and empty. Both sides of the streets, the right and left sides converge to become the same, fringed, forgotten and damaged. Socialism is supposed to create equity but it, unfortunately, creates disparity. Socialism is supposed to close the social-economic gaps but it widens them. Socialism is supposed to eradicate violence but it creates and supports it. Instead, socialism creates a border in Venezuela. Socialism is responsible for an underclass society. Venezuelans who were once poor and support President Chava were given money and some sort of position of power. They became known as the Chavistas. People, who once had money, now are poor, especially those who speak out against the Program. If you speak out against the red monster and are lucky not be murdered, tortured or have your family slaughtered in front of you, you spend eternity in solitude where the only thing that keeps you company are the dark, red-lit streets.

Los Caraqueños walk by one another as if they were shadows. Those who were always poor die without ever being noticed. Los Caraqueños walk by with their shoulders shrugged and head held to the ground or glued to their phone as to intentionally not glimpse at anyone other than themselves. Some may know that poverty exists and everyone is living it, though many know this is living an abundant life. Poverty has no place here – it's not a word and is neglected by its Spanish name, pobre. This is what many Caraqueños believe. It surrounds every one of them even when they do know but ignore it. Other than death, poverty is certain where life is not.

If you are not Venezuelan, you are an outsider looking in, as am I. I am an interloper and am only to see a glass half-empty. To Them, and to any Venezuelan, I am the intruder who is looked at indifferently, not because of my skin colour, religion, political ideology, status but just because I am North American. To them, instantly they presume I am better. I come from better conditions. Some are angry just for the fact that I am here. I am here to invade, to change, to persuade them that Venezuela must be like the United States – a capitalistic monster. Others want to embrace me just because I am North American. "Take me with you to show me where I can find opportunity or so that my dreams can become reality," they want to say. Then others – many more than I realise, don't care. They know their country is failing – that they too will or are part of the masses to trying to survive before dying. To these people, they have lost hope. They are a skeleton of their former self, just counting the days if today is their day to die. To that, I say, yes, I am an outsider looking in but putting myself in your shoes. Though I cannot ever possibly fathom the life you are a prisoner to live but I can walk a kilometre and live that life briefly and just briefly. However, I do not see the glass half-empty or half-full. I see the glass as it is. I see the glass as fragile needing to be fixed before it shatters. I also say, I'm no interloper in disguise. I am here to learn, to understand and experience a culture once well-known and travelled. I also say, losing hope is fire to the soul. Without it, They win. The virus becomes that much more deadly. It continues to consume and ravage everything and anything left of you and of Venezuela. The greatest tool against the virus – the red monster as it became to be known to tourists to save hope is your voice. Words shout loud and louder than you may think they do. All you have to do is give reason to your voice then it is able to listen. Then your voice is able to thrive and that cannot be ravaged and raped by the Program. Like a caged bird's voice thrills, so does your imprisoned voice thrill in what darkest hours you encounter.

It has been a matter of hours. Part of the room is disturbed where the other part of the room has been untouched. Carlos and Ezekiel were unaware of the time because they were caught up in their own heads to realise it's almost time to meet Julio and the others by poolside. It was safer for them to speak outside than inside. Inside they can hear you whereas outside, they hardly can hear you. Ezekiel enters from the bathroom to put on a clean shirt and socks to find Carlos blacked out from his medication. Suddenly, Carlos yells out words that to Ezekiel have no meaning and are somewhat disturbing.

Little does Ezekiel knows that Fernanda is in fact back in Caracas. She has been with the Victorias ever since the Program reformed her. She decided to reform to save herself and her family to avoid death. This information was also deciphered from the newspaper that Carlos routinely forgot to tell Ezekiel. Embedded in the information briefly discusses how she is vital in the next, soon-approaching assignment. Carlos, on the other hand, lives in his own prison of solitude, that is, his mind. He once again attempts to assemble a new puzzle, but not all of the pieces are there; some are intentionally missing from the assembly. One of the many adverse side effects of the negative reactant injections is that it has a tendency to alter past memories, but temporarily, of course. One of the positive side effects is to maintain healthy body shape, which this is how Carlos after all of these years of sporadically *keeping in shape*, he did not have to do much work because of this drug.

"No Carlito! You didn't take me. You took my little brother Simon. Don't you remember? You said in my interrogation that he was too valuable. That's why he was released. I wasn't nor was my family. So you released him," Carlos states as if he was Fernanda or she states if she was actually in the room.

"What are you talking about Fernanda? After I tortured you, to protect your family, you wanted to reform. That's what happened. I did not murder Simon. I murdered a lot of people but surely I did not go around murdering children or women for that matter."

"No. Don't you see? This is what you want to remember. You had a change of heart eventually. You came into the prison cell at an odd hour of the night to tell me that I must leave with my family. It's not going to be safe. Clever as you were, they never found out it was you who helped us escaped."

"Yes, that's what happened. I did not murder anymore. You wanted to be reformed but I wanted you to escape. So you and your family did. You and your family left that night – left Caracas – left Venezuela."

"That's an alternative reality Carlito. Yes, I was reformed but at the expense of my little brother being released. At the time it was not your call, all you did was to report it to Lt. Rodriguez and Major Maburro. Remember the ring. I overheard you stating that it's your ring your mom gave to you on your eighteenth birthday to celebrate a new life you will have with your own family someday. Then you said it's a symbol of not only your forgotten childhood but a symbol of what has been lost every day since then. That ring you carry in your pocket is a symbol of a life you could have had."

"No. No. It can't be true! Can it be true! Fernanda, I do not know anymore! Please you got to help me. My own sins are converging! I do not know what to do! Please help! Are you even here? Speak to me! Damn it! Speak to me! Are you here? Are you even listening? I did not torture anyone! I did not kill Simon or any child for that matter. This ring is just a piece of jewellery given to me on my eightieth birthday. It's no symbol. I carry it in my pocket because it did not fit on finger then and now it still doesn't. I always forget to get it resized. Everyone in my family has one. It's a tradition in some families. Please hear me. I did not murder Simon! I did not hurt you! I could not! You are the one who helped me in school. See, I'm forever in your debt. See, after all this time, I wanted to ask you to go to the nightclub but really I did not know how to say thank you, so I wanted to thank you by taking you to a night club or another place like that."

While the bathroom door closes behind Ezekiel, Carlos snaps out of this psychedelic trance, realising Ezekiel may have heard his entire conversation.

With a puzzled and traumatised look, Ezekiel states nonchalantly, "I just came to get a new shirt. I just came from taking a shower. I'll go now."

"How much did you hear of that?" Carlos responds stutteringly.

"You mean the ravenous ranting of just bizarreness, um, all, almost all of it. You know, actually, to come to think of it the water was running I just heard sounds. I thought nothing of it because you must have had the television or radio on. Though, as I said, I was in a shower, so I just heard sounds. But from what I heard while shaving, is that you have made a mistake to Fernanda and you are unsure of what is reality. So yea, nothing in particular. Though while I was shaving, I'm not even sure if I heard that." Ezekiel casually and calmly speaks.

"Yeah. That's pretty much it. Just listen to me. By tonight, I will be fine. All of my confusion will dissipate."

"Okay, bro. But I was going to ask, are you going to go like that to meet Julio and the others? You are not going to change or something because it is passed 7:00, bro."

"I thought we are meeting them at 7:30, no?"

Ezekiel snaps his fingers, "Wait you are right, Carlos. 7:30 does sound very familiar now. So I guess we will be on time then."

"Yeah. Yeah. Give me one moment. And I'll put a shirt on or something."

Ezekiel does not divulge further into Carlos' conversation, for Carlos has warned him that these manic episodes of wailing confusion will happen at least in the first night while he returns to Caracas. Ezekiel far encountered these moments and remembers far too well not to intervene in Carlos' crisis. Ezekiel is concerned nonetheless, that he may, in fact, be losing touch of reality. Perhaps, he thinks *it wasn't a bad idea after all, to have stayed put in the States.* This frame of thought is but remains stationary in the past that no longer can happen. They are finally here, in the *Capitol.* Whatever horrors or adventures are going to happen will happen. For Carlos, the horrors and adventures have long started but for Ezekiel, will be forever petrified or changed for that matter. The capitol doesn't discriminate whether you are not from Caracas, from the Americas or from any other part of the world. It craves on fear. It obsesses over it, much like children getting their way with others. If you have fear, it'll exploit it. Everyone has fear, so it exploits it regardless. It not only craves on fear, it lives on fear.

"Let's go, Ezekiel, it is almost time to talk with Julio."

"You have some nerve bro to tell me to go. You are the one who...never mind, I'm right behind you man."

Carlos decides to take all ten flights of stairs down to give Ezekiel a proper tour of the Venetur Alba Caracas. Its design is not special or more elaborate than any other five star Hilton Hotel from the late nineties. What is astonishing is the

Venezuelan historic painting around the lobby and around the marble path to the pool area. There are various pictures of Chava, of Bolivar and of course of Maburro. Maburro is the current president. Perhaps more people immortalise Chava more than they do Bolivar but Bolivar is right next to him. Chava had a mystic way of moving people. Every time he went on camera, being interviewed, touring parts of Venezuela to tourists or discussing anything to anybody, he made it a performance. He believed, to truly capture everyone's attention, the presenter has to put on a great performance every time. That's what he did – every time – put on a performance. This is not uncharacteristic of him to do so because if anyone actually knows Chava, he wanted to always be an actor, not join the military. However, once he joined the military, he was amazed and moved by the various uniforms they get to wear and the astonishing celebrations they get to participate in. To Chava, the military got to be his new stage, a performance that would later help him lead the Bolivarian Revolution. Simon Bolivar, on the other hand, is well respected and honoured as one of the greatest American Liberators that liberated Venezuela, Bolivia, Colombia, Panama, Ecuador and Peru. As a Venezuelan military leader, he liberated these six countries from under Spain's shadow, so to these countries, especially in Venezuela, he is an iconic legend.

"There he is in the distance. Typical Julio, always by the water. Hey, we are almost there."

"Yeah, I know. (Directed at someone else.) We are over here, okay." Julio states excitingly.

A feeling of uneasiness pours over Carlos' mind. In his thinking, it could be Fernanda.

"Yeah. I know. I see you."

"Are you going to be okay, bro? Because you are losing colour in your face?"

"Yes. I'm fine."

"Alright then, we are here."

"Carlos and E, I want you to meet Marissa. I'm unsure, Carlos if you know Marissa or not. It has been a long time since your return and I do not think you have met her before your leaving."

"No, I can't say I have. But it's nice to meet you, Marissa."

"It's nice to meet you too, CCS." Marissa gives him a hug and a kiss on the cheeks in return.

"Shall we order some beers?"

Ezekiel states as he gets the attention of the nearby server. "Hey *hermano, ocho cervezas las Soleras verde para la mesa!*"

"*Señor, no mas?*"

"*Luego,* Zulias."

"*Si, señor.*"

"I can't believe they do not have any Soleras. That isn't cool."

"*Hablas Española,* Ezekiel?" Marissa utters in surprise.

"No, *un poco.* I just know how to order beer. What? Every North American likes their beer."

Ezekiel, while waiting for the beer, without reservation downed the crisp slowly condensing glass of water. Everyone certainly knows drinkable water is scarce in Venezuela. Even Ezekiel knows. Though he wasn't particularly thirsty as everyone else sitting around the poolside tables, Ezekiel felt a sudden compulsion to drink the water anyway. It wouldn't be enough to quench the people's thirst but perhaps maybe sustain it for a few, short minutes. It would have to be enough. No water, no life, right? Drinkable water in Venezuela is as scarce as diamonds. People kill over little drinkable water that they find.

"Ah okay. So we'll speak English then," Marissa calmly responds.

"Yes! I agree. It will be much safer than speaking Spanish." Julio responds.

"So, what's this situation happening tomorrow around the Capitol?" Carlos says with revelation.

"While you guys get reacquainted with each other, Ezekiel and I are going to talk about why he is here," Marissa mentions.

"About tomorrow…the protests are in response to the failing Program's reach to continue to help Venezuelans. Well, I do not know how much *they* help or change to better the people. I do not know if you are aware of the lack of water flow from your shower?"

"Yes, I have noticed that Julio."

"Well, you see beyond this hotel and outside the immediate area of Caracas, there's no water, there's no food, there's no electricity, there's no bolivares, there's simply nothing anymore, CCS. Venezuela has become a barren, abandoned, abducted and raped prison. Where there is a chaotic prison, there's bound to be rampant riots. Riots unimaginably feed on the people's fear, which leaves them petrified. So this is why the protests are happening to get as many people fuelled as we can, for the soon-to-come revolution. At this point, the revolutions are inevitable. Yes, I have said it, revolutions with a 's' at the end."

"Okay. Before you move forward with this, let me say something…"

"*Lo siento mis amigos, aqui son sus cervezas*," states the server.

"*Gracias, mi pana*! What was I saying before? Ah yes. I was talking to Ezekiel about that, no water. When there's no water, there's no life. I imagine it got worse, but not like how you are describing it. Damn Julio, this is a problem but I don't think that there should be a revolution among the people, especially not now. They are not prepared. They are not ready. You know how much more bloodshed there will be this time. Certainly, this time the Red Scare will win and winning means the people will completely lose hope…and then what? Another 30 or 50 years of this shit solitude policed state?"

"Yes, it is a risk we unfortunately have to take. It's necessary. It is necessary chaos. Leo is in jail. Maria is being indicted. One by one all of our leaders are either being thrown in jail or being murdered, unknowingly. What else can we do? The revolutions have to happen. This is what the Victorias are discussing. This is what Marissa is here to confirm. I'm sorry to say, Carlos, it must happen."

"Hold on for a second, will you? In the newspaper, you mentioned 'Project Take out the Lazies, status unknown.' How about our assets in the military? Aren't they preparing to take control of the military and overthrow the ridged Chavistas from their positions?"

"Yes. It's true. We have not heard anything from them in a while. But we feel we cannot wait any longer. Besides, we do not have another president in line. The two are basically in jail and the other two are dead. The presidential line of succession has always not existed. Similarly, there isn't any legitimate president to succeed Maburro after the coup."

"The other two are dead?"

"Yes, unfortunately, CCS, they are dead."

"Well, that kind of sucks. But wait! Hold on! There's a provision, if I remember correctly, in Project Take out the Lazies that the military, once we had control of them, they would free the people's president if the people's president is in jail?"

"Yes, Carlos. This is true. Maria will be in jail any day now."

"So, this is sort of good news because she's not dead and we can move forward in stealth."

"But as I said, the Project is static. I do not know where Fernanda is. I have not had contact with her for four weeks. She is supposed to be back in the Capitol but I'm afraid she is either missing or lying low or worse. In either way, CCS, the V's do not want to wait any longer. The grip of the Program is worsening every day. Every day now, you are lucky to read or hear about it if you are not part of the chaos where *they* are just shooting people on location. You are lucky enough not to get caught up in the food riots or loitering to get food or any other necessity. You are lucky enough not to commit acts of violence yourself to find one partly filled bottle of water. I mean, Carlos, there's nothing. There are no clothes to buy, no shoes to wear. Businesses are not doing business because of the amended New Bolivarian Republic Decrees."

"Okay. Okay. Julio. Don't forget that like you, I have lived this experience like any Venezuelan. You could say I was actually in the mouth of the red monster. I have a suggestion, Julio and if Marissa agrees with it, then I think, we can postpone the revolutions for a little while more."

"Okay. I'm listening. What do you propose?"

"There are still high ranking generals in the Program that happen to be on our side. I know them. I can guarantee you I can get them in a private room and discuss where we are with Project Take out the Lazies."

"Well, CCS, if you can pull it off, I do not see why not. But we have to discuss it with Marissa first. But you will only have one day, Carlos! Do pull this through. Otherwise, the revolution will be starting. However, the protests are still on for tomorrow."

"Perfect. I can work with a day. And I understand that the protests must go on tomorrow. It's much-needed action among our people to remind them that change happens through liberation."

"So, Ezekiel, why come to Venezuela? What's so special about our country that made you come here, anyway?"

"Well, Marissa, this is a tough question to ask but one of which should be asked. I have been to other South American countries before. I have been to Chile, Argentina, Panama and Honduras. The Americas have been particularly interesting to me through their European rule, fighting for their independence and now their president day. I, however, research how education affects their culture, for better or for worse. For some time, while completing my doctorate, and after, I have worked with my government to correlate terrorism and education."

"So, I see that you have an interest in researching our education systems in the Americas...but why Venezuela? Why come now?"

"Other than its natural and historic beauty, I come to Venezuela to participate in doing my part to help understand how Venezuela got to where it is now. I'm also here to do my part to help Carlos with eliminating the Red Scare."

"So you want to help, even though you have no connections to our country – even though you can go back home and enjoy life fully than say any person living in Venezuela – you want to help us? I have to say, Ezekiel, it is a very noble cause for you to do this. I still don't understand why. I suppose I never will."

"Anyone can move people and persuade change through revolutionising their efforts but understanding how this will impact everyone, not just in the immediate but for the long term, is not done correctly. What I am discussing, Marissa is about properly educating people so that they can continue to establish and sustain their country. You see, I'm here to eventually give tools to your people so that they can educate each other. Above all, Marissa, I have this indescribable feeling like I should be here. I do not know why but I just feel I need to be here."

"You are more of an educationalist then?"

"Precisely. Marissa, let me ask you this…why are you interested in working with the opposition?"

"Ezekiel, it is not about so of my working with the opposition as it is doing what justice that needs to be done. If it were the opposite, where the Victorias were the Red Scare and the Program were the Opposition, I would be fighting for the Red Scare because that's the moral way. Remember this; I fight for the people and for the world. Our country, Venezuela, is desperately crying! Venezuela is not helping its people and certainly, it's not helping the world. Our country is failing to the point where it will not recover and once it completely crumbles, it will slightly impact the world, but shortly thereafter, Venezuela will be a footnote in history – forgotten and removed! There is one thing, however, that the Program did get right."

"What's that Marissa, what did the program get right?" Ezekiel says sarcastically.

"Ezekiel, the Program's attempt is to build connection among people and extinguish disconnection. If people are not or do not feel connected, then what's the point? But as we know, the Program has this sinister way of building a connection with people that once were decent ideologies of fulfilling deep-rooted relationships, which turned out to be corrupt. Instead, the Program continues to create this embedded line of division between *them versus us*."

"I have to say, Marissa, you nailed it. You certainly did. It is about forming connections and trust but without properly instilling this among all people equally, you have division – clash of views rather than views working side by side."

"Over time, Ezekiel, we will achieve this among our people. Hell, come to think of it, that may just be happening right now. To think about it, more and more people are coming together because of the Program's failure, right? Well, I mean, they are coming together as a result of not being unified. Sadly, though, they are coming together under extraneous circumstances and for the very wrong reasons."

"This is why, Marissa, people need to be given the tools I have attempted to describe, not now, not after, but always. It always has been rooted in education for better or for worse. I'm afraid, just like Carlos mentions, that almost all the time after the revolution, it will take years, Marissa, for Venezuela to restructure, so its survival and prosperity relies on its people collaborating – interdepending on each other."

Julio briskly interjects, "I'm sorry E, to cut the conversation short, but Marissa, may we have a word for a second?"

"Yes, Julio you may. Ezekiel, we will finish the conversation soon. I'll be back. This should not take more than a minute."

"Sure, Marissa, I'll just order more beer, everyone agrees?"

"Marissa, Carlos and I were discussing on holding off of the revolution until…we'll I'll let CCS talk to you about it. Carlos, would you mind?"

"No, Julio, I do not mind."

Julio apologises to Ezekiel. "My brother. I'm sorry. It will take about a minute."

"Yea, man. Don't sweat. It's all good. I'm ordering more beer for the table, so it's all good. Nah."

"Don't worry, okay?"

"Thanks, Ezekiel."

"Carlos, what is this new assignment you have?"

"So I have been thinking Marissa, I still know generals and other high ranking officials in the military and in the Program that are on our side, I could…"

"You are talking about Project Take out the Lazies? It's not going to work."

"Project Take Out the Lazies?" Carlos expounds inquisitively and suddenly.

"Damn, Marissa! Let me explain. I still know these assets well. I can get them in a private room and discuss where we are. Afterwards, if you do not like what they have to say, then you and the Opposition can move forward with the revolution."

"Alright, Carlos. I will give this leverage, only if you can get it done in one day."

"As I have said to Julio, a day is all I need."

"Fine. We are all on board then."

The darkness begins to set heavily around Caracas. Carlos Christian Santos begins to enter into another trance to the past somewhere. For him too, the past is as mysterious as anyone who enters his mind. He does not realise that the well-into-the-night conversations just closed. Everyone who is still outside are about to head inside or are already walking inside, unnoticeably digresses amongst himself or herself to why Venezuelans are not walking around Caracas during nightfall.

There's an unwritten and unspoken curfew – 'in before nightfall'. The crimes that take place heinously only unfold at night. These crimes are the boogieman. The boogieman is a legend that parents tell their children. It's an unfixed shadowy figure. It's a nonspecific embodiment only to reveal itself through children's worst fears. Caracas becomes this nightmare at night but children are not the only people petrified, everyone is. At night, Caracas is a playground for any boogieman to pervade, perverse and prey over. This monster does not just feed on fear. It enjoys it. It rapes your innocence. Once it does, you become boogieman-like – committing unthinkable crimes yourself. This legend exists because it is a product of the Program's failing attempt to destroy crime and corruption. The worst of all, in Caracas, it's not a legend – it's very real and something to be very terrified of.

There's no imagining it when it is the very reality that Venezuela weeps. The military or police don't manage Caracas, yet they may think they do but they do not. The criminals overrun Caracas. The criminals and the corrupt have the real power, not state actors or political officials. These servants have no power or authority. To them, it's an illusion.

Chapter 10

Lies, Deceit and Horror

The Grim Reaper lurks with its grimy, rusted, macabre scythe. It's always there, looking with its no face for its next victims to consume. There were too many deaths – too many corpses to count. They have fallen ferociously, feebly. Incapacitated by their own blood to shortly die dreadfully. They have dissipated into the black abyss. In the end, we all end up alone just like them. One by one they have fallen in a pervade of chaos – one by one they have fallen on its scythe – one by one they have fallen to the earth where they rest horribly – one by one the ground drank and chocked on the endless, pouring ribbons of their blood.

We have lost count of how many we buried during the last resistance struggle. There wasn't enough land to bury the bodies, so eventually; we started to burn them like our garbage. The bodies we did bury are somewhere but nowhere to be found. There are rows and rows of unmarked graves of the V's and of the Chavistas. Determining who's who is like a needle in a haystack – an impossible task. You just see rows and rows of disturbed earth and from there, you know – you know corpses, someone's corpse is buried well beneath the earth – beyond the polluted, red soil.

When we buried them, to save space in the ground, we buried them, one on top of the other. They were thrown in these mass graves without dropping a tear because there was no time to cry – no time to feel remorse or sadness – no time to have proper burials. Our tears really were dehydrated salt crystals unable to fall from our eyes. Better yet, our tears were sour dehydrated raisins, spoiled and rotten. They were buried one on top of the other like garbage bags. We discarded bodies every time one collapsed to the ground. Some think (to this day) that it's God's problem now. He has them or his counterpart does – the devil. We knew something had to have them because it could no longer be our problem. It was no longer our responsibility to attend to their deaths. Once they stopped breathing, it became God or Lucifer's problem. It wasn't even our responsibility to think about whom we have killed or were about to kill. It was our responsibility to follow *the kill orders* to protect the security of our country and this meant that we could not hesitate to complete these orders. Come to think of it hesitantly, if we wouldn't comply, we were soon to be on *the kill orders.*

The counts became worse at times. The corpses sat for days until they were buried or burned by them or us. Corpses lay on our land, sometimes weeks at a time before they were disposed of. When we disposed of them, they were well expired and well decayed. Their flesh glued to the ground seeped well into the soil. At times, we could not lift them, so we shovelled around them to make shallow graves. Those graves are seen today. Today, these graves are moulded skeletons of what used to be people. They are a figment of their former self, lying in the ground helplessly in unforeseen poses – poses that haunt the very minds of those who survived. They are eternally frozen in their last action of life before death caught up with them.

The stench of death became intolerable, even the critters or birds did not want to feast on them any longer – even the earth neglected them. Their stench wouldn't wash out of our uniforms or our pores. It clung to us like a calling. That death could come after us next. We, at any un-prescribed moment, could fall victim to the Grim Reapers' grimy, rusted, macabre scythe. Some would say, after a few shots of rum or vodka, *we smell death on our bodies because we are death.* In the local bar, *El Ultimo Lugar* (The Last Place) or in our quarters, we joked about death. Our joking became a twisted, dark rhyme:

> From where we see the fallen
> And from where we see their blood,
> For we know the Grim Reaper is comin'.
> It lurks in waiting.
> There's no hiding.
> For we know the Grim Reaper is comin'.
> No one leaves alive.
> No one is ever lucky.
> For we know the Grim Reaper is comin'.

Our joking was our escape from the dreaded reality we had no other choice but to live. Hell, we were better off than the Common People. We were well taken care of both financially and socially. This wasn't why we dreaded reality. We dreaded reality because death always lurks around us. It walks with us everywhere. We too were not immune to its virus. We thought we were infallible, even our superiors said it, especially Major Maburro and Commandant Chava. This was not one bit true. It was a harsh reality we rejected to accept much like the prevalent amorphous, death. We knew, however, that Commandant Chava did not mean we were infallible literally. He meant it as a figurative message, that our spirit guides the living military to continue to successfully lead Venezuela in glory for all people and that our spirit gives our living military the strength to not fear death. Though we knew the heart of this message and in turn, never questioned – loyal to the cause. This did not stop the anxiety that we felt. This did not stop the sadness of the loss of our brothers and sisters. This did not stop our fear of dying. The negative reactant injections we take daily seem not to function properly, so our dosage increased more through the killings and *kill orders* we confidently carried out. Soon, with the negative reactant injections, we felt nothing. Our feelings numbed but our joking and the sick, twisted rhyme remained. The shadow of our dreaded reality still existed. No amount of medication could eradicate the anxious feeling of death – our reality.

We became so used to death that it became a daily habit or a routine chore. Death or killing was routine like disposing of garbage. It's a mindless task. It requires no thought or attention. You just follow, discard, dump, bury or burn. This is how it was – routine. It required no awareness. We expected death, mass causalities every time the sun rises until the sun sets. We expected to walk around and trample over the dead as we struggled not to be one of the victims. Many of us were victims but those of us who were not victims were not so lucky. Death is merely an unexpired prescription that is prescribed to us all. It is only a matter of when we do die. When we die, we die alone. Those of us who died are probably the lucky ones. The survived have to live with every disgusting image, every vile action; live in contamination – in filth as a perpetrator or victim.

It was common for bystanders to get caught in the crossfires. They were not participating in the violence or against the violence. They were just causalities, walking home or walking somewhere other than where it occupied violence. San Cristobel and Caracas were the first cities to have witnessed and experienced the savage loss of bystanders. It did not long though (sometimes it took weeks, other times it took days or a matter of hours) for other cities to follow. They were non-discriminatory. Anybody will do. At least that was the general thought at the time between them and us. As long as someone's body fell to the ground. That's what mattered.

The forgotten fallen – that's what they are. They are men, women, children, old, young, students, professionals – anyone that still needs to matter. The fallen were buried well beneath the earth or were burned and their ashes scattered tenuously across the earth. The dead are people. People who are no longer here, people who are dead for believing in them, or us, or believed to be left alone. They are people who intentionally or unintentionally died. They are somewhere else now. For sure, they are no longer part of the living. They are no longer alive. Surely, they must be better in death than here, but then again, are any of us better off wherever we end up? Does life or death even matter? I mean what's the meaning of all of this chaos – to what anatomical degree? To promote an ideal that many seem to believe is false and unprovoked of lies and deceit. These unprovoked lies and falseness reign horrifyingly in our communities.

The earth has eaten rotten flesh. In a matter of months, it became uninhabitable. Our plains, *Los Llanos* became infertile. Nothing grows anymore. The soil is tainted with stale, mucky blood. The soil refuses to cultivate any crops. We thought if the rapture was going to come, it was already here. We were lucky if we could grow anything. With each passing fraction of time, our hunger intensified. Sometimes it was days before we had anything to eat, but before we could breathe, it seemed to feel like, that those days became weeks and those weeks became months. We grew hungrier and hungrier, so we ate worms, bugs, or whatever other critters we could find. Whatever we could scrape up – whatever we could salvage. We painfully digested them to keep alive, to keep fighting. When we finally grew something, we were satisfied – we satisfied our hunger. There was an unusual taste afterwards; a taste of eating the remains of our forgotten brothers and sisters. The crops grew on soil where death occurred, so you could say that death kept us company while we ate, for it was the unwanted pessimistic visitor none of use wanted socialising around. When any of us socialised with death, it was a poisonousness conversation that left us breathless. After one conversation with death, our souls were imprisoned in eternity. Death, in those conversations, hardly speaks it just takes. It takes the very words from our mouths before we could even spew one word. Death's conversations, you could say, were breath taking.

Though the Chavistas and the Victorias hardly ever see eye to eye, they are still *brothers* just because they are Venezuelan. To this day, after the resistance struggles and Bolivarian Revolutions, in the silence you hear the ground tremble from the forgotten fallen. That's their souls, some say, escaping from the red-flamed ashes of their remains to somehow warn all of us that death is rejecting people. Even in death our *brothers* do not rest. Their enslaved souls tell us a time where peace is met without violence, without bloodshed and without suffering. Though all we have to do is listen, listen to compromise. Both the Victorias and Chavistas wanted the same ideals for its people – security, prosperity and freedom but they had different views on how to achieve these ideals. Their enslaved souls also frantically trample the ground, again, to warn us to cease the revolutions because, in the end, death is not freedom to end or begin life anew but a prison to it. Their souls screech this time; *cease before more of our brothers are forgotten historical names. Cease before more bloodshed taints our hands and contaminates our lands and waters. Cease for a future our kids and their kids' kids would want to wake up to.* Their voices regrettably are faded footnotes in history; always overlooked and never carefully read. They are, nonetheless, eternally forgotten.

The decaying flesh caused our air to impetuously growl and rumble, releasing poisonous water, at least that's what it felt like when the clouds cried in agony as sulphur drenched over our plains and over our bodies. The smell of sulphur lingers as a contagious virus, not desiring to disperse. It affected our trees, Uva de Playas. It suffocated them. Every time we were outside, we could feel the thickness of the air laced with poison. If we did not die in battle then certainly we died from the elements. Each time we stood in the rain our faces, arms, legs – whatever exposed skin was deformed. We shortly became something else – something hideous – something resembling our wickedness. Some say, this poisonous Red Scare gas has been happening since the inception of the 4-F Program, not when the earth erected masses of sacrilegious graves. Of course, this did not actually happen, but to us, when we were in the rain, it felt like piousness to us.

What was worse than watching our brothers helplessly fight through each day when there was no hope of surviving? We could not help them. After a few days, we all forgot why we were fighting – why any of us should continue the Bolivarian revolutions or resistance struggles. What is the point when the Grim Reaper takes our brothers and sisters every day because of these conflicts? Who should be responsible for all of these deaths? Are we to blame our primate selves for committing these heinous conflicts or do we blame God for allowing such suffering and vileness to plague the earth and our lives? What evilness have we contracted to just promote an idea many of us are willing to die over, undoubtedly? What country are we creating when we educate our children that they must choose to be like them or us and then tell them to pick up a gun and fight? Have we come to realise that in the end, all we feel is nothing because we become so used to the misery of the Grim Reaper's scythe? Is it silliness to live when death is our physician? Have the conflicts deformed our souls and stolen our minds? Have we no regret for what we have done and what every generation after is responsible for? Have we yet forgotten our humanity that we have become people without it? Are we both the real monsters and heroes? Perhaps we all are to blame for what we have created and allowed to nourish. Then again, what else do we know other than what we live and learn? Simply, what is the meaning of life when God does not answer our prayers? Are we, in fact, none or all of these things?

The butterflies do not fly around our country anymore but they used to though, in another lifetime. Perhaps the butterflies are not here because of the stench of death and all of the dead around here. It was not long before Venezuela became barren – inhospitable to life – desolate to any sustenance. Today, it is polluted with fear and isolated by the Red Scare. What runs rampant are not the butterflies but decay and death.

Taking someone's life, that was frightening at first, became enjoyable to some. Taking a life is as if we have committed original sin once more. The light in their eyes turns off. Their heartbeat slowly stops pumping. Their limbs permanently begin to stick together. Their lungs vulnerably gasp for life. Then, there's a moment before they are about to die that they realise they are weak against death. The Grim Reaper wastes no time and rapes the soul from their eyes. It eternally captivates their soul in its abyss of nothingness.

Perhaps the butterflies no longer fly around here anymore because they smell the Grim Reaper's scythe chiming in the cool Venezuelan breeze, echoing the rattling sound of death.

Captain Santos stands on *Balcón del Pueblo. Balcón del Pueblo* overlooks Caracas from afar. The air is much cleaner up there. It's thin too but not too thin where it would be hard to breathe. Captain Santos stands here sometimes to clear his head from battle or from a victory. Today, he's up there to clear his head for choices he is about to make. From up there, things look smaller and vague. He begins to take in the pleasant perfume of nature's smells. He knows he has to inform his men to dismantle the protests and riots of the Victorias later today. Though at some point, Captain Santos believed in non-violence against them but far too many of his men have died, which is not cool. He thinks today is the day, where the missions of President Chava and Deputy Frost will rain without hesitation.

Captain Santos' trusted Adjutant, Sergeant Ruiz lagged fifteen seconds behind to arrive on *Balcón del Pueblo*. Ruiz likes to think that he gives Santos a head start but it is Santos who strives not to make Ruiz look out of shape because he doesn't run as often as he should.

"Hey, sir. You just got lucky today that's all."

"Sergeant Ruiz, you always state this every time we run up here."

"But do not forget Santos, I always run two more kilometres than you just to get to the starting point."

"I suppose you are correct, Ruiz," Santos sarcastically mentions.

Sergeant Ruiz walks near Captain Santos to view the pandemic, yet majestic Caracas.

"I can see why we come here. She's a beauty, isn't she? I mean, what's more beautiful than the luscious green mountains, the skyscraper giants and over there, there she lays – her golden dome shines – our princess, the National Assembly. Then over there, there's her pink queen, the Presidential House." Ruiz patriotically motions to Santos.

"Yes, Ruiz. I come up here to view our beloved Caracas that our beloved liberator, Bolivar fought for. Today, it is our job to continue his vision, so that his spirit remains everlasting among us as our humble Commandant announces every day. These are chaotic times. Uncertainty threatens our capital; the uncertainty that the Victorias give our people false hope. However, after today, there will not be any more uncertainty from them. Today is the day where they will never be resurrected again. Today is the day we begin peace again. Today is the day our great country prospers once again."

"Sir, I do not mean to question your leadership, but they continue to come back like an unwanted peasant wanting food. We have already captured many of their leaders and yet, they still manage to resist and recruit the Common People. I hate to say this sir, but about eight to ten years ago, from what we were taught, our Commandant disbanded the Victorias and now suddenly, they are emerging. Is there even an end in sight?"

"Normally, I would demote you for that comment if you were any other soldier but you are not. I, however, understand the merit of your concern. But today is different. I am going after the head of their organisation, Maria Elizabeth and the directors. Without her and the directors, the organisation will seise to exist. Then it will be a matter of time before the Common People will start to fall in order and begin to restore our beloved country, Venezuela in the image of Bolivar."

"Great! We have been trying to find their location for months now. Every time we have a lead, it often happens to be false. They move before we get to them. We always thought we had a mole or moles somewhere in our military and the intelligence we collect always was compromised. I mean, Santos, they move around more than my wife changes her mind about what to wear or where to spend our time."

"You were always funny, Ruiz. In seriousness, yes, you are correct. There were moles in our military that we have taken care of but even then, the human intelligence did not seem to match with the digital intelligence we had. That is up until now. We have found the last mole and we have corrected the corrupt servers and bugged network. This is why you are here, Sergeant Ruiz. Before you *release* the mole, you are instructed to torture him to send a message to the Victorias, that they are exposed and the Bolivarian Guardias and the 4-F Program is coming after them. Of course, while you do this, they will get the message far too late."

"Yes sir, as long as this will put an end to any more of our brothers dying. There have been far too many of our brothers and sisters forgotten and unrightfully removed from their life. They have all died prematurely. Our country cannot handle any more deaths."

"Your concern is noted. You already know how I feel about our *brothers'* death. I don't have to explain to you how that makes me feel and the immense anger and hatred I feel because of death. This is why the mission, Operation Burnout is initiated today. I have been planning this day for a long time. The spirits of our enteral brothers and sisters speak to me that today is the day. After today, there will be no more deaths – just peace."

"Well then, our country is in very capable hands. Today will change the very future of our country. Today is our victory."

"Yes it is, Sergeant Ruiz. Shall we attend to our guest then, the mole that is? Before we go, however, you know why when we run up here what we have to do?" Santos states sincerely.

"Forgivingly, sir, I know why we are up here. It is not to converse about our next assignment, continuing to follow the *kill orders* or to clear our heads from the savage death of our beloved soldiers. We are up here to commemorate the ones we call *brothers,* who have tragically given their lives to the cause of the 4-F Program, who have fallen from the Victorias' sword, savagely."

"Yes. That is why we are up here – to ensure that they are not forgotten footnotes in history. As you see below you, I have chiselled ten of the fifteen names last night. Will you help me engrave the last of the fifteen names of those who have tragically fallen yesterday afternoon?"

"Of course, sir. It is my duty," Ruiz sorrowfully states as he painfully decompresses his tears from falling from his eyes.

Every Guardia, no matter which branch they serve under comes to *Balcón del Pueblo* and its surroundings to commemorate the Fallen Ones by adding their rank and surname to an unending list of dead soldiers.

Carefully, both Santos and Ruiz chisel the following names in the ridged, suborned concrete ground. The names are always written in the order of when they have fallen.

"Let their names forever be immortalised here. Let their spirit forever guide us to further the New Bolivarian Republic of Venezuela. You are not alone. Soon, all of us will be reunited to celebrate our great, prosperous country with Commandant Chava," Captain Santos chants before he and Ruiz chisel.

Sergeant Ramos

Lieutenant Edwards

Warrant Officer Lopez

Petty Officer First Class Nunez

Tech Sergeant Cruz

"These are all great men and women who have given their lives to preserve Venezuela under the leadership of our beloved Commandant Chava," Ruiz utters humbly.

The location is remote where Adjutant Sergeant Ruiz and Captain Santos are travelling. Somewhere in the dark, desolated corners of Caracas there lies a dormant, barren and negated warehouse. Warehouse 4 is where people come to disappear. The people who disappear from here are not missed by society. Society would never know that they have existed. This would be true for Rebel Eugenia Southerland Suarez, a director of the V's.

The unmarked, red car pulled up to Warehouse 4. Neither Santos nor Ruiz are new to Warehouse 4, for whom better to be acquainted with the warehouse than these two soldiers.

The industrial, vast warehouse used to produce vehicles and other small machinery for the military until it closed its doors in 1995. The warehouse closed to move to a more prominent size location, closer to the training facility of the new recruits. This warehouse obtained its name from the fourth warehouse built under Commandant Chava in 1991. The warehouse kept its name but its new purpose is unknown to the Common People. All they know is that it is just another neglected deteriorating building. People who committed treason or people who are sentenced to be released are guests in Warehouse 4. Military personnel who are in a position to extract intelligence from these people come here.

Inside, it is cold from freedom. Though atypical of Caracas to be sunny today, the warehouse sees little of it. Broken, blacking windows encase the walls and ceiling. Dim and dysfunctional lights seem to keep it dark and frightening. Reddish oil and water drip casually on the wrecked, abused floor as it laughs throughout the facility insanely. Rusted, diseased ridden metal beams madly support the facility as to keep it from collapsing to uncountable pieces. Infinite sized cracks fill the fainted concrete floors as it travels to the far, unnoticeable edges of the facility. The smell is suffocating to those who are unfamiliar with the stench of rancid mist and mould. The only faint sounds heard in Warehouse 4 are the cracked minds of the released, silent to the rest of the country and the world.

"Jesus Christ, Captain! You did not tell me the mole was a woman. Fuck! Shit! Christ! You know, I do not like confronting women but you know me boss, I do it anyway."

"Sergeant, you are the best interrogator I know and I have witnessed you work on countless occasions. If there is one interrogator who can extract the slightest intelligence from any treasonable person, you are the one. I did not want to tell you anyway that the mole is a woman until we got here. It is sort of a surprise. I wanted to keep you in suspense if you will."

"You are both fucking insane and bat shit crazy. Talking about mutilating a woman and this drone asshole monster is going to do it anyway. I have to give it to you – you are both cracked individuals," scornfully yelled Rebel Eugenia.

"She has spunk on her, doesn't she?" Confidently sates Ruiz.

"At least, a thank you is in order, for not tying me to a beam or chair or something dilapidated as your moral compasses. Though I would try to leave I know there would be nowhere for me to go to and I know the perimeter of the compound is buried with land mines."

"Very clever girl," states Santos.

"She's a smart one. I will give her that Captain."

"You can do what you wish to me but I won't tell you a shred of information without putting up a fight or die trying. Just to let you know, I also have studied both of you – how you think and how you behave. What you didn't think that we, the Victorias, were not capable of doing our homework? How else you think we have survived as long as we did. And don't get me wrong. We will continue to survive."

"Same bullshit story! All of you guys always same the same thing. It's like give it a rest already," sordidly mentions Ruiz.

"Alright! Sergeant! That's enough with the comments! At least, treat the lady with some respect. She deserves it –we all do. It doesn't matter which side we fight for – we fight with honour and respect. Don't forget this, Ruiz. I do not want to have to remind you again."

"Affirmative, sir. You are correct. There is no need to disrespect or dishonour anyone," apologetically, Ruiz spoke.

"Nicolas Anthony Ruiz born on April 3, 1984. Your mother died when you were fifteen from pancreatic cancer. Your father was a dyslexic who used to abuse you. Every time you got an answer incorrect or made some type of mistake, minor or not, he used to sit you down at a table, tie your hands together and beat you with a leather strap repeatedly on your back. You would probably say, *no. Stop. I won't make the mistake again.* This wasn't enough for your father. He wanted to take your dignity away. That was until one day, probably in your last year of school, you had enough. He was about to hit you with that worn-tired-exhausted looking leather strap. Boy, you hated that strap. But you did not let that happen. Instead, you did something about it. You dislocated his legs and strangled him with your biceps until he nearly stopped breathing. The National Police came that day. This is what you told them. Once your father came to, laying on the gurney, he said, *you are finally a real man and not a weak helpless boy.* Hey, at least, this is what you told the police and from the numerous filed police reports from your estranged neighbours and from your poor mom before she died. What really happened to you, though?"

"Oh! Congratulations are in order! Wow! You have managed to hack into the police database. But the thing is, you may think you know who I am but you are sorely mistaken. You know nothing! You little…" Ruiz angrily responded.

"What? Did I hit a nerve? See, I know who you are. You joined the military as a segregate for your pain. It is a way for you to compensate for you wanting to kill your dad or you wanting your mom to still be alive. See, you were more than abused. Your father took the very thing away from you. Without your dignity, you are a monster. What probably really happened, you were a victim of sexual sadism. Your father got off abusing you." Eugenia responded in kind.

"Shut the fuck up! You know nothing about me." Ruiz pulls out his handgun.

"Now, think about what you are about to do, Ruiz." Commandingly utters Santos.

"Bravo for the general and poorly defined psychoanalysis. I am really going to enjoy torturing you. Afterwards, no one, not even your precious Victorias will miss you when you are released from this earth. Fuck this shit!" he says, holstering his handgun.

Ruiz begins to roll-up his camouflage battle dress uniform sleeves halfway to his elbows. He is about to begin his torture. While he meticulously rolls up his selves he thinks about the dark and unthinkable ways he is about to torture Eugenia. He may begin with putting little rusted, infected pins underneath her fingernails. Thoughts like his begin to light up his eyes creatively.

"Can I trust you, sergeant, to not kill her until you extract intelligence from her?"

"Affirmative, sir. You can trust me."

"Then I am going to go and take a visit to the Victorias base of operations with a few men. More are already in position waiting for my command."

"Well then, I have everything settled here."

"Don't you see by now Eugenia? We have been several paces ahead of you and your organisations. The point of your visit here is to send a message to them. There is no resurrection of the V's. Today, the resistance struggles end. No more of our people are going to die," Santos stated loudly and angrily as he walks away to join his fellow comrades on the raid to initiate Operation Burnout.

"I'm going to give you five seconds to run. One – two –three – ..." Ruiz utters insanely to Suarez.

While in the unmarked black SUV, Carlos finds himself banging on the steering wheel repeating, *you leave me; you leave me*, a song by Prince Royce.

Y Te me vas, Te Me Vas. Como hoja que el viento se lleva sin mirar atras. Y Te me vas y Te me vas. Como gota de lluvia que al cielo no regresara. (And you leave me. You leave me like a leaf that the wind blows away without looking back. And you leave me. You leave me like a raindrop that won't return to the sky). Carlos with troubled thoughts and great anxiety with his right foot on the break looks at himself in the rear-view mirror and reflects on his uncertainty about himself and who he has become. He does not question the merit of his action, rather the chaos that has been unravelling throughout the capital and his country. He remarks his thoughts, nonetheless, to God rather than Fernanda. Fernanda vanished from his mind, an isolated, dissuaded memory along with the rest of his childhood – undeniably displaced.

Yet again, God, my thoughts pour out to you much like the widespread, plagued chaos inhabiting in our country. The Program and our code of conduct states we have to believe in you. That while believing and entrusting you, we will know what to do. Of all of this, is it worth it? The chaos created by the Rebels, will it end? I do not particularly believe in you, God. I do not know why. I do accept that you watch over the Guardias and the spirit of the fallen ones. Many of our soldiers have fallen victim to the Grim Reaper. I particularly do not care if the Rebels, the V's, as they are named, die. However, but the Common people, God, why them? They are the ones who suffer – leaving behind broken families and displaced children – children, many of which are screened to serve with the Guardias. Sadly, many of them are not taken in, so they are unlucky. What happens to them? What future do they have when the Victorias attempt to dismantle the 4-F Program and the New Bolivarian Republic? There has to be a better way than to live in fear that death lives and hovers over our shoulders, isn't there?

This is what I have become. This is what the program had made me into, God. Are you happy now? I have killed for you. I have lost count how many Rebel lives I have taken and perhaps the innocent lives I have also taken. I am about to add a few more to the list of those who I have killed. I have become, perhaps a monster. A vile beast, all because of the opposition disagreeing with the Chavistas. There is enough food, water, supplies and resources, isn't there,

God? Ah, but you want me to think in this way but I do not. I know who I am and who I have become. I am, Captain Carlos Christian Santos. My national identification number is 02-04-01-23.

In the chaos, there is order. I envision this but I do not know how to accomplish this when the Rebels retaliate against us. This is silly for me to think because there is one way. To have order once again, God, Operation Burnout is a go. I just hope that you are listening. At least, if not to me, then guide the Guardias through the purpose of this mission. Disband the resurrected Victorias. At least, listen to the outcries of our men then. Our country craves peace otherwise the dead will rise, and so, the rapture begins. Operation Burnout will stop that from happening.

Tears struggle to come from Carlos' eyes and they do not. After the conversation with himself, and apparently, with God, he takes another dose of his negative reactant injection and puts the vehicle in gear.

While Santos drives, the environment surrounding him vaguely fades away much like his emotions and whatever is left of his reality. He types in the coordinates to the V's base of operations into the other vehicle following behind his. A few minutes later, they arrive at a similar warehouse at Warehouse 4.

Captain Santos stumbles out of the SUV favouring his right leg. He leaves the driver side door open. One of the Guardias witnessed his almost falling on the muddy, red-stained ground.

"Sir! Sir! Are you okay?" shouted Lt. Martinez, while running to his aid.

"Lady, I'm fine. It is my stupid leg again. It must have fallen asleep while I was driving here. I should be careful next time with the cruise control," He shouted in response, not noticing it was Lt. Martinez.

"Oh, Martinez. I did not know that was you. Yes. I am fine. It is nice to see you again. I haven't seen you since the raid on Barrio 4," Santos respectfully responds.

"Yes, sir. It has been awhile. But I am happy to be called in to participate in Operation Burnout," Martinez states.

"Men, attention! Is everyone in place?"

"Yes, Captain Santos. As instructed, our men are positioned around the warehouse. We have men around the compound following a five-kilometre radius. Also, sir, as instructed, there are sharpshooters concealed in the mountainous-part surrounding the warehouse and sharpshooters are concealed on top of these buildings," utter Sargent Major Jimenez, crisply.

"Thank you, for debriefing me, Sargent Jimenez. Well done. I do not have to ask that the place has been vetted. I do not want any more of our soldiers dying today. Is this clear?"

"Yes, sir!"

"You, Lopez. Have air support ready. We are most likely going to blow up this warehouse. Everyone – have your radios on. No one enters until my command," Santos ordered.

"Yes, sir!"

Captain Santos enters the barren, desolated warehouse cautiously and skilfully, not making a sound. Somehow, in his cat-like manoeuvres, *they* were waiting for him as he turned around the other corner.

"There's no need for your weapon here," sounded a feminine, stern voice from afar.

Without any reservation and without Carlos' reaction, fifty to a hundred Victorias swarmed around him like butterflies.

"What is this trickery? What nonsense we have here." Santos stated puzzlingly but harshly.

"I would not do that if I were you. We kindly ask that you put your radio and gun away. We have been expecting you, Carlos Christian Santos." The same feminine voice responded again but more clearly.

"Whoever you are, show yourself, or I will…"

Before Santos could finish his sentence, out from the sunlight the woman appeared.

"Welcome to one of our homes. We have been watching you carefully Carlos. Today, we wanted you to find us because today we hope to change your mind and begin to think for yourself and not what some government program tells you to think."

"Who the hell are you?"

"I'm sorry. My name is Maria Elizabeth. I am one of the leaders of the Victorias, or as the Chavistas put it, one of the Rebels. I see you are favouring your right leg. Your pale face and heavy eyes indicate you have not been sleeping much. Perhaps the drugs you are taking caused all of this. Tell me, is one of the things you want to feel most is your emotions."

"I do not know who you are lady or how you know about our medicine. But I assure you, I feel more than you can fathom."

"Tell me, Carlos, have you ever wondered why you ended up with the Guardias? Have you ever wondered exactly if what you are doing is in fact even benefiting everyone in the community?"

"Listen, Maria. I do not know where you are going with this but if you think you are here to use psychological warfare on me then you are entirely clueless. And please, stop calling me Carlos!"

"There is no trick here. I am just trying to allow you to open your mind once again. I tell you what. If you give me this leverage to speak to you and show you who we are and what you are really fighting for, your men can come in here and take me, but I ask no one dies."

"Maria!" Someone shouted.

"Well then…since I do not want any more of my men to die, or be injured today…you have yourself a negotiation, Maria."

"Walk and listen to me, Carlos."

While Carlos, Maria and many of the Victorias walk around the warehouse, Maria begins to give a memorable speech to Carlos.

"This is the era of proclamation, reconstruction and transparency we seek. We have not thought this would be a living history; though, we are creators of living this history. Our existence testifies, when there is a will there is a way. Persevering through years of failed policy, not of ideology or concept, but of direction and focus, we embark towards Venezuela anew. As we do, it is absolute we not abdicate our past, we not numb our provocations and we not forget what is to come, Carlos."

"Where are you going with this speech Maria?"

"Like the Chavistas, we too believe that courageous, dissident and outspoken Venezuelans have paved this era we begin entering. Alas, they are not here today because of their noble and selfless actions. Their spirits remain in our memories and our hearts as we continue their efforts of a better country. Their noble and selfless actions testify that we must shout our words for everyone to hear and we must exhibit our actions greatly for everyone to witness. We live in their past while striding forward to promote a common vision their efforts sweated for. As we do, it's necessary we remember who they are, what they have accomplished and what mistakes they have endured. Our past illustrates where we are today and how we arrived there. Our past provides answers to a future we not only want but we also have to build collectively. Our past is our teacher. It teaches that failed policy is policy without specific direction and clear focus. Our past teaches us which mistakes we have made, so that future generations, our children and their children, don't have to endure further violence and bloodshed. As we bear our past, we proclaim Venezuela, we all know exists. All I am asking of you, Carlos, is to remember your past."

"You have yet to convince me, Maria. I see no point in this whatsoever," Santos uttered strictly.

"Perhaps seeing this may help you open your mind more, Carlos."

"I will indulge you for this one last time. Remember, my patience is growing thin, Maria."

"Watch the videos and listen to my words. I assure you, Carlos, that these videos are not fabricated. In fact, these are recordings from your missions. Not all of them, but we pieced together what we think you may remember."

"Fine, Maria," Carlos shouts unnervingly.

"Four million people in Caracas alone live in shambles – houses made from steel, concrete, wood – whatever can be found. These are *glued* on top of each other in the mountain. This is what the underprivileged call home. There's hardly any access to clean water, as much of the water in Venezuela is tainted or polluted. Not just that the underprivileged can't find clean water to drink, no one can. If one does, he or she is likely to pay four times as much than the regulated price. No water; no life. It's a phrase every Venezuelan states commonly. Many Venezuelans cannot find, let alone have drinkable water. This is a direct result of years of improper education. Now, I leave you with this Carlos, when is a policed state a secure state?"

After viewing the videos of his missions, most of which were from his first ones. Somewhere in the depth of his mind, Carlos senses that two forces create violence, not just one and that most of the violence has been ordered by the Chavistas. The V's have not committed such violence, only attempt at peaceful protests…until the Chavistas begun targeting the opposition without prudence and warrant. Even then, the opposition hesitates to retaliate in extreme conditions.

"I hope you begin to see what's actually in front of you. To help you begin to think for yourself, you must consider stopping the negative reactant injections. I hope by me showing you these videos some of your scorned nerves activate the little memories in your synapses what you know to be just and unjust."

"I cannot say. However, I will give you this latitude. I will wait to order the Guardias to breach in here so that you and your people can attempt to escape. Mind you, Maria we have been expecting you."

"And so, have we, Carlos. Before we go, I want to give you our creed, Spirit of Liberation. This may help in your quest to see what's in front of you and to discover for yourself, Carlos, the truth; what is moral and what is not. We will meet again."

Fog suffocates Santos and permeates throughout the entire compound. A few seconds later, the warehouse is barren and lost just as Carlos entered it a few minutes ago.

Without any reservations, Carlos radios his men to ambush the entire compound. Carlos says to himself as he exits the compound, *let the games begin Maria. Let's see who is the better opponent.*

"Hey, Captain Santos!" Ruiz responds loudly as if Santos suddenly became deaf and lost in his mind.

A common side effect of his medication is losing track of time for a few seconds. Though, has it been a few seconds or more?

"Yes, Sergeant!"

"Well, our intention was for her to get away but I made sure she was scared. That was our message, Captain. Too many people died today, both of us and of them. You have said this was the message to let her go on the brink of death. Don't you agree?"

"Ruiz, I do. In fact, there has been far too many deaths this week that plague our country, shit in Caracas alone the death toll is massive. Tomorrow is another day of death. So, let's save the killing for then, Ruiz."

Santos begins to read the document Maria gave to him as they exit. While he feels through his pockets, he does not recall having possession of the document or remembers what it was. Nonetheless, Carlos takes a brief look at it. It reads:

We must stand together. We must make noise. We must always remain strong. Our act of valour will dissolve the dictator regime. When we lose hope, we remind ourselves, the courage that Simon Bolivar had for South America, lives on in us. We carry the spirit of liberation. We hold the torch of resistance. We walk with dignity. We owe it to our family and our friends that each bloodshed will be remembered for what we do to end civil unrest and restore a country for the people, peacefully and humbly.

This is not the time to give up. This is not the time to give in. Certainly, this is not the time to fail. Our voices will be heard. We are united for a common cause to restore hope that Venezuela is our fight. It is our country, for the people. With hope, political corruption ends. With hope, we succeed. Today, we prevail. In this peril time, Venezuelans will remain strong.

To initiate change, to proclaim our liberties and to restore security, we must take the path that is less travelled by. On this path, we meet courage, resolution and victory. These are the greatest truths given to us by the spirit of our supporters. These truths guide us. These truths give us breath to stride forward. These truths bind us to walk together in chaotic times.

They will strive to tire us. They will strive to beat us. They will strive to defeat us. In the end, we will not subvert. Our promise, we will not falter. We will not give up on Venezuela because we are the hope. We are the future Venezuela has. That is our promise, through peace and humility is winning.

We humbly take this oath as the Victorias

At the end of the document, a V hand sign is drawn to indicate their symbol.

In greater despair than conversing with Maria or of refusal to accept his discomforting feelings, he rips up the creed and jams the four pieces roughly back into is left pocket. The thought would yet be discerning for Captain Santos to a choice he would eventually make, fighting for the Red Scare or fighting to cure it.

Darkness, death, evil, chaos, are one and the same but the difference is in what we call it. After having seen their faces, which are the Boogieman, the Baron Samedi or the Grim Reaper are all the same. The Red Scare keeps these nightmarish creatures a reality. Carlos Christian Santos fights this. Does he become part of the cure or part of the disease?

Sergeant Ruiz begins to speak something to Captain Santos, perhaps to criticise friendly regarding his sluggish behaviour. The words fade intensely as Carlos Christian Santos begins to wake up to the present. The memory darkens with fury while it crumbles with rage and might be revisited another time, but brokenly, or might be lost forever as a missing piece puzzle fighting together.

Chapter 11
When There Is a Will There Is a Way

DEATH SEEKS POLITICAL ASYLUM OR REFUGE IN MASSACRE PROTESTS IN VENEZUELA BUT CHAOS IS NOT LIKELY HONOURING SUCH REQUESTS

By, Joanna Stephanie San Cristobal, Venezuela February 24

If you are reading this, then like many others, I am probably already dead in the protest for change, freedom, security and peace. The only hope we have is for others to read our messages and watch our videos, even those will be appropriated and destroyed by the government. When you read or listen, please share, so the world knows the truth of Maburro, the Red Scare and our totalitarian government. The people must continue our hope for a better city, a better country and a better world.

REPORTING FROM SAN CRISTOBAL, VENEZUELA: Signs read: *freedom does not exist here. The government has exploited the teachings of God. A policed state is a dictator state. Free the opposition. There is no food. No water, no life. There is only corruption. What voice do we have? We won't rest until we are safe.* That is what is left of them. Pieces of these signs and others scattered across the empty streets, avenues and highways of ransacked, mobbed cities.

The sun did not awake today. Rain wept hysterically from the sky in the early morning hours but this did not stop anybody from leaving their homes. A blanket of grey still travels across the bitter afternoon sky. The angrily awaited wind dissipates, what is left is the grey omnipresent tear gas, fragmented bullets and red-flamed ashy fire. Blood stains these streets. There is so much blood even Lady Macbeth cannot wash out.

What happened should not be the question asked but the question, why did it happen should be the question asked. Though the horror happened, this horror is only one shred of its darkness and psychopathy.

Innocent bodies of men, women and children lay stiff and cold wondering why they died from a government that is supposed to protect them. Something evil, vile and monstrous pillaged what was peace and murdered these innocent people.

Disturbed silence occupies the cities wondering what just happened in the early morning hours of Venezuela. The dead would tell you what happened objectively if they could. Sadly, though, if they could, the words from their lips are eternally stapled together. The survived could also tell you what happened objectively but a rusted, dull blade cut the words from their tongues.

Chaos has a face. It is the provocations of the Red Scare. After today, world, the face of chaos could not be any clearer. It's vile, hideous, deformed, wicked, grim, animalistic and disgusted. Simply, it is the virus inhospitable to life and it disgusts humanity.

Hundreds of thousands of commoners stampede the streets of San Cristobal and neighbouring cities and towns today. From afar, they looked like little coloured dots surrounding almost every street and stopping traffic. No one in traffic was angry. In fact, people got out of their cars to join the protests – to join peace and change.

The leaders of the opposition group, student political parties and others who are just exhausted from the government's lies coordinated these protests. They hope there would not be causalities but they knew it was probable. They were not expecting a massacre from the military. Within minutes of their gathering, *they* came and heavily armed as if it were a battleground – as if it were war. *They* were at the ready and as soon as *they* exited from their vehicles, we knew who *they* were, the Guardias.

Heavy black boots grossly polished stormed the ground in riot gear. These are not men who wear these boots. These are parasitic machines that blindly and deafly follow orders. They have no consciousness they can call their own. The only consciousness they have is a collective one programmed by the government. This program only knows one thought: *at any cost protect the Chavistas and their ideological cause.*

We were not warned while these patristic machines pervaded around us. They were in perfect alignment, protecting each other and not us, the commoners. We, the commoners only knew of peace, so we innocently walked up to each Guardia to hand them flowers. The flowers were meant to replace their bullets with breathable air. Out of evilness or anxiety, no one knows for sure, but the program told the machines to fire because it was the order. There was no warning, not even God could have intervened. Unarmed people dropped madly from their feet like butterflies falling from the sky from a poisonous vapour. Clearly, the poisonous vapour was not the bullets but the inhumans behind the guns.

People stood frozen. People panicked. People screamed. People ran. People stayed. We did not know what a massacre was until today. Thousands of people died and hundreds of people injured. Then the rest of us, who did not die, our innocence were raped from us. We will not be able to function the same. However, *they* walked away without any scratches or injuries. *They* walked away unharmed.

We came peacefully but *they* came violently. We stood on our knees screaming for them to stop. We screamed peace but we were silenced as they stood gigantically over us. Our last memory was the scattered, broken shots of gunfire before we were violently and grossly laid to rest.

It is certain that after today's chaotic attacks from the Red Scare, Saint Christopher is not in San Cristobal. It is certain that the Red Scare desires turmoil. After our protests today, our cities, like San Cristobal, is in turmoil. Chaos is not likely to honour death's request of asylum or refugee.

"Hey, Carlos! What are you reading and watching over there? I have not heard anything from you since last night after you said we were leaving Caracas and would return later after the protests."

Carlos desperately and painstakingly strives to keep his sorrows bottled. Too many Venezuelans to count have died in this morning's protests. A video and news article just went viral exploiting the true face of the government. In his desperate attempt to conceal his emotions, tears involuntary fall from his sore eyes. His words poorly mask his sadness in his conversation with Ezekiel.

"Ezekiel! I'm fine." Carlos unnoticeably wipes the little tears from his eyes with his index finger.

"Obviously, bro, things are not fine with you. Something is going on. I have not seen you this sad since you first told me why you came to the United States."

"My sorrow is that obvious, Ezekiel. I must be really losing touch with reality."

"Yes, my friend. I can read your face like a book. You want to tell me what's going on? Or should I guess from the video you have just watched?"

"No, no. It is quite all right, Ezekiel. You do not have to guess. Please don't. I do not need one of your lectures right now. It is easier if I just tell you what has just happened. I have to tell you regardless."

"Then, shoot. I'm listening."

"You may want to choose a better word then shoot right now. But…don't answer that. The thing is the protests just occurred throughout every major city in my country. The protests began peacefully but that was up until *they* had arrived. There were mass causalities. All of a sudden, the military started to fire at unarmed commoners. I guess they felt provoked when the commoners gave those flowers and told them, here is a flower drop your gun. The military may also have felt threatened by the signs. These signs were nonthreatening anyway. The signs spoke the truth. So in the end, maybe the military did not like that. Either way, *something* gave them the order to shoot. Here, it is easier for me to show you the video. It will be easier for you to watch than to read the news article."

"Okay, Carlos," states Ezekiel as he leans over Carlos' right shoulder. Ezekiel takes the phone once the video begins to play. With earphones in his ear, he begins to listen intensely and watch the already lived and unending horror.

Carlos begins to think to himself as he runs his hand through his hair and interlaces his hands together. He does this repeatedly back and forth. It's a coping mechanism for Carlos to understand what just had happened. While he begins to think what the point is of his returning to his country, once again, he breathes deeply in and out reciting prime numbers up to 151. This helps him to not go back into the past. He thinks he was better in the United States. He has no family. Well, his family believes he is still missing or dead. He cannot return home to them. They would not recognise who he is. Carlos thinks similarly. He believes he would not recognise his family. There is no meaning anyway he wonders. Through this thinking, Carlos may return to some charted time in the past, but does he?

Carlos soundlessly whispers in his head. *My life has been screwed up, God. I am not even sure if what I am doing will help my country. I should have stayed in the United States, as a ghost living out the rest of my dreaded life. I have done things, some very unspeakable things. Then I have done things that my family would be proud of. I can no longer recall the past from the present anymore. There is such chaos. Once again, innocent people are dying. Dying from being shot, dying from starvation, dying from no will to live, dying from thirst, dying from the virus and dying from insecurity. I want to remember the times when we were all happy. I no longer want to remember all of this pain. Our country is changing but for the worst. My presence here may mean nothing. For our people, it gets worse and worse every day. The government fails to acknowledge this. Hell, the people fail to acknowledge that it is getting worse. At one point in my life, I knew these were great times. At least, I was well taken care of. I have to say, the Program did not lie about that. We were well taken care of. Then I saw what happens when someone goes against the Program. In return, you get nothing. It wastes you away until there is nothing left of your sanity. That's the thing God, death, famine and plague surrounds us. It is the Common People who get hurt the most. Everything that we had here is gone. There's no family. There's no freedom. There's no security. There's no food. There's no water. There is only cold and red. Why am I here? Why are any of us here? There are only why questions. Yet these questions are impossible to find answers for because one group of people tells you something and then another group of people tell you something else, but after all, of those conversations, you believe in something completely different. In the end, there is no truth. Truth is a fabrication, much like the fabric on our clothes. You may think the fabric is real but you are really not sure. How can you be sure? I want to remember when everything was what it used to be. Today, I cannot tell what this really is. I want to believe things will get better. I suppose I have joined the Victorias in a quest to restore hope and a country the people want but I'm not sure of that anymore. Perhaps, I have joined the Victorias in search of myself because I believed the Program fulfilled my identity. Maybe they did. But, all of that is nonsense...the women, the children, the innocent, God...they still continue to die just from peace. I see that through our peace, the Red Scare continues to be more violent and deadly. Oh, there is no end, is there? I say God, and yet there is no God. God left and isn't returning. I suppose I say God because there has to be something else. Something else has to answer for our wickedness, surely we don't.*

2,3,5,7,11,13,17,19,23,29,31,37,41,43,47,53...

Carlos' eyes begin to dilate and he continues to silently count. Involuntarily, he rocks back and forth in his seat. Ezekiel notices his peculiar behaviour just in time before another manic-panic attack occurs.

"Hey man! Snap out of it. Have you been thinking about the Grim Brothers' Fairy tales again? Oh, wait! You are about to ask one of the sexy flight attendants for their phone number. You dog, you," Ezekiel states jokingly as he taps Carlos on his chest.

"What! What do you mean bro? It's none of those things. Well…I have to admit the flight attendants are fine. That's beside the point, Ezekiel. Did you finish the video or not?"

With a long pause and dreaded sigh, Ezekiel remarks, "I have to say; at the end of the video it hits the nail right on its head. I mean, whoever created this video for sure got my attention. It was very creative to add the part where people are walking away from the massacre with sown duct tape over their mouths with the words *Solitude*."

With a puzzling look, Carlos hesitates then mentions, "You know that this is a real video. That, in fact, this just happened. This is why we left Caracas at the time we did. Don't worry, we will return just in time for my speech with the generals and political officials."

"Lighten up will you. You sound constipated. It's as if you hadn't had a proper bowel movement for several months. Yes. I know it is quite real. It's quite daunting to see all those people just shot by the Guardias, especially Emmanuel Jose. He's no older than fourteen. I do not know my friend what is to come after all this. He (remarked about Emmanuel) was just a boy giving *them a* letter he wrote. He briefly said, in English subtitles nonetheless, *this gift is to you from God that the freedom we ask is for us all to live in solidarity, not in violence*. It's such a disgrace. I can see why you had tears. As I said Carlos, I just don't know anymore."

"Pretty funny with the comments are you? But yes, the video is quite real and disturbing. This just happened. You have to remember though that this video can only speak of one immeasurable piece of the horror we face from the Red Scare."

"Yes, bro. I understand, but at the same time, I cannot wrap my head around the fact that this has happened and is very, very likely to continue. What is Venezuela to do when its people truly live in a prisoned state."

"Unfortunately, I do not have any answer to your question. I can tell you that the Opposition and I are working around the clock to put an end to this virus."

"What virus?" Ezekiel inquisitively asks as if something new is happening that he was not informed of.

"What I mean is the Opposition and I are trying to avoid another long civil war. We are trying to avoid another conflict. To do this, we have to carefully remove the current corrupt people in power and replace them with people of moral intention. Even then, this is a bandage. Strategically, we must focus on developing our education."

Ezekiel was not paying much attention to what Carlos was just stating, as he was very much fascinated with watching the plane land. However, he did selectively and clearly hear the last statement about education.

"You know me and education, my friend. I don't think you and I should have this conversation as we are about to land. By the way, you have not told me exactly where we are going. Though my point is education and I will say this much about it…"

Carlos was about to interject, but again he is reminded that it is better not to interrupt North Americans when they are in the middle of pontificating their ideas.

"To properly educate our youth for a tomorrow they ought to live in and for a tomorrow that is sustainable, we cannot ignore these factors: Social Emotional Learning, Social-Welfare Capacity Reform, Adaptive Fluidity Leadership and Restorative and Reflective Practice. It is only through a holistic framework that we can properly or begin to properly educate our youth for a tomorrow they will have responsibility over."

"Please, Ezekiel, I know you mean well. I just have a nagging headache much like my mom telling me to be careful riding my bike to Jonny's house. I do want to hear it but I have to wrap my head around the violence once again, which for that reason I left and now have returned to encounter."

After seeing Ezekiel's face, Carlos knew he had put him in a position of awkwardness. Deep down in his mind, he knew that he unintentionally hurt Ezekiel's feelings. For, after all, this is why Ezekiel is here to understand how the Venezuelan education systems have created terroristic movements on its people. Ezekiel is also in Venezuela to present a legal petition for the South American allies and the United Nations to intervene on behalf of the Venezuelan people who have been constantly shunned with violence and treachery. Carlos repents his actions in the following manner: "Okay my brother. I have been off my game ever since I got here. I should not be taking it out on you. After all, you are here to help my country. I immensely appreciate your help more than you will ever know. I should have worded my previous comment a little differently. What I really want to say Ezekiel, despite my headache, is that our conversation must wait because we are about to leave the airplane and gather our bags. However, Father Jonas Fria will particularly enjoy your views and ideas of education. This is who we are going to see, Father Jonas Fria. He's actually not my father, though. That's a different story. He lives on a farm called the Farm. It's not the Farm I told you about where my training was some years ago in a previous life. This Farm is more like a safe haven and shortly you will see how so."

As Ezekiel and Carlos stand up ready to leave the aircraft, Ezekiel puts his left arm on Carlos' shoulder before uttering the following words, "Look, bro. I know what I was getting myself into way before we left Philadelphia. I knew you will be unrelentingly having mixed thoughts and feelings, so I do not take your previous comments personally. All right? Besides, I should have known from your pale skin and the bags under your eyes something was troubling you after you wanted me to see the video. So, I should be the one to say sorry."

"Let us both call it a truce then?"

Carlos and Ezekiel departed the Laser plane and headed to pick up their checked baggage. The Jose Antonio airport in Barcelona, Anzoátegui is small. Many of the airports other than the one in Caracas are small because these are national airports. These airports also have a few flights that fly to and out of them per day. There are few planes that don't fly anymore because Venezuelans do not have the money or the time to take flights anymore. For a one-person round trip ticket, it would cost around 80,000 bolivares, which is equivalent to several weeks of one's working salary. After the plane lands, you would have to walk about two to three metres from the plane to the airport terminal. Once inside, there is one carousel for people to obtain their checked luggage. Usually, this takes some time either because the aircraft crew is lazy or because the carousel is not working. In the case of the carousel not working, it is utter chaos. The crew just piles the luggage in unkempt rows for people to take. Of course, the passengers would have to check the luggage tag number that they put on their bag. For every Venezuelan, this is normal. For Carlos and Ezekiel though, they were not so lucky to encounter the normal airport situation.

In the Jose Antonio airport terminal, a voice on the announcement speaker sounded the following words: *Ezekiel Ian Masefield, please go to the nearest and available crew member to check the status of your luggage.* A few seconds later, the same feminine, calm voice spoke the exact same words over the loudspeaker but hastily this time.

Carlos amazed at the message and thought it must be some sort of mistake.

"Okay, Ezekiel, the announcement said you have to see one of the crew members to get your bag. I'm sure everything is fine. Relax. I am coming with you."

Ezekiel's mind fills with irrational thought. These thoughts form from the little patience he has left. These thoughts take over his speech. He must be careful not to say things too loud that could provoke the Program or otherwise, he may not be so lucky.

"I do not believe this. What they think, I am carrying some type of weapon in my bag. They must think I am that stupid. All I am carrying in the bag is food and supplies. Hey Carlos! You asked me to bring the food and supplies but I don't know for whom. Is this really legal to do? Do they really think I am some sort of terrorist? I think I am smart enough to know that if I wanted to take out the government, it wouldn't be what I have in my bag," Ezekiel responds to Carlos out of frustration and fear.

"I'll do the speaking. Everything will be alright."

"I'm sure everything will be fine. I just want my bag back." Ezekiel states with anxiety and perplexedly.

Carlos approaches one of the crewmembers that happens to be a Guardia and calmly says, "*Mi hermano. Tienes el eqipaje de mi amigo. Mi amigo es de Norte America. El no habala Español. Solo iinglés.*" (My brother. You have my friend's luggage. My friend is from North America. He does not speak Spanish, only English.)

With a disdainful chilling look at Carlos' absent hazel eyes, Soldier Reyes speaks English to his friend. His unpleasant and sneer face suggests his lack of desire to speak with anyone as if he was disturbed from not doing anything. The Guardias like to do nothing but when they have to do something it is as if they were being disturbed – uprooted from the ground like nature's children. Carlos couldn't help but notice that Reye's chilling and uneasy look was more than his contention not to speak. Somehow, Carlos knew that Soldier Reyes hated him for resigning from the Guardias. This is impossible because many Guardias do not know former Guardias for the simple fact that many of them are around the ages 17 to 19. "Merico, who are you? Why are you here?" States Reyes with discontent.

Ezekiel nervously states (his nervousness is not from Reyes' presence, or that he is a Guardian, but his nervousness is from going to prison), "Well, sir, I was asked to come here because you have my bag. I don't know why you have it."

"Ezekiel, is it? Every so often, we have to inspect people's luggage. Because you have a big bag here, we suspected that you might be bringing something into our country that you can't. We don't see people around here with large bags like yours. We don't get outsiders like you either."

"Okay. But, I don't have anything that may be dangerous in there. It's just clothes and some canned food and toiletries. Besides, I wouldn't be here if I did have something in my bag that I'm not supposed to have. I arrived from North America to Caracas with this bag," Ezekiel states puzzlingly.

Carlos interjects, uttering somewhat angrily, "This is unusual for the military to check a person's bag after having been scanned by the machine. Is it because he is from the United States?"

"Thank you for your concern. We have to check your bag anyway. And you sir (looking over at Carlos), who do you think you are? We are not just checking his bag. As you can see, I just got done inspecting another woman's bag because the machine showed some odd-shaped things. Next time, be careful what you say, Merico."

Carlos said nothing further to avoid a confrontation that may leave him detained for several hours. He did not want this because certainly *they* could find out that he is Captain Santos uncharacteristically aiding the Rebels, the Opposition group called the Victorias. In compromise, he nonchalantly took two paces back where he was before and put his hands in his lightly tanned kakis.

"This should not take too long. We want you to go on your way. If you will, please follow me downstairs to the loading bay. Your bag is there, obviously. I was just sent to go get you." Reyes says commandingly and heavily as if he wanted to continue to do nothing.

Ezekiel looked back at Carlos with a troubled and annoyed face. He silently mouthed to him, *fuck this shit.* In response, Carlos mouthed, *just walk. I am behind you.* The three men walked down to the loading bay. The loading bay is underneath the terminal. It looks like a typical basement of a warehouse, grim, grimy and dim.

"So Ezekiel, what brings you to Venezuela?" Reyes asks.

"I'm here to see some friends, experience the culture, taste some food, go to some clubs, go to the Chino Y Nacho concert and hopefully meet some beautiful Venezuelan chicks," he answers casually.

"I am only asking not to make conversation just to see if your answers match to what is in your bag," Reyes states condescendingly.

"I am kind of confused about how my answers to why I am here may help you understand what is in my bag and why I have the things that I do, Reyes."

Carlos interjects, "Reyes the questions you are asking my friend here has no merit. I think you are fishing for something that doesn't exist. I ask that you please get along with the inspection, so we can go."

"I wasn't asking you, Merico. These questions are quite important, Carlos. You may care for your friend but if you let your friend speak, the inspection will go a lot faster and easier for the two of you. Now, Ezekiel, can you tell me exactly what you remember what is in your bag before we go to the table and open it up?" Reyes tries to utter with control as he struggles not to become angry with Carlos. Reyes' discontent of actual work does not help him keep calm.

"Yeah, sure I can. So, as I have tried to state earlier what is in my bag are my clothes. You know the nice kind of clothes to attract the woman or for going out with friends and their family. What else is in my bag? There's some food such as dried milk, butter, syrup, cookies, canned vegetables, canned fruit, probably some candies like chocolate. For toiletries, toothpaste, toothbrush, toilet paper, maybe dental floss. For supplies, batteries, pens, pencils, paper and my friend's video games he lent me. Probably, some of the clothes are not mine such as packaged socks, underwear and undershirts."

"Thank you for your cooperation. Now if you can put these yellow and orange safety jackets on. You have to wear them when you are down here because of safety rules that I don't know about."

Closer and closer as they approached the bottom of the stairs the more it darkened and the more it loudened. Down in the loading bay, the sounds are tormented souls desperately crying in agony. They cry for release. They come and go and the workers who work down here are numb to these sounds as they have long forgotten and tuned them off from their hearing. In actuality, the sounds are from planes refuelling, loading, unloading and getting fixed. While they approach the table where Ezekiel's bag luridly rests its aching body from torture, Carlos notices more heavily armed Guardias. They all look the same – evil, monstrous and ready for battle. Ezekiel's bag, like all bags, are thrown around, beaten and banged on moving planes and cargo vehicles until they finally end up back in the hands of their owners. These are merely bags but helpless victims that have died unexpectedly and prematurely. They horridly rest in the cold, bare ground. They lie stiff and bare. The rotting victims are not frightening to see but what is frightening is how they died.

"Okay, Ezekiel. Let's make this quick, it's about my lunchtime. Can you please identify if this is your bag or not?" Reyes says hungrily.

"Yes. It is mine. I recognise the silver airplane symbol pointing up. I also see that my nametag is still on my bag. It says, Ezekiel Ian Masefield."

"Can you show me some ID, perhaps your passport?"

He hands him his passport. Reyes intently checks his photo and his face to see if they match. Ezekiel's passport photo is nearly as identical to his present-day face. Ezekiel has short wavy dirty-blond hair that sluggishly and messily stands up much like people who have had too many drinks at bars. Though, there is a subtle difference in his hair colour from the photo to the present day. It is so subtle that no one would ever notice unless they were looking to find a difference. The difference is that today, Ezekiel has sporadic tints of grey in his hair. Grey formed from the stress of his getting older. His philosophical, stern hazel eyes stare intently into space gazing over a world that is both troubled and free. He has a muscular face that on the surface is strong and complex, but well beyond its surface, his face is a bighearted-softy much like a detective coming off as stern, but in his heart, he cares for the justice he seeks for others who are voiceless. His complexion is fair and toned not revealing any characteristics about the life he leads personally and professionally, which could be secretive, not of choice, but out of necessity.

"Thank you for confirming your identity. Now, I am going to open your bag. When I do, can you kindly confirm that these are your possessions?"

"Sure, Reyes. As you have said, let's make this quick. I know you are hungry and so are we. Let's get on with the inspection."

Reyes madly puts on red utility gloves as if he was getting ready to diffuse a bomb or as if he is expecting to find some evidence of some criminal offence. He chaotically and heatedly begins tossing the contents of his bag and rudely slamming them on the table.

"Okay, Mr Masefield. Is this all of your things? Everything you have indicated to me is pretty much here. This is correct, isn't?"

"Yes. These are my contents from my bag. Now, can you please put it back and give my bag back to me," Ezekiel responds respectfully to Reyes.

"I think you are mistaken. The inspection is over. It's my lunch. You can put your own bag back together. If this is a problem, I can always have you detained. Trust me, you want to leave here. So, it is your choice, leave or be detained, Ezekiel," Reyes says ignorantly and exhaustedly.

Carlos Christian Santos finally snaps at Soldier Reyes. He doesn't care if he gets detained and if *they* discover who he *actually* is, and how he turned his back on the *Guardias*. His frustration how Reyes has acted became so intense that he could no longer control the words spewing out from his mouth. He acts on emotions instead of thought. He knows better. His training, torture, teachings and hostile programming from the *Harvest* prepared him much better than this. The Guardias has taught him to never act on emotions but always on rationality, thought and instinct. Acting on emotion is irrational and reveals weakness. However, none of his training mattered here. What mattered is that his friend was disrespected. The *Guardias* always teaches respect and somehow and for some disregarded reason, Reyes intentionally had forgotten this, perhaps from not wanting to do work or just because for some peculiar reason he knows what Captain Santos had done. Either way, that anyone may look at Reyes' actions are but disrespect, he cannot be touched. He is a *Guardia*. The commandment is – all Guardias protect their own people. Captain Santos knows this but still proceeded with his heated and emotional comment, despite the repercussions that might follow.

"Don't try to stop me, Ezekiel. Reyes needs a lesson on respect. Hey, *mi hermano*. This is not very Venezuelan like of you to treat anyone like this. This is very disrespectful. I'm sure your parents have taught you much better. Hey, Merico, I'm talking to you. This is not fine. You have asked us to come down here and insisted to inspect our bag. Now, you don't want to put his things back. This is very rude, *mano*. I am very disappointed," Carlos exclaims at Reyes as he casually walks away as if he was speaking to someone else. Surely, he wasn't speaking to him.

"Excuse me, Captain Santos. Who do you think you are talking to?" Reyes angrily states as he swiftly makes an about-face with his hands clench as fists.

"What did you call me?" Carlos mentions confusingly.

"What you cannot hear me over this noise? I said, Carlos, who do you think you are talking to?" Reyes says even louder and more furious as before.

"All I am saying bro, you do not have to be disrespectful, that is all. Your disrespect disgraces the uniform you wear. I also think you should check your attitude and look at yourself in the mirror. It is not going to get you far," Carlos harshly screams across the echoed basement.

Another *Guardia* appears. This one is older and mature and in return, his camouflage battledress uniform sags as he marches.

"Is there a problem, Reyes? Is there a problem gentleman?" (Directed at Carlos and Ezekiel)

Soldier Reyes utters condemningly not at the mature Guardia, but at Carlos, "Sir, I have this from here. There is no problem. This Merico here is a little emotional. But everything is taken care of. They were just leaving."

"All right, Reyes. I trust you have everything under control here. Gentlemen, I hope you have a great day," the mature *Guardia* states lazily as she marches away.

"Ezekiel, whatever your friend may think he is starting, he better be careful. Remember, we are always watching. Consider this as your only warning. If Carlos tries to pull any of this monkey business again, he will not be so lucky. Be careful. Anything can happen. Mistakes and accidents happen all of the time in Venezuela. We do not have the time to investigate all of them," Reyes impatiently and eagerly responds as he fades into the darkness.

"He thinks he can call me Merico and get away with it? He is sadly mistaken!" Carlos responds.

Ezekiel responds in concern while grabbing a hold of Carlos' right arm, "Come on, my brother. It is not worth it. Let's go."

Carlos and Ezekiel walk away back towards the light. Carlos shortly thereafter drives away in the rented car to Father Jonas Fria. Approximately, in an hour and fifteen minutes both Carlos Christian Santos and Ezekiel Ian Masefield arrive at the Farm where Father Jonas Fria, his wife, Aunt Adriel Fria (though she is always referred to as Ma) and the children who are called the Saved, are expecting them. A Venezuelan barbeque awaits them. The potent smell of burning wood and cooking meats permeates the breathable air, which Carlos and Ezekiel will soon taste.

Carlos turns onto an unmarked dirt road that once was smoothed and naked but now it is rough and disturbed. Certainly, this road is not the road less travelled by. It is quite the opposite. It is the road well-travelled by and by many others. There are no two roads here that diverge, only one that if you doubt to look back, you cannot turn away. You must continue to stay. The roads used to be wide and straight but now they are narrow and bendy. If it were not for the sunlight, for sure he would be lost just like in horror movies. Like horror movies, they would not able to survive. There is nothing but frail, brittle, decaying corn stalks surrounding them. The more Carlos drives, the more it appears that the cornstalks are closing in on them. They used to be luscious, abundant, green and yellow but because of the drought, they are decaying and dying. Since Carlos can remember, much of the agriculture and livestock in the Tiger city of Anzoátegui have been rotting, frantically searching for water that doesn't exist, not even tainted water exists, just dried up like a raisin in the sun-parched and withered ground.

The red dirt road stretching for kilometres and kilometres has probably over hundreds of different deformed size potholes. While Carlos continues his drive to the Farm, the red dirt escapes from the well-beaten road and scattered tenuously around them creates a blanket of thick powder. This thick red powder suffocates every living thing around. The good thing is that they are not outside. From the red, thick blanket powder, a whirlwind of poisonous red vapour forms. The poison swarms tenaciously engulfing and devouring everything in its presence. Its omnipresence is nothing less than a chaotic disaster. Carlos is careful enough not to drive too fast around the narrow, winding curves. He swerves around the deeply entrenched potholes. Though, it is a failed attempt.

Bump, bump, bump. Owe, owe, owe, there *goes a few more potholes*, Ezekiel says to himself as he and Carlos bounce in and out of their seats like a poorly designed roller coaster.

"Jesus Christ Carlos. Are you trying to get us killed? Can you be even more of a maniac? Hey! I'm sure you want to make it there in one piece as much as I do."

"Oops. Sorry about this. Yeah. Don't complain to me. It is not my driving. It is these God-forsaken potholes that the earth has yet to smooth over with freshly cultivated red dirt."

"I'll make sure to send the message to God then. You're crazy you know that?"

"Yeah. I'm crazy just like Maburro. Just like the Program. Will you stop your whining already?" Carlos utters jokingly as Ezekiel laughs alongside him.

"How much longer until we arrive? Everything looks the same around here. I fear we are lost and you don't want to admit this. This wouldn't be the first time that we were lost and you refused to admit it."

"Look, bro. If we were lost, or better say, if I get us lost, I wouldn't know whether we are or are not lost. You are right. Everything around here is the same. Who knows if we are going around in circles? Ha – ha – ha."

"Really funny, Carlos. Really funny to say some shit like this. You know I'm in a foreign country, a country that is nonetheless indifferent to North Americans," Ezekiel responds sincerely.

"Relax, dude. We are not lost. I would not ever do that to you. Look! We are almost here. You see the clear horizon up ahead. That's Father Jonas' Farm. They are expecting us. They are very friendly. You will see."

Within three minutes of their friendly banter, they arrive at the Farm – a safe haven not only for the Saved but also for anyone who stays. Some stay. Others make the Farm their own while working to keep it producing nourishment. The children especially work to keep the Farm alive. As Ezekiel and Carlos got out of the car, they saw the Farm as it is. The Farm stood paradoxical. Its face is dichotomous. The Farm is the true nature of Venezuela, its virus and its 4-F Program. The Farm is both unproductive and productive – producing assorted meats, poultries, fruits and vegetables. The Farm is both uncultivable and cultivable. It is both, infertile and fertile – baring abundant subsistence for the Saved and for the inhabitants of the Tiger. The Farm is barren, disarranged, disarrayed, tousled, vulgar, marred and depleted in areas. Then in other areas, it is fruitful, kempt, exuberant, plentiful, luscious, profitable and robust. The Farm in appearance is unending due do its few thousand acres. Most of the land is shaggy and stagnant weeds occupy the pasture like interlopers squat the land as their territory. There aren't enough workers to tend to all of the farmland. The Farm, to Ezekiel, reminds him of the dustbowl the Joad family in *The Grapes of Wrath,* were moving out west to avoid – a paradise they never found just as Moses never found. Their car, dusty, stained, ruined and decayed by now, pulled up next to the worn white Dodge pickup truck and the fatigued dark blue Ford Escape.

Father Jonas Fria stood tall glaring in the high noon sun with Bolivar Jr., the grandpa golden-brown retriever dog. From their limp, due to years of working on the Farm, they walked tiresomely and laboriously down the fatigued, worn out, sweaty, stained road. In time, working on the Farm takes its toll. Both the dog and Father Jonas resemble in age and personality. They both have fought to survive for many years and they have lived through many adventurous years. Time has caught up with their biological clocks though. Soon their time will stop ticking. This does not stop them from continuing their work on the Farm. With open arms, a large simile, an un-tucked shirt and soiled, faded blue jeans, Father Jonas and Bolivar Jr. came running to Carlos and his friend Ezekiel to welcome them to their home.

"Buenas tardes, Padre. Encantado. Este es mi amigo, Ezekiel. El es de Norte America. No hablas Español, solo ingles."

("Good afternoon, Father. This is my friend Ezekiel. He is from North America. He does not speak Spanish, only English.")

"Let's not be rude Carlito. We have to speak English, so your friend can understand us and participate in the conversations. It's not uncommon anymore we have many people from the States visiting us these days. It's nice to have them when they do visit," Father Jonas states ecstatically.

"Of course, Father. This is why I have told you we are coming here."

"I must have forgotten that's all. Ma though continues to remind me at my age that you are coming and you were bringing a friend. Enough already. Now, it is nice to meet you, sir. It is an honour for us to have you as our guest. Please, make yourself at home," he says, the last of it directed towards Ezekiel).

"Well, sir. It is nice to meet you. Thank you for inviting me to your home. I am grateful to be a guest here. I also have heard a lot about you," Ezekiel states friendly and jokingly as he shakes Father Jonas' right scarred blackened hand.

"I hope little Carlos here has not told you all of my secrets now. If he did, I am going to have to kill you and you will be what we are having for dinner instead of the meats we are preparing for the barbeque. Hey. I'm just kidding. I hope I did not scare you."

"Ha—ha-ha. No, you did not. I can use a little humour anyway. It has been a long journey to come and meet you and your family here."

"Come in. Come in. Leave your bags. Lincoln and Jefferson will get your bags for you. Here, I want to show you around," humbly, Father Jonas states.

"Are you sure? I can grab them myself."

"Nonsense, Ezekiel you are our guest."

"Now, Father. We are only here for the night then we have to travel back to Caracas tomorrow evening for my meeting with the generals and politicians," Carlos states to remind Father Jonas not to be too hospitable if that's at all possible.

"Let's save the politics for later. It's time to have fun. Jefferson...Lincoln (yelling away from Carlos and Ezekiel and towards the sky), can you come by the car to pick up our guests' bags?"

A sudden cold, chilling breeze passes over Ezekiel. He silently thinks, *this cannot possibly be good. I fear this is only the beginning. Things are going to continue to get worse.* His thoughts are not related to his being on the Farm, but his being in Venezuela. It is the same chilling, cold breeze he felt while departing from Philadelphia. Yet, it has come back to perhaps to warn him or tell him something important. But despite this, Ezekiel brushes it off to enjoy the hospitality of Father Jonas. He thinks nothing of the chilling, cold breeze again.

"What took you so long, Jefferson and Lincoln? Our guests are waiting," Father Jonas pleasantly states.

Because they know little English, they respond using words they recently learned. Father Jonas speaks English when there are guests on the Farm. The children knew that. This is why, among other reasons, they are taught English, so that they can speak to guests in the common world language. To the children living on the Farm, any visitor they receive that speaks English is a luxury they desperately desire. They believe English speakers come from a *world* of opportunity that they are unfortunate not to have, especially someone from the United States.

"Sorry, Father. We did not hear."

"We were working."

"We can get the bags now."

Both Jefferson and Lincoln state one after the other. Their bright similes indicate their joy of having the opportunity to speak with someone for the United States.

"It is okay. The bags are outside."

"I want you two both to meet Ma. You may not remember her from your last visit, Carlito. You were just a kid at the time. If you remember Ma, she is always doing something – shopping, cooking, working on the Farm with the kids and reviewing the finances."

"I cannot remember that I do. That is Ma. I know that my mother and father would visit you and I stayed with you a few times. But it wasn't until your name came up. The Victorias told me about you and I thought it would be the perfect time to visit you, given all that is happening right now in the cities. You know…the political protests, the civil unrest, my search."

"Yes, yes, Carlos. It does not matter why you are you, but that you are. I cannot say how good it is to see you. Because when I do, you want to jump into politics. You are no different than your father. This is a story for another time. I want you to meet Ma. That is all," Father says with concern.

"I'm sorry Father. It is just that…"

"You do not have to explain to me. Ezekiel, you have quite the friend here."

"He is quite the friend all right. He likes to always talk about business…nothing fun or personal," Ezekiel utters loudly so that Carlos could hear him.

While they approached the entrance of the doorway, Ma appeared. Ma has a dark complexion. Her exhausted demeanour suggests she has gotten back from being in town. It is evident to both Carlos and Ezekiel that she has eaten her fair share of *arepas*. While they enter, they see that the house is well kept, but the kitchen is in disarray. Groceries in bags still lay frantically on the counter. Empty milk containers are spread out across the floor. Different cut meats, poultries and vegetables are packaged on the counter ready to be cooked. The disorder of the kitchen much like the disorganised condition of the Farm mirrors the various unfinished tasks the Jonas family has started, but either put off or forgot to finish. The melody of *Pasan los Dias* by Guaco plays as Carlos, Ezekiel, Father Jonas and Bolivar enter the house. Ma's words are as charming as angels every time she speaks. Any time she speaks, her words uplift everyone's spirits. It was so when she briefly speaks to Carlos, Ezekiel, Father Jonas and the children.

"Forgive me and the mess in here. I did not get the chance to tidy up the house. I did not expect to be in town as long as I did selling milk. We sold all of it. We did not make much. We don't do it for the money. We do it to help the people. I'm sure you don't want to hear this. So, you must be Ezekiel. It's nice to meet you. You can see I speak English fine. No thanks to the government Programs anyway. (Ma briefly pauses) Carlos told me. I did not forget you were visiting. I know Father does. Anyway, come here," Ma utters with kindness to Carlos and Ezekiel as she gives both of them a hug and two kisses one for each cheek.

Carlos and Ezekiel respond, "It is nice to meet you too. Thank you for allowing us to stay the night."

"It's not a problem at all. Thank you for coming here. Please, enjoy yourselves. This is your home. Jonas, we need to talk about this week's sales and numbers. Also, later we have to talk about getting some more supplies later this week," she tells Father Jonas.

"Of course. We can talk tomorrow night," Father Jonas sates.

"Okay. I'm sorry I have to run. If you need anything, the children can get it for you. Many of them do not know English. But, someone will help you if you need anything," utters Ma charmingly to Ezekiel and to everyone else. Though, her remarks were intended for Ezekiel as a way of apologising for her abruptness.

Ma looks over at Jefferson and Lincoln entering the house before she leaves from the rear door to state, "Thank you, gentlemen. When you have the chance, you can introduce Carlos and his friend to the other children here. Enjoy. I hate to run. There are many things to do on the Farm. I hope though to see you all some later time. Maybe tonight I will. Bye."

Carlos and Ezekiel explore the Farm and the house. Carlos assists the children in preparing the Venezuelan barbeque they will have tonight. Adjacent to where the grilling happens, Father Jonas is struggling to stand near Ezekiel and walks over, breathing heavily, to engage in a philosophical conversation about life on the Farm. Their conversations are unsettlingly for Father Jonas and Ezekiel. While the red blowing dust around the Farm distorts their sight, they both begin to gain insight on an unfamiliar and familiar world.

Ezekiel, with a half-empty beer bottle, ponders what his life would be like if he wasn't in a country that is divided by freedom and oppression. He battles with himself to make sense of what he experiences.

Perhaps what these children only know is working on a farm and living in makeshifts houses around the land. They only know of this life. We would call them indentured servants or child labourers. It is much more than that though. From my brief observations, being here for only a few short but long hours, I can only surmise that if these children were not here then they would perhaps be another victim of the Red Scare – a criminal – a Guardia – a druggy – homeless – or fighting to make ends meet. Maybe I am wrong about the Farm. Maybe the children are better here than out there. I cannot help but see children wearing soiled clothes or whatever they could find and stitch together as clothes, walking around barefoot, with poor dental hygiene, missing and rotting teeth. Some of these children, who are younger than me, are parent. The children can see what the world is only through their environment – bearing a limited perspective. But somehow, they know life is better than in their country and not grim. From the broken stories they are told by others, they imagine a world not filled with ghouls, goblins, demons, witches and wickedness. These inexplicable monsters are very much real here, that the children or anyone else for that matter cannot escape because their country is a prison of solitude. The children here do not eat what I eat because there isn't enough of it. They eat whatever their parents can scrape up or whatever leftovers there are. In my brief observations, I can say that despite the adversity, these children face knowingly or unknowingly, among them there is a sense of community. Perhaps through their solidarity among each other, is the hope and happiness they feel. When asked, 'how is life here,' they respond, 'we are grateful for what Father Jonas and Ma provide for us. Without them, we would be somewhere else – somewhere harder for us to live. They do the best that they can for us. We don't complain because we know what little we have here. We are saved. Maybe someday, we can save others just like they saved us.'

In my short conversations with them, every child says they are happy and appreciate that they can call something a home, their home. I see a world here that I am beginning to travel but have little experience of. I know one thing is certain. Though these children may be happy here on the Farm and are saved, this may be the only life they will experience during troubled times their country is currently undergoing. The Farm is a place where the ghouls, goblins, demons, witches and wickedness are all forgotten about. It is a place of hope – of communion – of safety. Father Jonas is the Saviour of these children.

Father Jonas, with a heavy cool, crisp glass of whisky over the rocks, out of curiosity stumbles up to Ezekiel and taps his left shoulder in the hopes to have a conversation.

"What are you looking at, *mi pana*, Ezekiel?"

"Hark, who's there?" Ezekiel utters astoundingly.

"I didn't mean to startle you."

"Oh. Nothing. I was just looking beyond the pasture."

"What did you say? I do not understand you."

"I mean to say, I was looking out towards the little homes around your Farm here. Then I saw children coming from these homes. Forgive me, Father. I call people who are younger than me children."

"I see what you mean. You probably want to know who they are and what they are doing here?"

"Well…since you have asked, yes."

"I do not know how to exactly explain it to you. I mean, I do not know where to begin, Ezekiel. I have been doing this for a long time that is, managing this Farm you see here. Before the Farm, I used to work with the Chavistas as an oil manager at one of their plants in Bolivar state. After a while…I do not know…I guess I had a change of heart. So, Ma and I ventured out to have a farm."

"I do not mean to be rude when I say father, but you realise you have children working on your Farm. I probably can understand that maybe you have taken them in or something like this? From my too few conversations with them, it sounds like they work here."

"I understand, or I think I understand the question here. You know, you are not the first person to ask me about this. You see, I try to take as many children off the streets as I am able to. As you know, Venezuela is no United States or European Union. We don't have programs for children who are homeless or who are lost. So, Ma and I took it upon us, to try to change the current situation we're in. We wanted to try to do something. So, we decided to transform the land you see before you into a farm. But, it became much more than that. It became a safe haven. It is the Farm where anyone is welcomed. It is a place where people can have a life without fear – without punishment – without insecurity."

"So, you have been taking children off of the streets for a long time and giving them and their families a place to live. I am beginning to understand. Forgive me, Father. I come from a different world where it is unspeakable for children to work. I guess I am beginning to understand."

"I think…I know where you are going with this. Perhaps, it is better for me to explain. Yes, the teenagers do work on the Farm. The adults train them and they will train the children. They do not do any work. They won't when they are incapable of doing or do not know how to do. Their parents and the teenagers work to build their character, to build a sense of reasonability and to create something where they have ownership in. Let me think of the common English word…ah, yes…there is no sweatshop here. I assure you, they earn their keep. The adults and the younger adults too, do earn money for their work because they take apart in running the daily operations of the Farm. Of course, I pay them little. I only can. There's food and supplies for them. No one here is kept a prisoner. In fact, some of the children's parents work other jobs, off the Farm, to provide more for their family. I hope this is clear for you now, Ezekiel?"

"Thank you for explaining this to me. It is much clearer to me now. So you must be some sort of saint for doing all of this for people who are really strangers."

"I want you to listen very carefully to me, Ezekiel," Father Jonas states in a drunken manner while the alcohol begins to take control of his mind and body.

He must of have had slightly more than one tall cool, crisp glass of whisky before conversing with Ezekiel. His thoughts at the moment are still rational. Ezekiel, on the other hand, has not indulged in the alcohol as well as Father Jonas has.

"Sure I'm listening, just give me a second," Ezekiel states intriguingly as he briskly walks over to the rusted, tinted pale of beer.

There are still small lumps of ice, but mostly water in the pale of beer. While he reaches in the arctic water to fish for another green bottle of *Zulia*, Father Jonas begins to speak. The Farm faintly hears the ghostly sound of beer bottles opening. The Farm is also intrigued to listen to Father Jonas.

When Ezekiel bends back up, at the corner of his eye he sees a worn, grey beaten football rolling to his feet. He picks up the football that was once black and white, to give back to one of the children standing innocently near him.

"Listen here, son! I am far from a saint. I do the things I do because it was sort of my wife's and I dream to do – to start the Farm. But, it has been very difficult to keep up the Farm. I am not saying that we are going to close the Farm or anything like this. Hell, it will be here well after death comes for me. It is just getting harder to find resources to upkeep everything and I am afraid because of the unending drought, that our crops will become so frail that they will die, and then our livestock too might follow."

"Okay, Father I sort of, understand. You are worried, right? Well, I'm sure there will be rain soon. But, I cannot help with the state of the country and the lack of resources that are becoming more normal and more prolific," Ezekiel states puzzlingly.

"Well, I too hope it rains as well. This doesn't concern me. What concerns me is that you are here. And, I think I know why you are here. Hell, you know why you are here. You have to make sure that whatever happens, happens. The

Opposition must prevail. I do not know what Carlos has planned but you have to make sure that it prevails. The Opposition may be our last hope, but perhaps not. I'm afraid, if the people do not act, then monsters like Maburro will continue to control their lives. I fear for the worst if the Opposition fails. I fear we will be in this situation that will continue to get worse. When it does get worse, the people will be too far gone – too far lost – too far dehumanised to know that it is worse."

"Father forgive me for my forwardness in advance. But, I do not know how much you know or what you think you may know why I am here…let's get the record straight, I am trying to compile factual evidence for my legal petition for international aid and for our South American allies to impose sanctions. I am also here to continue my work in international education, as such, I am composing several news articles that will be brought to the full attention of the world, exposing Venezuela as the country it is, under a hostile and sadistic government under Maburro's leadership and command," Ezekiel exclaims respectfully and somewhat awkwardly, as he did not fully understand Father's previous response.

"Okay, okay. Let me put it in these words for you. Do whatever you can to make sure Carlos is successful tomorrow."

"Okay, Father. I will do what I can."

"Good then, my son."

After a long discomforting pause, Father Jonas begins to have a disconcerting but truthful conversation that Ezekiel strives to change. In his effort, though, he tried but has nearly failed.

"I am afraid Ezekiel that death has sent its messengers and it is far too late for any of us to run. There's no escaping," Father Jonas states seriously.

"You mean he, Death has sent sickness, sorrows and sleeplessness as his messengers," inanely utters Ezekiel to echo the Brothers Grimm fairy-tale, *Death's Messengers.*

"Or, perhaps you mean the Baron Samedi himself?"

"What nonsense are you spewing boy? No. This is serious, so I hope you listen, or you too will be missing…missing the meaning, I mean."

"Okay. No need to get bent out of shape, Father. I was trying to make a joke."

"Okay, then. What I meant was, that well before Chava died people have failed to realise that death was inevitable because the Program did not do any good. As you see, it is getting worse – death, war, famine, earthquakes, false prophets, holocaust, deteriorating education. You can even say that the dead are waking up from their graves. But what do I know? I am an old fool who runs a farm."

"No, no I see your point, Father. So, death is people who died over the years and are increasing as the protests continue. War, is the previous one Venezuela entered to bring Chava to power and the probable war that will come soon – perhaps tomorrow – next month – or next year. Famine is the lack of food the government and whatever private companies are left, cannot produce. Also, the unending droughts that have been occurring…we cannot forget that."

"I do not want to be rude, Ezekiel, but I understand that you understand me. Thank you for not considering me crazy or as one of the crazy criminals that manage the cities of Venezuela and who make the actual decisions of our country."

"If I can ask you, sir, for you to explain something more to me, that will be awesome. Can you?"

"Well…sure. I guess. But what do you want me to explain for you?"

Ezekiel hesitates for a moment as his current train of thought passes him. He begins to state, "Oh yes. This is what I was talking about. Can you please explain to mean what you mean by the lack of education? I know that in South and Latin America the education system needs to be overhauled. I presume it will be similar for Venezuela, given my knowledge so far of the country's history and its current affairs."

Father Jonas takes the last sip of his whiskey. He then grabs the last bit of ice in the rusted tin pale to put in his glass. Afterwards, he takes out his dented, aged flask from his pocket pours himself another drink over melted rocks before speaking the following,

"Indeed, I remember now. Carlos was telling me about how you are the expert of education. Isn't that right, my son? But, but before you answer me, let me explain. There is no good or bad in the world. Okay, okay you are going to argue, but let me explain. I'll say education has to do with this. Yes. You agree that people make choices that have both negative and positive consequences but there is really no good or bad. It is a matter of perception and perspective. Let me also say this, education teaches people and of those teachings, people learn and through their learning, they make choices, and through their choices there are consequences, and from those consequences, we determine good and bad. How we determine what is good and bad well…through our teachings, our environments, and how we perceive our actions and the perspectives it has on us. Good and bad is relative. But you must know in the age I am in now, and the revelations I have had, what matters is how we feel and what we feel. Now, the Program has created or taught people to be people without these feelings – with some not knowing who they are, what they are doing, who they have become, and the consequences of their choices."

"I do not know how to proceed with what you have just said. I do not know if I should be angry or not. I know I am baffled."

"What do you mean, Ezekiel?"

"Well, I guess I am confused."

"Look here, this is what I mean. People only know what they are taught and if they are not given any opportunity to learn for themselves they will become the product of whoever or whatever is teaching them."

"So you are saying, how people are educated determines what they may be and if they are not given any opportunity to learn from their mistakes and that their actions have consequences, then they will become people, let's say, unjust people?"

"Well, to comprise, which I believe is what English speakers say, then yes. Sure, why not." Father Jonas utters before taking another sip of this drink.

"But I hope you agree, Father, that education is important in any country, and if it is not the priority then we are sorely mistaken. We also create communities that are not democratic when education is not the priority. Moreover, if we do not consider where people come from, who their families are, their communities, who we are educating and the schools in which they go to then people are not actually learning."

Father Jonas, before he loses consciousness, falling on a black lawn chair that used to be white, from too many whiskies on the rocks, he utters his last words, "I agree. As you see, on the Farm, I do the best I can to educate the Saved. I do the best I can where the world has forgotten about my country, Venezuela and these children."

"So, I see you have met Jonas. He is quite the person, uh?" Carlos seriously and jokingly states to Ezekiel as he looks over at a passed-out Father Jonas.

"You can say that again, my friend."

"How did your conversation go with him anyway?"

Ezekiel did not want to get too much into his conversation with Father Jonas as he continues to struggle to understand what he meant in some of his comments. It is puzzling to him because he does not know whether to take the conversation seriously. After all, Father Jonas either had too many drinks or couldn't control his liquor any longer. To Ezekiel, people like Father Jonas means well, but when the liquor becomes a beast inside of them, then their words can be unreliable.

"Well Carlos, in the beginning the conversation was fine but then it just got weird. He ended up talking about death and how he tries to educate people here. But our entire conversation wasn't all like this."

"From what I can recall, Father Jonas tries to be philosophical when he drinks, but it is his way of having fun and making new guests such as yourself feel comfortable – to feel like you are at home."

"Okay then. Is he going to be fine?" Ezekiel responds with concern.

"Who? Father Jonas? Yeah. He is going to be quite fine. He never misses a Venezuelan barbeque. Besides, he gets likes this. He will wake up in a few minutes ready to eat and converse again. Come on, now. The food is almost ready."

The smell of cooking meats on burning cider wood pleasantly wakes up Father Jonas and lures the children and Ma out and from what they were doing. The pungent and savoury aromas intensify around the fire indicating that the blacked, crispy, juicy, tender, succulent meats are ready to be enjoyed and devoured. Hunger, warmth, conversations, laughter, music, stories and games dance around the fire. Carlos and Ezekiel participated in these festivities, but they do not remember much from what has happened. Somehow, either the darkness of the virus has stolen these memories or the alcohol they have consumed did. As the night darkens and looms around the Farm, the conversations, laughter, music stories and games fade, so do Carlos and Ezekiel fade into sleep to wake up to Simon Bolivar Airport in Caracas.

"Yo. Holy shit, dude." Ezekiel exclaims to Carlos as if he just have had remembered something important.

"Yeah. Yeah. I'm up. I'm up. What is it, bro? Damn!" Carlos insanely mentions to Ezekiel while glancing over his turned over black wristwatch. He too remembers where he is – back to the Monster and what he has to do – secretly negotiate with generals and political officials to peacefully end the tyranny of the Red Scare, if at all possible.

"That's right; we are here already, back in Caracas. Or in your words, we are back in the belly of the beast. Back to where *it* all began – the virus – the Red Scare."

"Unfortunately, we are back *here*. As I have said previously and certainly by now numbing, but remember to follow my lead. Even though the protests have ended, for now, the darkness, the evilness, the vileness, the plague, the agony, the horror and the defeat still occupies us. You can smell it getting off of the plane. It is a very bad smell, my friend. It reeks of forgotten memories."

"Yes, Merico! I understand!" Ezekiel utters with exhaustion and tiredness.

"I see that Venezuela is having an effect on you?"

"Well, I guess Venezuela is."

"Listen. When we get to the meeting, I want you to relax. There will be Chavista military there but they are not Chavista anymore. They want a new government and the generals are important for this to happen, being that the military has the control."

"Yes. I understand. But, how are we going to get to the meeting?"

"This is not a problem, Ezekiel. That's not the question you should be asking either. We are very close to the meeting place. We also have a car waiting for us. The question you should be asking is whether Venezuela will have a future people want to wake up to tomorrow."

"Okay, bro."

The protests have ended. The riots have been disbanded. The National Guards have driven away. The dead have been buried. The blood has been washed out. The roads have been sanitised. The people are silent. For now, they are certain that Caracas, like the rest of Venezuela, is a prison of solitude – a perfect environment for the Red Scare to multiply. Though somehow, in some unrealistic way, the sky is still red. Death continues to pervade the streets with people. The wind recklessly blisters fragments of forgetfulness. The earth sorrowfully and mercifully cries for peace. Nature is frail, brittle and brown. Nothing is the same, for it is an interloper in masks. These masks conceal the true identity of the horror. People continue to wear these masks. These masks are the people's unrelenting ignorance of the Program's desire to keep them silenced. Carlos Christian Santos and Ezekiel Ian Masefield feel the unwanted change as the black, tinted car stops in traffic on the anarchic Simon Bolivar Blvd but must continue onward in their journey to the meeting.

Carlos and Ezekiel enter in a remote place with an unmarked building just outside the Capital. When the time is precedent, a meeting is called. One of the Opposition leaders, Leo Lopez was responsible for creating the Clandestine Council of Common Opinions. This Council consists of twelve members: two generals of each branch of service: Army, Navy and Air Force, three members of the Victorias and three political officials of whom which are Chavista. While Carlos and Ezekiel walk in the dim-lit, empty room, all the members with either a bottle of beer or glass of rum and coke in their hands have gathered around, impatiently waiting for their final guests to show. Carlos enters first, Ezekiel right behind him. The two light brown heavy doors slam behind Ezekiel echoing throughout the vast, warm room. The Counsel looks over and without a passing heartbeat, they are silenced synchronously.

"Welcome, Generals Luis Santiago and Dante Joseph of the Army, Generals Marina Isabella and Mateo Samuel of the Navy, Generals Christopher Daniel and Sofia Valentine of the Air Force, Julio Marcus, Marissa Juliette, Marino Esteban, Politician Lucinda Rose, Politician Lucas Javier and Politician Amelia Nicole," Carlos utters confidently and sternly by looking at their various nametags.

"There he is!" Julio Marcus says happily as if a moment later he would have to clean up the tension off of the floor.

"Thank you, JMS for the introduction."

Various voices say welcome almost at the same time to welcome Carlos. Many of them do not know each other until they meet for meetings such as the one commencing. Many of them are strangers but are strangely familiar with each other's work with the Opposition. They cannot know each other and are strangers for the reason it is a clandestine organisation. If the Program ever discovered that there are intruders within it and these intruders knew each other and have been working publically with each other, then forget any hope to better the country, the Venezuelan people outcry. The nametags that they wear are not their real names except for Julio Marcus and Marissa Juliette. It is just a name to most of them. When they rarely meet, their names change to preserve the secrecy of what they do.

"My name is…well it does not matter. Many of you know me as one person and others here may know me by another name. So, my name has no importance. What is certain though, I am here for the reason why all of you are here, to eliminate the reign of the virus we live, we breathe, we eat, we drink and we sallow. Granted that I do not know who any of you are, except for Julio and Marissa, but if I am here then they have spoken to you about my previous work." Carlos utters profoundly to get their attention.

"Sir. I want to thank you for coming, but what information do you have for us that will possibly end the reign of the 4-F Program peacefully," asks one of the politicians.

"That is the question isn't what information do I have that will end the 4-F Program? It is not much about the information as it is about what all of you have to do."

"What is it we have to do?" asks one military officer commandingly.

"Thank you for your candour, General Dante Joseph. All of you are wondering the same idea, what is left for us to do. Well, from this point, all of you have been participating in what seems to be fragmented operations such as establishing backdoor negotiations with our allied countries, restoring humane efforts in our slums, forming austerity measures in consultation with other country's military to dismantle any connection with terroristic groups, or terroristic groups that want to harm us, clandestinely reforming our education, justice and economic systems through small but important laws and amendments. All of our disjointed efforts are not so disjointed. They have been small, but important pieces leading up to the moment we now face – eliminating the Red Scare. To do this, however, the current heads cultivating it must be taken care of."

"So, all this time, sir we have been planning another coupe?" General Mariana utters loudly.

"It is more than another coupe or another series of discussions or consultancy protocols. It was about transformation. For example, butterflies do not transform overnight. They transform in a series of days and in stages. Change happens this way too, but slower. Otherwise, if we have frantically and impulsively cut off the heads of the virus, the virus would grow back more fiercely and at alarmingly rates. You would not walk into battle unprotected. You would not walk into the National Assembly unprepared and without your briefs. You would not walk up to a girl or guy at a club and tell him or her you want a dance. No, you would slowly talk to him or her as wrapping a present. This is what we have done over the past few years. However, it has been unknown to all of you specifically what you have done in your respected positions and is still to be unknown."

"What happens now?" Politician Amelia Nicole asks unnervingly

The remote, occupied room enters into a parade of voices endless stating their opinions. The words cannot be recognised as the voices are herding sounds converging together. Each are worried about what has to come next. Others are unsure if the work they have done separately and in isolation has had any effect on the 4-F Program, or has the 4-F Program has grown much stronger and vile over the years just to continue to protect the virus it breeds and cultivates?

Ezekiel Ian Masefield could no longer stand in the shadows and continue listening to these chaotic whispers while nothing is being resolved.

"Excuse me, ladies and gentlemen! Silence. My name is Dr Ezekiel Ian Masefield from the States."

Voices faded in distant echoes as the words from Ezekiel's mouth gets their attention, perhaps because he is from North America or perhaps he announced himself as a doctor. The following is the speech Ezekiel gave to the Venezuelan officials who were appointed to this Clandestine Council of Common Opinions as the hope and light of Venezuela and for its people. He recounts an important historic shift when the Opposition took the majority control of the National Assembly on December 7, 2015.

The 2015 elections to the National Assembly begin an era we sought to believe but unrealistic to attain. This is the era of proclamation, reconstruction and transparency we seek. On December 7, 2015, as we stood and waited to cast our votes, this dream came to fruition. We had not thought this would be a living history; though, we are creators of living this history. Our winning testifies that when there is a will there is a way. Persevering through years of failed policy, not of ideology or concept, but of direction and focus, we embark towards a New Bolivarian Republic, Venezuela anew. As we do, it is absolute we not abdicate our past, we not numb our provocations and we not forget what is to come.

Courageous dissident and outspoken Venezuelans have paved this era we begin entering; alas, they are not here today because of their noble and selfless actions. Their spirits remain in our memories and our hearts as we continue their efforts of a New Bolivarian Republic. Their noble and selfless actions testify that we must shout our words for everyone to hear and we must exhibit our actions greatly for everyone to witness. We live in their past while striding forward to promote a common vision their efforts sweated for. As we do, it's necessary we remember who they are, what they have accomplished and what mistakes they have endured. Our past illustrates where we are today and how we arrived there. Our past provides answers to a future we not only want but also we have to build collectively. Our past is our teacher. It teaches that failed policy is a policy without specific direction and clear focus. Our past teaches us which mistakes we have made, so that future generations, our children and their children, don't have to endure further violence and bloodshed. As we bear our past, we proclaim Venezuela, a New Bolivarian Republic, we all know exists.

The difference then from today is that this vision of Venezuela anew has always existed, but more individuals understand what that is.

Venezuela has the propensity to be steadfast, ingenious and prosperous to its people, to South America and to the world. To get here, we must reconstruct our policy, our position and our approach of how to get there. We cannot get there by division. Our past teaches us that by dividing we create rebellions that much of the time our people do not know what they are fighting for. Reconstruction is progress, but progress is long and complicated. However, we have to and will rebuild Venezuela correctly and collectively. As we do, it's not going to be easy; it never is easy. Our rebellions, though some short and some long, teach Venezuelans who want to live in sovereignty.

We must allow ourselves to connect with our past to avoid another fatal, but avoidable rebellion, pushing reconstruction farther away. We must collaborate, discuss and refute our doctrines, our ideas and our policies with the Chavistas and with the Common People; otherwise, we have not heeded our past. We simply cannot allow our well intentions to be enclosed in darkness. When we collaborate, discuss and refute our doctrines, our ideas and our policies, they become transparent.

The Chavistas have failed in communicating their doctrines, their ideas and their policies because they were not transparent to the Common People. We cannot fail to be transparent either. No transparency precursor's corruption. It's easy to forget what our purpose is and why we have such a purpose when we assume authority. This is exactly what has happened since Venezuela began extracting oil and began expanding economically under the Perez administration, which would later continue under the Chavez administration to our present, the Maburro administration. Over thirty years, Venezuela toiled in corruption while the Common People have been exploited.

Remorsefully, it takes at least sixty years to deconstruct corruption, reconstruct the economy and educate the Common People. As we do, we create a future of transparency and our shared vision.

Fellow Venezuelans of the Clandestine Counsel of Common Opinions and Venezuelans of the public, it is our obligation to proclaim, reconstruct and translucent our doctrines, our ideas and our policies. For we fail to settle common ground with all of our political parties, then this meeting fails at not abdicating our past, not numbing our provocations and not forgetting what is to come. We then continue to promote a failed Venezuelan state. As we do, we sustain failed policy and we lose direction and focus.

Instead, work together to pick up the rubble and rebuild collectively and correctly, this New Bolivarian Republic, Venezuela anew. We cannot forget this as forgetting is grave in itself. We are here to remind ourselves of the final chapter that is to come, that will finally eradicate the Red Scare, but we simply cannot forget the work we have already done. The election in 2015 was a significant historic event that got us to this point today – to continue our work for a better Venezuela, a Venezuela anew. We may just be the last hope for a future we all want for our children and the future that is emerging.

While it is true, there are no staples, there is no water, there is no electricity, there are no rights, but there is chaos, violence and death today. People are murdering others to find the last staples they can, to cut in front in line, or because they are driving too slowly. Our bolivares are not worth the paper they are printed on. Hell, there is no paper to print them on any more, so we cannot wipe our ass with the paper any longer. These are the realities of the dying program trying not to die. We, though, have begun witnessing change, though unnoticed to the public from our secret inner government workings. It is coming together.

If we quit now then we are giving our children and ourselves a perception to die. Here you are. Here is your prescription to die. We cannot give up. We cannot fail when we are so close to giving Venezuela back to its people – back to ourselves – our communities – our children – our future. What remains is we have to look back on ourselves and ask the question who are we willing to be – another product of the program or our true being who wants peace? Let's commemorate this day a V Day – the day of the Victorias.

The council thinks these remarks over and privately converse with each other that Ezekiel and Carlos may be right. They cannot give up now. Perhaps the fragmented and isolated operations they were conducting in the past and current years have been slowly transforming Venezuela anew and eliminating the cultivation and spread of the Red Scare.

Carlos and Ezekiel stepped aside to view the council's deliberation. Carlos intently holds his right side, which has gone unnoticed before. The pain intensifies as he nonchalantly bends over to see blood blanketing his lower part of his shirt. The faint, distorted sound they heard before walking inside was gunfire meant for Carlos. Somehow, the Red Scare, the Chavistas and Maburro have found Carlos, but how? Some of the bullets must have recoiled onto Ezekiel hitting him in his back. The sound of gunfire wasn't heard. The butterflies haven't flown away. Carlos points to Ezekiel with a draped bloody hand, but Ezekiel is perplexed about the situation and is unable to register any response. Are any of these real or perhaps phantom pains? What is certain is time – broken, misplaced time.

Maburro begins to flood his head stating; *you think we did not anticipate your arrival and your initiatives to destroy the Red Scare. We always knew you would return. It is a shame really, Carlos. You should have not betrayed us as for your friend, Ezekiel, he is as good as dead too – another insignificant, unnamed casualty.*

The walls begin to crumble. Voices begin to fade away. The room begins to disappear. The people including Ezekiel Ian Masefield begin to vanish. Carlos enters into another time somewhere in the past, but this time the past in which he is entering is chaotic, jumbled and unstable. These are broken incomplete memories. Carlos is unsure if any of his memories are real. He feels like he does not exist as his mind departs him. Unlike other times when he enters the past, the past memories were constant, but not this time. Snapshots of random memories perforate his mind. These memories are fragments of forgotten pasts that were removed without permission.

Chapter 12

Uncharted Past, Uncharted Reality or Uncharted Mind?

Every day when Carlito wakes up, his life starts from scratch; rather every moment when Carlos Christian Santos or CCS awakes, he begins his life from scratch. For him, his life is anew. It is as if his mind is a computer program, restarted, rebooted or deleted when he awakes. It's a new moment he attempts to piece together but the puzzle is jumbled and the pieces may not fully be there. He attempts to figure out his past and present memories. In so doing, he has become distraught and uncharacteristically becomes inept. Carlito, Carlos Christian Santos – CCS, or Captain Santos' mind has difficulty in distinguishing what may be real or illusions.

In his attempt to assure himself that he is alive and in fact, the reality he is a part of is real, he has written a partial journal of some events. Like his mind, the memories he wrote down are incomplete and misplaced. These events are not complete due to his forgetting or his being distracted.

The journal was not written at the time of the events happening. Carlos Christian Santos began writing down whatever memories he could remember during his dehumanised military training, so he wouldn't forget his past, which held his humanity. He attempted to write the specific memory at the time of remembering it. Though it was days and at times months before Carlos wrote down another fragmented, deprogrammed memory, he began to partially remember. Every time he wrote, the memory came to him in broken streams, partial information, or clips of random scenes spliced together. The Program shortly discovered his writings and confiscated the journal from his possession, much like confiscating his mind from him. His journal was eventually destroyed, burned and buried like all other cadets' personal possessions. No such materials were allowed as they showed weakness and materialism.

Who are we then without our memories? Who are we then when we cannot trust ourselves?

Maybe in October 2003

Carlito is in his sophomore year at *El Colegio Cristiano de Academicos Medias*. At some moment, before the start of school, while Rafael meets up with Carlito, Carlito stares at Fernanda from across the hallway. Fernanda does not know he is staring at her.

The school is like many private schools in Venezuela, better than the public ones, but the building and the resources are worn. The multiple coloured tile linoleum floors are fading. The grey-blue and gold-yellow paint begins to chip from the walls. The shine from the blue, grey and red lockers have already dissipated. The wooden classroom doors are splintering and the hinges begin to squeak.

"Hey, Carlito. Hey, Merico. What are you doing bro?" Rafael said jokingly while his mouth is half-full of an *arepa*.

"Hey, bro. Why do I always see you eating *arepas*, anyway?"

"Do not be a gringo! Do not change the story, Merico. But, besides, you never know when we won't have any more left with these new government programs coming soon."

"So, as you keep eating them, you are going to be a fat ass just like Chava," Carlito says jokingly.

"Hey man! Merico! Who are you looking at? Oh, wait! Is that? No! It cannot be! Ah, but it is. It is Fernanda. Bro. Just ask her already and stop being a gringo, Merico."

"It's complicated."

"No, it is not, Carlito. Wait, I think she is coming over to you. This is perfect. This is your chance. I can see why you like her. Who would not with that jet black hair and..."

"No, it is not."

"Yes, it is. Wait! What are we talking about?" Rafael utters confusingly.

"All that I am saying is the Fernanda thing is not complicated."

"*Hola*, Rafael," Fernanda says.

"Hi, Fernanda. How are you?"

"I'm well. Thank you. Do you mind, if I ask Carlito a question?"

"No, I do not mind. I was just leaving to go to my class. You know how Mrs Alvarez gets when we come in right when the bell rings. She's worse than our mothers. Always saying to be on time is foolish, to be late is a fool. She says something like this. I usually am not paying any attention."

"I do not know who that is."

"Carlito can fill you in. Sometimes she can be a tool."

"Well then. See you guys."

"Carlos, I do not seem to be getting this math chapter on quadratic functions. I do not understand the whole U shape they make. Can you help me after school? We do not have math together, but I think your class just finished that chapter."

"Sure, Fernanda. I will. We can just sit in English when it is over today. Mr Suarez always likes to get out by the bell. I think, he thinks every day is a Friday night and goes out and has a few drinks. How else would you explain his drunk-like behaviour every morning? I don't blame the guy, not really desiring to want to teach English to an only Spanish speaking culture."

"Yeah. I see that. He's always funny in the morning. Then in the afternoon, he's not. He's somebody else in the afternoon. I guess he is not what he is (Fernanda begins to think about something else, but cannot quite remember). So, I will see you at last period."

"Bye, Fernanda."

Ah. My diosa hermosa…I just can…Why God – can I just tell her how pretty she is? What is wrong with me? Today, after school is a perfect time for me to just come out and say how much I like her. I may not get another chance again. I believe it is fate that brought us together. She's the one. I just know it. You know how you feel different about someone. I mean, you know that you just don't want to be just friends. You know something more can happen between the two of you. Okay. I am physically attracted to her. Many guys in my school are. But they don't see her in the same light as how I see her. They just want one thing then they move on to the next pretty girl they see. Fernanda and I…it's just different. I cannot explain it. She is truly my angel. She saved me. She makes me a better person. And I just know that I make her a better person too. It is more than love at first sight…it just has to be. Maybe, Rafael is right. I should just ask her already. I have the time to do so today, after school. You only get one chance and this may be the only chance I have. Well, God…here goes nothing.

Maybe in August 2003

It was the summer before Carlos Christian Santos met Fernanda. It was also during the time when the 4-F Program was growing into what it would later become a hideous, infectious monster – a callous program. Carlos is in a nightclub celebrating with his friends, not just because it is almost the start of school, but also because it is a typical Saturday night.

"Hey Carlos, the night is young. Let's get some more beer?"

"Okay, but are you alright? Because you just broke up with your girlfriend that you were dating for a while, Dante?"

"The best remedy I say is more liquor."

"That's the truth," Carlos inanely utters.

"I will come with you Carlito," Jorge says loudly over the music.

"Are you going to be okay with Dante, Jonny?" Carlos asks.

"Yeah. Do not worry. More liquor makes dancing more enjoyable," Jonny says.

"You know I do not like being called Carlito, Dante."

"I'm just playing around Merico. Lighten up. I wanted to ask you something anyway."

"Sure, Merico. What's up?"

"There's a lot of talk about the government changing things for the poor and for everyone else. *They* say everything is going to be better. However, I do not know, with this regulation of products and wages. Wouldn't regulations and government appropriations do more harm than good, economically? It seems the government will have its hand in everything."

"Look. We are here to have fun. This is why we came here. It is like what we always do my friend. We have to trust the government because *they* have our best intentions at heart. Chava said it himself. We do not worry because we are Venezuelan. Tonight, we continue our happiness. If anything, my *pana*, things are getting cheaper. This is always a good thing, at least. More liquor and more *arepas*, right?"

"You are right, Carlito. Let's have fun then," Dante says while Carlos signals over to the bartender for four more Soleras and four more *Cacique* with coke.

Romeo Santos fills the room as more people flood the dance floor. *Inocente* (innocent) is playing. *Sábado salí en la noche, me pase con par de tragos, pero no se como diablos, hay fragancia en mi camisa, y una mancha de pintalabios.* (Saturday night, I went out.

I had a couple of drinks, but I don't know how on Earth there's perfume on my shirt and a lipstick stain).

Carlos and his friends continue to dance and drink, but for Carlos, he may have had a few extra drinks, so he eventually falls asleep shit faced at Dante's house. The morning after a hangover is not fun, but dancing, drinking and partying with friends on a Saturday makes the hangover worth it. For Carlos and for his friends partying and getting drunk is worth it, because mama and grandma make the best *desayuno*.

At some point in the night, before everyone fell shit faced at Dante's house, Jorge reflected on the government's new programs.

Dante! He is going to be fine. He will find another girl to date. He always does. We are Venezuelan. That is what we do. I am worried though what fate does our country have under the new program. I fear it is not going to be good. I mean, sure on paper the programs seem to benefit the people, but they will not. Who does not want to help the poor? End world hunger? End poverty? Educate all? Give a future to everyone? Provide for all? These are great ideas and some of the promises the government is making. I just do not know if the government is going by it the correct way. There is also an agenda I see too. Little kids are being taught to love the president and socialism is the way. Then they are given free stuff. I am pretty sure that's not educating anyone. Then again, who will argue over low prices and government run programs? Though I do know one thing as long as we have our shopping malls, smartphones, liquor, music and arepas, we are then happy. But are we really? We used to care about what little we have, we are happy. I hope this stays that way.

Maybe in January 2008 to March 2009

Before we graduated from the program, that is before we became lieutenants, we had to participate in a supervised mission determined by our training officers. I had to participate in a raid. I was tasked with leading a team of current soldiers in occupying high school students who would be potential soldiers for us, *the Guardias*. For the past several months we were authorised to set up surveillance around schools. We thought it was just another exercise. This one was, but it was realistic. With the information we gathered, we documented students' behaviour, their conversations and filtered the ones who did not fit our profile. Today is when we would collect our information. In the matter, I did not have any choice.

188

If I did not participate in this mission to become a lieutenant then I would have been released like others before who did not comply. I did the unthinkable. I became an unwilling participant.

I would not forget leading this mission. I did not want to do it. This, however, faded in time. I would not forget their voices pleading not to take them. I would not forget the horrible choices I made, which led me down the path to becoming Santos. I would not forget I sold my soul to the devil. I would not forget I became a person without humanity. Though I did not rape any women and children like some of the other soldiers, but I did murder, torture and violated my fair share.

"Cadet Santos. Are you ready for tonight? No more of this fucking up shit. No more hesitating. No more Merico shit. You understand me?"

"Yes, sir. I understand. I will carry out the orders that have been discharged to me. I will complete this last assignment that will confirm me as Lieutenant Santos."

"Very well, Cadet. Fall out and pack up. We head out soon."

"Yes, sir. I will see my team in one hour."

The heavy, camouflage vehicle drove off into the dusk lit sky. The darkness in the sky is still young. It slowly takes over the light as the clouds stretch over the moon. Quite is but a feeble warning for the students who were about to be taken by the Program.

Cadet Santos, his team and his supervisor entered the school where the students would be studying. Voices shortly overflow their ears, crying, *stop, what are you doing, let me go, who are you, why are you doing this, you monsters, someone help, please help*. However, these voices are deaf. No one is around to hear their cries except for the Guardias – that is the boogiemen striping them away from their life. This is all too familiar to Carlos. He erased this particular time in his memory but tonight the memory, broken and unrecognisable, attempts to revive itself. Carlos is hesitant, but it didn't last long. Before the mission, a drug called negative reactant was injected into his system. It is now in his body and assuming control of his mind.

"Cadet. Let's go. Finish tying these students up and let's fall out. And for God's sake, someone shut them up!"

"Yes, sir. But, I hear something down the hall there. Should we investigate it?"

"Well, you are leading this mission. It is then your call. What do you want your soldiers to do?"

Before Cadet Carlos could utter his command, the faint voice that appeared to be heard from far away came in. He must have heard one of the children screaming.

"Soldier, what did I say about allowing these children to scream for so long? You should have just taped their mouths shouts. Now, look at what we have done. You have, because of your idiotic and foolish actions brought upon us an unwanted visitor," Cadet Santos barks at one soldier.

"Well sir, Supervisor Luiz over here said the building is empty except for the children we were supposed to take," the soldier anxiously states.

"This does not matter now, Cadet. Take care of this."

"But sir."

"Are you refusing a direct order, Cadet Santos."

"Ah, no sir. I just need the silencer."

Cadet Santos fires his gun. The gun was loaded with rubber bullets. These bullets were meant to temporarily paralyse a combatant so that a memory inhibitor can be injected into the body of the combatant. Unknown to Cadet Santos at the time, he did not fire rubber bullets. Before firing his gun, he asked God to forgive him, not for just about shooting a person but also for the person he wants to reject becoming, but cannot. There's only silence in his mind, not God's voice before Cadet Santos pulled the trigger.

"Well done, Cadet Santos for becoming Lieutenant. Let's get the rest of these students in the vehicle. And do not worry about the body over there. We will take care of this waste!"

"Yes, sir. Let's get back and celebrate," Santos states confidently as to mask his true perplex feelings.

Cadet Santos' conscious, whatever is left of it, strives to echo what may be the last words of the young dying teacher.

We are zombies going about our lives. We have no awareness of others or ourselves. Do we then know what has been happening around us? Are we then blind to the signs in front of our eyes? Are we then deaf to our brothers' and sisters' cries? Do we then not feel anything when we witness the savage loss of our humanity? Do we then not think what has become of us? Do we then not smell the rotting flesh of our communities and ourselves? Do we then not taste others' and our calamities? If we are then zombies, we have no awareness, so too we are just bodies lying cold in the ground.

In sometime between the past and present maybe February 2001 to July 2015

The stale burning sulphur lingering ubiquitously in the dusk lit sky still can be smelled vibrantly. Water and other abundant sustenance became scarce commodities. The plains, *Los Llanos* became infertile. Much of the land also became inhabitable. The 4-F Program is just a virus disguised as providing its people of life, liberty and prosperity. It is certain the butterflies no longer fly around here anymore.

We have become complacent that this virus is life. It is not certain if we will live to see and experience the next day. The virus is inhospitable to life. We have lost hope. We have given up. Most of us have become parasitic machines to the virus. We lurk in waiting that our number will be called. Once our number is called, death is here. Death this time did not send its messengers that are sickness, tiredness and pain because the virus is its sole messenger. We did not recognise it because we have abandoned our humanity. We were told not to fear death.

They are always watching us. When you think you're safe – in your house – with your friends they always find ways to track you. You are never safe from the Red Scare. That's what started out as a virus – an epidemic – a plague that was going to eradicate poverty and restore equity to all. This virus was disguised as and still is, the 4-F Program. We assume no responsibility for its existence. We refused to acknowledge its presence. We have failed collectively and individually to stop the spread of it, so we become used to it. We became complacent to its toxic symptoms. We tried to change it at one time. Though, to this day, some still attempt to eradicate or at least find a cure to the unending red monster. The doubt remains, how can we when we live in a prison of solitude? All is left are faded historic footnotes waiting to be read but are always glanced over and then forgotten. What remains are these last footnotes. They read:

Our voices have been imprisoned.

Our actions have been forgotten.

Our eyes have been fooled.

Our ears have been poisoned.

Our hands have been tied.

We are anonymous to the world – to our country – to our communities – and to ourselves.

We wept peace, but none came.

We blindly followed our leaders without any direction or any grain.

We deafly hear the impoverished but no aid is provided.

We screamed for change, but are brutally silenced.

To what end do we dare to hope when God has been abandoned.

To what end do we dare to live when death is our physician.

Underneath the smoky, burnt ash and red, fragmented ruble of chaos, uncertainty, failure and immorality, a barren, incomplete book half-buried on the tired beaten, unpaved, tainted ground is turned to a random page. The pages are half torn and covered in burnt ash. Perhaps this book is the incomplete word of the imprisoned, or a journal belonging to the rabid, raped souls of the horridly resting dead. Nonetheless, these pieces of writings, however, read the following unspoken, silenced words:

Man is both hero and villain. They are tied by these dichotomous structures with thin, worn ropes. Man can cross either side of these ropes by walking on a bridge. Underneath the bridge is the abyss of chaos. When man is blinded, has lost direction and has no purpose, he walks towards the villain. When man has purpose, direction and sees man walk towards the hero. When man is stuck in the middle of the bridge for too long, the thin, worn ropes break. The bridge crumbles from under his feet and into the abyss of chaos he goes. He later emerges as the villain. Man collectively and individually paves the bridge, but ultimately decides which end of the ropes to walk towards. This is not to say that man does not have collective responsibility, he does. Man must then support each man and guide him to equilibrium. To do so, successfully, man must first reflect upon himself, which man has he become, villain or hero. Man's teachings, values and beliefs may shape his past thinking and may influence him to be hero or villain, but it is man's observation, reflection and action that shapes who he is to become. So, the question when walking across the bridge isn't who man is, for sure man is both hero and villain, but the question then is who is man to become, hero or villain?

While the disturbed Venezuelan earth has partially dug up an incomplete journal filled with broken memories, the events of its past still rest uneasily. In this journal, the world witnesses the savage loss of innocence but also witnesses the collective will and hope of people. This is all told by Carlos Christian Santos and Ezekiel Ian Masefield. The question they have is, will the world listen?